A Book Of

BUSINESS
MATHEMATICS

B.B.M. Semester - I
As Per Savitribai Phule Pune University's Revised Syllabus
Effective from June 2013

Prof. A. V. Rayarikar
M.Sc. (Maths.), M.Sc. (Stats.), M.Phil (Maths.)
Former - Head of Mathematics Department,
Modern College, Pune – 5.

Prof. P. G. Dixit
M.Sc., M.Phil (Stats.)
Head of Statistics Department,
Modern College, Pune – 5.

NIRALI
PRAKASHAN
ADVANCEMENT OF KNOWLEDGE

N2928

B.B.M. BUSINESS MATHEMATICS (SEMESTER – I)   ISBN 978-93-5164-639-6

Third Edition   :   July 2015

©   :   Authors

Published By :
NIRALI PRAKASHAN
Abhyudaya Pragati, 1312, Shivaji Nagar,
Off J.M. Road, PUNE – 411005
Tel - (020) 25512336/37/39, Fax - (020) 25511379
Email : niralipune@pragationline.com

☞ DISTRIBUTION CENTRES

PUNE

Nirali Prakashan : 119, Budhwar Peth, Jogeshwari Mandir Lane, Pune 411002, Maharashtra
Tel : (020) 2445 2044, 66022708, Fax : (020) 2445 1538
Email : bookorder@pragationline.com, niralilocal@pragationline.com

Nirali Prakashan : S. No. 28/27, Dhyari, Near Pari Company, Pune 411041
Tel : (020) 24690204 Fax : (020) 24690316
Email : dhyari@pragationline.com, bookorder@pragationline.com

MUMBAI

Nirali Prakashan : 385, S.V.P. Road, Rasdhara Co-op. Hsg. Society Ltd.,
Girgaum, Mumbai 400004, Maharashtra
Tel : (022) 2385 6339 / 2386 9976, Fax : (022) 2386 9976
Email : niralimumbai@pragationline.com

☞ DISTRIBUTION BRANCHES

JALGAON

Nirali Prakashan : 34, V. V. Golani Market, Navi Peth, Jalgaon 425001,
Maharashtra, Tel : (0257) 222 0395, Mob : 94234 91860

KOLHAPUR

Nirali Prakashan : New Mahadvar Road, Kedar Plaza, 1st Floor Opp. IDBI Bank
Kolhapur 416 012, Maharashtra. Mob : 9850046155

NAGPUR

Pratibha Book Distributors : Above Maratha Mandir, Shop No. 3, First Floor,
Rani Jhanshi Square, Sitabuldi, Nagpur 440012, Maharashtra
Tel : (0712) 254 7129

DELHI

Nirali Prakashan : 4593/21, Basement, Aggarwal Lane 15, Ansari Road, Daryaganj
Near Times of India Building, New Delhi 110002
Mob : 08505972553

BENGALURU

Pragati Book House : House No. 1, Sanjeevappa Lane, Avenue Road Cross,
Opp. Rice Church, Bengaluru – 560002.
Tel : (080) 64513344, 64513355,Mob : 9880582331, 9845021552
Email:bharatsavla@yahoo.com

CHENNAI

Pragati Books : 9/1, Montieth Road, Behind Taas Mahal, Egmore,
Chennai 600008 Tamil Nadu, Tel : (044) 6518 3535,
Mob : 94440 01782 / 98450 21552 / 98805 82331,
Email : bharatsavla@yahoo.com

niralipune@pragationline.com | www.pragationline.com

Also find us on ⓕ www.facebook.com/niralibooks

Preface ...

We have great pleasure in presenting this text book on **'Business Mathematics'** to the students of B.B.M. (Semester – I). This book is written according to the new revised syllabus of University of Pune to be implemented from June 2013.

We have taken utmost care to present the matter systematically. The book contains several selected solved examples and an ample number of graded problems in the exercises.

We are thankful to **Shri Dineshbhai Furia, Shri Jignesh Furia, Shri M. P. Munde**, Mrs. Anagha Medhekar, Mr. Santosh Bare, Mrs. Anjali Muley and the staff of Nirali Prakashan, for the great efforts that they have taken to publish the book in time.

We welcome valuable suggestions from our colleagues' and readers for the improvement of the book.

PUNE
JULY 2013

AUTHORS

Syllabus ...

1. Ratio, Proportion and Percentage

Ratio, Definition, Continued ratio, Inverse ratio, Proportion, Continued proportion, Direct proportion, Inverse proportion, Variance, Inverse variation, Joint variation, Percentage – Meaning and Computations of percentages.

2. Profit and Loss

Terms and formula, Trade discount, Cash discount, Problems involving cost price, Selling price, Trade discount and Cast discount. Introduction to commission and brokerage, Problems on commission and brokerage, Concept and Treatment of depreciation.

3. Interest

Simple interest, Compound interest (reducing balance and flat interest rate of interest), Equated Monthly Installments (EMI), Principles of hire-purchase.

4. Shares and Dividends

Concept and examples of shares, Stock exchange, Face value, Market value, Dividend, Equity shares, Preference shares, Bonus shares, Delete examples.

5. Matrices and Determinants (Upto order 3 only)

Multivariable data, Definition of matrix, Types of matrices, Algebra of matrices, Determinants, Adjoint of a matrix, Inverse of a matrix via adjoint matrix, Homogenous system of linear equations, Condition for uniqueness for the homogeneous system, Solution of non-homogeneous system of linear equations (not more than three variables). Condition for existence and uniqueness of solution, Solution using inverse of the coefficient matrix, Problems associated with the above.

6. Functions

(To identify and define the relationships that exist among business variables).

Introduction, Definition of function, constants, variables, continuous real variable, Domain or interval, Types of functions, One valued function, Explicit function, Algebraic functions, Polynomial functions, Absolute value function, Inverse function, Rational and Irratational function, Monotone function, Even and odd function, Supply/Demand function, Cost function, Total revenue function, Profit function, Production function, Utility function, Consumption function.

•••

Contents ...

•••

Unit **1**...

Ratio, Proportion and Percentage

Contents ...

Learning Objectives:

Ratio, Proportion, Direct Proportion, Continued proportion, Inverse proportion, Continued ratio variation, Joint variation, Inverse variation, Percentage.

Chapter Objectives ...

To understand the concept of ratio properties and percentage in business.

1.1 Ratio

In day-to-day life, we come across several situations in which we have to make comparisons among quantities e.g. salaries of persons, prices of commodities, sales of different firms etc.

In mathematics, the operations of subtraction and division are mainly used for comparison. When two quantities are compared by division, we use **ratio.**

Suppose that a firm having sale of ₹ 40 crores in a year made a profit of ₹ 13 crores and another firm having sale of ₹ 60 crores in that year made a profit of ₹ 16 crores. Therefore, do we infer that the performance of second firm is better ? Taking the quotient profit / sales we can compare the performance of the two firms. (Note that this is one of the criteria for judging the performance of a firm). In other words, we are using ratio (of profit to sales) to compare the performance of the two companies, and then our conclusion is that the performance of first firm is better than that of the second $\left(\because \dfrac{13}{40} > \dfrac{16}{60} \right).$

From the above illustration, it is clear that, we can find the ratio of two quantities of the same type. Moreover, the unit for measurement must be same.

Thus, we have a formal definition.

Definition : *If 'a' and 'b' are magnitudes of same kind, expressed in same units, then the quotient $\dfrac{a}{b}$ is called the ratio of 'a' to 'b' and it is denoted by a : b.*

Note :

(i)   Ratio is a pure number i.e. it has no units.

(ii)   In the ratio a : b, a is called antecedent and b is called consequent.

(iii)   If we multiply the numerator and denominator in any ratio by the same (non-zero) number, the ratio remains the same.

     i.e. $\dfrac{a}{b} = \dfrac{ma}{mb}$ (m ≠ 0)

From this it is clear that, the antecedent and consequent in a ratio may not be actual quantities. It also indicates that, if the ratio of two quantities is a : b, the actual quantities should be taken as xa and xb (x ≠ 0).

Continued Ratio : *It is the relation between the magnitudes of three or more quantities of the same kind.*

The continued ratio of three similar quantities a, b, c is denoted by a : b : c.

Illustrative Examples

Example 1.1 : *Two numbers are in the ratio 7 : 8 and their sum is 195. Find the numbers.*

Solution : Let the numbers be 7x and 8x.

∴   7x + 8x = 195

i.e   15x = 195

∴   x = 13

∴   Required numbers are 91 and 104.

Example 1.2 : *If a : b = 4 : 7 and b : c = 9 : 5, find a : c.*

Solution : $\dfrac{a}{b} = \dfrac{4}{7}$

∴   7a = 4b

∴ $a = \dfrac{4b}{7}$

Again, $\dfrac{b}{c} = \dfrac{9}{5}$

∴   5b = 9c

∴ $c = \dfrac{5b}{9}$

∴ $\dfrac{a}{c} = \dfrac{\frac{4}{7}b}{\frac{5}{9}b} = \dfrac{36}{35}$ i.e. a : c = 36 : 35.

Example 1.3 : *The sum of present ages of 3 persons is 66 years. Five years ago, their ages were in the ratio 4 : 6 : 7. Find their present ages.*   **(April 2015)**

Solution : Let the ages of three persons, five years ago be 4x, 6x and 7x years respectively.

∴ Their present ages are 4x + 5, 6x + 5 and 7x + 5.

From the information given,

$$(4x + 5) + (6x + 5) + (7x + 5) = 66$$

∴ $$17x + 15 = 66$$

∴ $$17x = 51$$

∴ $$x = 3$$

∴ Present ages are 4x + 5, 6x + 5 and 7x + 5.

i.e. 17, 23 and 26 years respectively.

Example 1.4 : *The monthly salaries of two persons are in the ratio 3 : 5. If each receives an increase of ₹ 200 in monthly salary, the new ratio is 13 : 21. Find their original salaries.* **(Oct. 2013)**

Solution : Let the original salaries be ₹ 3x and ₹ 5x.

Due to increase in salaries, the revised salaries are ₹ (3x + 200) and ₹ (5x + 200). It is given that

$$\frac{3x + 200}{5x + 200} = \frac{13}{21}$$

∴ $$63x + 4200 = 65x + 2600$$

∴ $$2x = 1600$$

∴ $$x = 800$$

∴ Original salaries were ₹ 2,400 and ₹ 4,000.

Example 1.5 : *The ratio of prices of two houses was 4 : 5. Two years later, when the price of first had risen by 10% and that of the second by ₹6,000, the ratio became 11 : 15. Find the new prices of the houses.*

Solution : Let the original prices be ₹ 4x and ₹ 5x. Two years later, the price of first house increased to ₹ $4x + \dfrac{4x}{10}$ and that of the second to ₹ (5x + 6,000).

∴ Ratio of new prices,

$$\frac{4x + \dfrac{4x}{10}}{5x + 6000} = \frac{11}{15} \text{ (given)}$$

∴ $$15\left(4x + \frac{4x}{10}\right) = 11\,(5x + 6000)$$

∴ $$60x + 6x = 55x + 66000$$

∴ $$11x = 66000$$

∴ $$x = 6000$$

$\therefore$ New prices of the houses are $4x + \dfrac{4x}{10}$ and $5x + 6000$

i.e. $24000 + 2400$ and $30000 + 6000$

i.e. ₹ 26400 and ₹ 36000.

Example 1.6 : *Incomes of P, Q, R are in the ratio 2 : 3 : 4 and their expenditures are in the ratio 5 : 7 : 9. If P saves (1/5)^{th} of his income, find the ratio of their savings.***(April 2015)**

Solution : Let the incomes of P, Q, R be ₹ $2x$, $3x$, $4x$ respectively. (Note that, we cannot take $5x$, $7x$, $9x$. Why ?)

$\therefore$ Their savings will be ₹ $2x - 5y$, $3x - 7y$, $4x - 9y$ respectively.

But it is given that P saves $1/5^{th}$ of his income i.e. ₹ $\dfrac{2x}{5}$.

Thus, $2x - 5y \;=\; \dfrac{2x}{5}$

$\therefore$ $10x - 25y \;=\; 2x$

$\therefore$ $8x \;=\; 25y$

$\therefore$ $x \;=\; \dfrac{25}{8}\, y$

$\therefore$ Savings of P, Q, R will be $\dfrac{50}{8}\, y - 5y$, $\dfrac{75}{8}\, y - 7y$, and $\dfrac{100}{8}\, y - 9y$ respectively,

i.e. $\dfrac{10}{8}\, y$, $\dfrac{19}{8}\, y$ and $\dfrac{28}{8}\, y$ respectively.

$\therefore$ Ratio of savings is $10 : 19 : 28$.

1.2 Proportion   (April 2015)

If two ratios are equal, then the four quantities given by them are said to be in *proportion.* i.e. if the ratios a : b and c : d are equal, then a, b, c, d are said to be in proportion and we write a : b :: c : d. Here, b and c are called *means* while a and d are called *extremes,* further d is called 4th proportional to a, b and c.

Note : If a, b, c, d are in proportion, then,

$$\dfrac{a}{b} \;=\; \dfrac{c}{d}$$

$\therefore$ $ad \;=\; bc$

i.e.   Product of extremes = Product of means

Continued Proportion (Oct. 2014, April 2015) : If a, b, c are three quantities of the same kind and if a/b = b/c, then a, b, c are said to be in *continued proportion.*

In this case, b is called mean proportional to a and c.

Note that $b^2 = ac$.

The concept of continued proportion can also be extended to more than three quantities of the same kind.

Direct Proportion : Petrol costs ₹ 11 per litre. If a person buys 3 litres of petrol, clearly he has to pay ₹ 33. Thus, as the consumption of petrol increases, expenditure on it also increases. Similarly, if the consumption is less, expenditure is also less.

Thus, we have a relation between two variables viz., consumption of petrol and expenditure on it. They are said to be in *direct proportion.*

Definition : Direct Proportion (Oct. 2014, April 2015) : *When two variables are so related that an increase (or reduction) in one causes an increase (or reduction) in the other in same ratio then the proportion is called direct proportion.*

Inverse Proportion (Oct. 2014, April 2015) : Suppose that a man completes a job in 15 days working 4 hours per day. Then we know that if the job is to be completed in 10 days, he will have to work 6 hours per day. Thus, if the job is to be completed in lesser days, the man has to work more everyday.

In this illustration, number of days and working hours are two variables such that if number of hours is increased, number of days is decreased in the same ratio. Also if number of hours is decreased, the number of days is increased in the same ratio. This type of variation is called inverse variation and two variables are said to be in **inverse proportion,** since in this case, one ratio is reciprocal of the other as shown below :

No. of days	Working hours
15	4
10	6
$\dfrac{15}{10} = \left(\dfrac{3}{2}\right) = \dfrac{1}{\frac{4}{6}}$	

Definition : *If two variables are so related that, an increase (or reduction) in one causes a reduction (or increase) in the same ratio in the other, then they are said to be in inverse proportion.*

1.3 Variation   (Oct. 2013)

If two variables x and y are in direct proportion, we write it as $x \propto y$, then, $x = ky$, where k is called constant of proportionality.

If a value of x and corresponding value of y are known, then this constant can be obtained at once.

For a circle, circumference $\propto$ radius is an illustration of direct variation.

Inverse Variation (Oct. 2013, 2014) : If x and y are two variables such that x varies directly as $\dfrac{1}{y}$, then we say that x varies inversely as y and write,

$$x \propto \frac{1}{y}$$

then, $x = \dfrac{k}{y}$ where k is constant of proportionality.

If a value of x and corresponding value of y are known, then this constant can be obtained at once.

Joint Variation (Oct. 2013, 2014) :

1.   A variable x is said to vary jointly with respect to the variables y and z, if it varies as their product i.e. if

$$x \propto yz$$

then, $x = kyz$

e.g. We know that area of a triangle varies jointly as its base and altitude.

2.   A variable x is said to vary directly as y and inversely as z, if it varies as $\dfrac{y}{z}$.

i.e. $x \propto \dfrac{y}{z}$

then, $x = \dfrac{ky}{z}$

Illustrative Examples

Type 1 :

Example 1.7 : *Find x, if (i) 6 : 15 :: 2 : x, (ii) 15 : 27 :: x : 45.*

Solution : (i) 6 : 15 :: 2 : x

i.e. $\dfrac{6}{15} = \dfrac{2}{x}$

i.e. $6x = 30$

∴ $x = 5$

(ii) 15 : 27 :: x : 45

i.e. $\dfrac{15}{27} = \dfrac{x}{45}$

i.e. $\dfrac{5}{9} = \dfrac{x}{45}$

∴ $\dfrac{45 \times 5}{9} = x$

∴ $x = 25$

Example 1.8 : *Find fourth proportional to 6, 8, 10.*

Solution : Let x be the fourth proportional.

∴　　6 : 8 :: 10 : x

i.e.　　　　　　　　　$\dfrac{6}{8} = \dfrac{10}{x}$

i.e.　　　　　　　　　$6x = 80$

　　　　　　　　　　$x = \dfrac{40}{3} = 13.3333$

Example 1.9 : *Ages of Madhav, Ajit, and Dilip are in continued proportion. If Madhav is 4 years old and Dilip is 9 years old, what is the age of Ajit ?*

Solution : Let Ajit be x years old.

∴　　4 : x :: x : 9 (since they are in continued proportion)

i.e.　　　　　　　　　$\dfrac{4}{x} = \dfrac{x}{9}$

i.e.　　　　　　　　　$x^2 = 36$

∴　　　　　　　　　　$x = 6$

Hence, the age of Ajit is 6 years.

Type 2 :

Example 1.10 : *If sugar costs ₹8 per kg, how many tonnes can be bought for ₹48,000 ?*

Solution : The price of sugar and quantity purchased are in direct proportion.

∴　　If x kg sugar can be bought for ₹ 48,000.

　　　　　　　　　　$\dfrac{8}{1} = \dfrac{48000}{x}$

∴　　　　　　　　　　$x = 6,000 \text{ kg}$

i.e.　　　　　　　　　$x = 6 \text{ tonnes}$

Type 3 :

Example 1.11 : *A student finishes a book by reading 30 pages per day in 16 days. If he wants to finish the book in 12 days, how many pages should be read everyday ?*

Solution : We know that the number of pages read and the number of days required are in inverse proportion.

Let x be the number of pages that he has to read everyday to finish the book in 12 days.

	No. of pages	No. of days
Original data	30	16
New data	x	12

Because of inverse proportion,

$$\dfrac{x}{30} = \dfrac{1}{12 \, / \, 16}$$

$$\therefore \qquad \frac{x}{30} = \frac{4}{3}$$

$\therefore \qquad x = 40$

$\therefore$ He has to read 40 pages per day.

Type 4 :

Example 1.12 : *If 75 persons can perform a piece of work in 12 days of 10 hours each, how many persons could perform a piece of work twice as large in half the number of days, working 8 hours daily ?*

Solution : In this type of problems, we prepare a table as follows :

Variables	Original Set	New Set	Type of Variation
Persons	75	x	....
Work	1	2	Direct
Days	12	6	Inverse
Hours	10	8	Inverse

Note that the proportions are decided with respect to the unknown x i.e. we know that when the work is more, number of persons required is more, so that proportion is direct. When number of days is reduced, number of persons required will be more so that the proportion is inverse and so on.

Then we have a concise formula as follows :

$$\frac{x}{\text{Original quantity}} = \frac{2}{1} \times \frac{12}{6} \times \frac{10}{8}$$

i.e. $\qquad\qquad\qquad \dfrac{x}{75} = 5$

$\therefore \qquad\qquad\qquad x = 375$

Note that on the R.H.S., we take the product of ratios : new value / original value and original value / new value depending on the type of variation.

The ratio new value / original value is taken for direct variation and original value / new value for inverse variation.

Example 1.13 : *20 men require 25 days to dig a trench 50 m long, 20 m broad and 1 m deep. How many days will be required for 60 men to dig a trench 90 m long, 60 m broad, and 1/3 m deep ?*

Solution :

Variables	Original Set	New Set	Proportion
Men	20	60	Inverse
Days	25	x	....
Length	50	90	Direct
Breadth	20	60	Direct
Depth	1	1/3	Direct

$$\therefore \qquad \frac{x}{25} = \frac{20}{60} \times \frac{90}{50} \times \frac{60}{20} \times \frac{1/3}{1}$$

$$\therefore \qquad \frac{x}{25} = \frac{9}{5} \times \frac{1}{3}$$

$$\therefore \qquad x = 15$$

Hence 15 days will be required.

Type 5 :

Example 1.14 : *If* $A \propto B$ *and* $A = 4$ *when* $B = 6$, *find the value of* A *when* $B = 27$.

Solution : $\qquad A \propto B;$ ... (1)

$\therefore \qquad A = kB$

When $A = 4$, and $B = 6$,

$\therefore \qquad 4 = 6k \qquad\qquad \therefore \quad k = \dfrac{2}{3} B$

$\therefore$ from (1) $\qquad A = \dfrac{2}{3} B$

$\therefore$ when $\qquad B = 27$

$\qquad A = \dfrac{2}{3} \times 27 \qquad\qquad \therefore \quad A = 18$

Example 1.15 : *If* x *varies directly as* y *and inversely as* z *and* $x = 12$ *when* $y = 9$ *and* $z = 16$, *find* y *when* $x = 9$ *and* $z = 24$.

Solution : $\qquad x \propto y \qquad\qquad$ and $\qquad x \propto \dfrac{1}{z}$

$\therefore \qquad x \propto \dfrac{y}{z} \qquad\qquad \therefore \quad x = \dfrac{ky}{z}$ ... (1)

When $x = 12$, $y = 9$, $z = 16$,

$\qquad 12 = \dfrac{9k}{16} \qquad\qquad \therefore \quad k = \dfrac{64}{3}$

$\therefore$ from (1), $\qquad x = 64\dfrac{y}{3}$

When $x = 9$, $z = 24$,

$\therefore \qquad 9 = \dfrac{64 y}{3} \times 24 \qquad\qquad \therefore \quad y = \dfrac{81}{8}$

Example 1.16 : *A diamond worth ₹25,600 is accidentally broken into two pieces whose weights are in the ratio 3 : 5. The value of the diamond varies as the square of the weight. Calculate the loss due to the breakage.*

Solution : Let c denote the cost and w denote the weight of diamond. Then,

$$c \propto w^2$$

$\therefore \qquad c = kw^2$ ... (1)

where k is constant of proportionality.

Let weight of the diamond be 8 gm.

$$25{,}600 = k\,(64)$$

$$\therefore \qquad\qquad k = 400$$

$\therefore$ (1) gives $c = 400\,w^2$ ... (2)

Due to breakage, the two pieces now weigh 3 gm and 5 gm respectively.

The cost of the diamond weighing 3 gm is

$$c = 400\,(9) = 3{,}600$$

Similarly, the cost of the diamond weighing 5 gm is

$$c = 400\,(25) \qquad\qquad \therefore \quad c = 10{,}000$$

$\therefore$ The total cost of the two pieces

$$= 3{,}600 + 10{,}000 = 13{,}600$$

$\therefore$ Loss $= 25{,}600 - 13{,}600$

i.e.   Loss $= ₹\,12{,}000$

Exercise 1.1

1. Fill in the blanks :

(i) A person was getting a salary of ₹ 37500 in 2005. His salary increased to ₹ 41,500 in 2007 ..... Ratio of salary in 2007 to the salary in 2005 is ......

(ii) Arvind has ₹ 8 while Sameer has 40 paise.

  $\therefore$ Ratio of amount with Arvind to that of Sameer is ......

(iii) If x : y = 5 : 7 and x = 30, then y = ...

(iv) A has ₹ 3,200 and B has ₹ 2,600

  $\therefore$ B has ...... times the amount with A.

(v) Manish has 3 bananas and Hari has 7 dozen bananas.

  $\therefore$ Ratio of Manish's bananas to that of Hari is ......

(vi) Ratio of two numbers is 4 : 7. The bigger number is 147. Hence the smaller number is ......

(vii) Ratio of two numbers is 3 : 5 and the sum of the numbers is 232. Hence, the bigger number is ......

(viii) The ratio of length to breadth of a rectangle is 8 : 3. If the perimeter of the rectangle is 352 cm, then the sides of the rectangle are ......

2. Monthly incomes of A and B are in the ratio 9 : 11 and those of B and C are in the ratio 13 : 10. If monthly income of C is ₹ 1,430, then find the incomes of A and B.

3. If 8, x and 50 are in continued proportion, then find x.

4. If numerator and denominator in a ratio are each increased by same non-zero constant, the ratio remains the same. What can you say about the ratio ?

5. An alloy of gold and copper weighing 100 gm contains 97 gm of gold. How much gold should be added to the alloy to increase the percentage of gold to 98 ?

6.   If an article is sold at 25% profit, find the ratio of cost price to selling price.

7.   Sand and cement are in the ratio 6 : 5 in a mixture weighing 671 kg. How much sand must be added to the mixture so as to make the ratio 8 : 5 ?

8.   A and B are two alloys of gold and copper prepared by mixing them in the ratio 3 : 2 and 5 : 8 respectively. If equal quantities of the alloys are melted to form a third alloy, then find the ratio of the gold to copper in the new alloy.

Answers 1.1

(1) (i) 83 : 75, (ii) 20 : 1, (iii) 42, (iv) $\frac{13}{16}$, (v) 1 : 28, (vi) 84, (vii) 145, (viii) 128 cm, 48 cm.

(2) Income of A ₹ 1521, Income of B ₹ 1,859.

(3) x = 20   (4) 1 : 1

(5) 50 gm   (6) 4 : 5

(7) 122 kg   (8) 32 : 33

1.4 Percentage

It is a special type of ratio, in which the consequent (denominator) is 100. When a ratio is expressed in this form, the numerator is said to express the percentage. Thus $\frac{x}{100}$ denotes x%. Consider the illustration studied in earlier section, in which profits of two firms were compared. The ratio of profit to sales of the first firm is $\frac{13}{40}$ = $\frac{32.5}{100}$ and the ratio for other firm is $\frac{16}{60}$ = $\frac{\frac{80}{3}}{100}$. In other words, the percentage profits of the two firms are 32.5 and $\frac{\frac{80}{3}}{100}$. Hence, according to this criterion, the performance of first firm is better than that of the second.

Note that with the help of percentage, we could compare the performance of the two companies very easily.

Remarks :

1.   As percentage is a ratio, it has no units.

2.   Percentages are very useful in profit and loss, commission and brokerage, simple interest, compound interest etc.

3.   If we want to find x% of a quantity, we should multiply the quantity by $\frac{x}{100}$, in other words, x% of Y = Y $\times \frac{x}{100}$

e.g. 3% of 58 = 58 $\times \frac{3}{100}$ = 1.74.

4.   If we want to write a given fraction in percentages, we should multiply the fraction by 100.

e.g. $\frac{3}{4} = \frac{3}{4} \times 100\% = 75\%$.

Illustrative Examples

Example 1.17 : *The population of a city according to 1971 census was 84,500 and it rose to 1,11,200 in 1981. Find the percentage increase in the population.*

Solution : The increase in population = 1,11,200 – 84,500 = 26,700.

This growth is w.r.t. original population 84,500.

on 84,500, increase is 26,700 $\frac{100}{84500} \times 26700 = 31.6$

∴   on 100, the increase is 31.6 (approx.)

∴   The percentage increase in population over the decade is 31.6 (approx.)

Example 1.18 : *A salesman gets 5% commission in his sales. If he gets a commission of ₹870 in a month, find his sales in that month.*

Solution : For a commission of ₹ 5, sales are ₹ 100.

∴   For a commission of ₹ 870, sales are ₹ 17,400 $\frac{870}{5} \times 100 = 17,400$.

∴   His sales in that month are ₹ 17,400.

Example 1.19 : *The price ₹ 50 of an article was increased by 12%. As a result, consumption decreased by 10%. Find the percentage increase or decrease in the original income.*

Solution : Suppose that the original consumption is 100 articles.

Due to 12% rise, the article now costs ₹ 56

Original price 100, new price ₹ 112 $\left(\frac{80}{100} \times 112\right) = 89.6$

∴   Original price ₹ 50, new price ₹ 56

Due to 10% reduction in number of articles, now the consumption is 90 articles.

∴   New income = 90 × 56 = ₹ 5,040

∴   There is an increase of ₹ (5,040 – 5,000) = ₹ 40.

For original income of ₹ 5,000, increase ₹ 40.

∴   For original income of ₹ 100, increase ₹ $\frac{8}{10}$.

Thus, there is an increase of 0.8% in the original income.

Example 1.20 : *In a school, there are 12% girls. If 5 boys and 15 girls are newly admitted to the school, the percentage of girls becomes 15. What is the total strength of the school ?*

Solution : Let the original strength of the school be x.

$$\text{Number of girls} = \frac{12\,x}{100}$$

$$\text{After new admissions, number of girls} = \frac{12\,x}{100} + 15$$

$$\text{Revised strength of the school} = x + 20$$

$$\therefore \quad \text{Revised percentage of girls} = \frac{\dfrac{12\,x}{100} + 15}{x + 20} \times 100$$

$$= \frac{12\,x + 1500}{x + 20}$$

But the percentage is given to be 15.

$$\therefore \qquad \frac{12\,x + 1500}{x + 20} = 15$$

$$\therefore \qquad 12\,x + 1500 = 15\,x + 300$$

$$\therefore \qquad 3\,x = 1200$$

$$\therefore \qquad x = 400$$

∴ Original strength of the school is 400.

Example 1.21 : *A sold a car to B at 15% profit. B sold the car to C at 5% profit for ₹48,300. Find the price at which A has purchased the car.*

Solution : Suppose that A purchased the car for ₹ x. Since his profit is 15% i.e. $\dfrac{15\,x}{100}$ he has sold the car to B for

$$₹\left(x + \frac{15\,x}{100}\right) = ₹\frac{115\,x}{100}$$

B takes a profit of 5% on this.

For C.P. ₹ 100, S.P. is ₹ 105

For C.P. ₹ $\dfrac{115\,x}{100}$, S.P. is ₹ $\dfrac{483\,x}{400}$

$$\frac{115\,x}{100} \times \frac{105}{100} = \frac{483\,x}{400}$$

Thus,

$$\frac{483}{400}\,x = 48{,}300$$

$$\therefore \qquad \frac{x}{400} = 100$$

$$\therefore \qquad x = 40{,}000$$

∴ A had purchased the car for ₹ 40,000.

Example 1.22 : *Rates of electricity charges increased by 25%. In order to keep expenses on electricity at the same level, by what per cent a family should reduce its consumption of electricity ?*

Solution : Let the original consumption of electricity be 100 units and rate be Re. 1 per unit.

∴   Original bill = 100×1 = ₹ 100

Due to the increase in the rates, new rate is ₹ 1.25 per unit.

Let the new consumption be x units.

∴   Revised expenditure = $1.25 \times x$ = $₹ \frac{5}{4} x$

As the family wants to maintain expenditure at original level,

$$\frac{5}{4} x = 100$$

∴ $x = 80$

Thus, the family should reduce its consumption by 20%.

Example 1.23 : *Price of sugar increased by 10% as a result of which a person gets 1 kg. less in ₹88. Find the original rate.*

Solution : Let the original rate be ₹ x per kg. In ₹ 88, the person would get $\frac{88}{x}$ kg.

Due to increase, the new rate is $x + \frac{x}{10} = \frac{11\,x}{10}$

∴ In ₹ 88, the person would get $\frac{88}{\frac{11\,x}{10}} = \frac{80}{x}$

By given information, $\frac{88}{x} - \frac{80}{x} = 1$

∴ $x = 8$

Thus, the original rate of sugar is ₹ 8 per kg.

Exercise 1.2

1. Fill in the blanks :

    (i) $\left(\frac{2}{5}\right)^{th}$ of an amount = ... % of that amount.

    (ii)   A person having income of ₹ 1,640 spends ₹ 1,230, therefore, his expenses are ...... % of his income.

    (iii) A student scores 42 marks out of 60. ∴ His percentage score is ......

    (iv)   A clerk writes 9 in place of 90. ∴ He committees an error of ...... %

2. Population of a city in a specific year was 80,000. There was rise of 10% for each of the next 3 years. Find the population at the end of 3 years.

3. A company declares a dividend of 20% on its equity shares. If a share whose face value is ₹ 10, is purchased for ₹ 30, what is the percentage return on the investment ?

4. Electricity rates increased by 5%, as a result of which there was a fall of 8% in the electricity consumption. If the total revenue of electricity board decreased by ₹ 6,80,000, find the revenue of the board.

5.   In an examination, a student got 28% of total marks and failed as he got 80 marks less than the total required. Another student passed by securing 38% of the total marks, when he had scored 20 marks more than the required total. How many marks were required for passing ?

6.   A person gave 20% of his total amount to his son. Of the remainder, he gave 50% to his wife and 30% of the remainder to each of three daughters. The remaining amount of ₹ 3,416 was donated to a charity trust. Find the total amount and share each one got.

7.   An alloy of gold and silver weighs 50 gm. It contains 80% gold. How much gold should be added to the alloy so that percentage of gold is increased to 90 ?

8.   Which investment gives a better return :
     5% stock at 75, subject to 30% income-tax or 4% stock at 90, tax free ?
     (Assume the face value of share to be ₹ 100.)

9.   Monthly incomes of A and B are in the ratio 9 : 7 and those of B and C in the ratio 3 : 2. If 10% of A's income exceeds 15% of C's income by ₹ 90, find the incomes of A, B and C.

10. A person invests some amount and loses 10% in the first year but in the next year, he gains 20% of what he had at the end of the first year. If there is an increase of ₹ 1,440 in his capital at the end of two years, find his original capital.

Answers 1.2

(1) (i) 40, (ii) 75, (iii) 70, (iv) 90.
(2) 1,06,480.
(3) 6.66
(4) 2 crores
(5) 360
(6) ₹ 85,400, ₹ 17,080, ₹ 34,160, ₹ 10,248
(7) 50 gm
(8) 5% stock at 75
(9) ₹ 4,050, ₹ 3,150, ₹ 2,100
(10) ₹ 18,000.

Miscellaneous Exercise 1

1.   Find the value of x, if (i) x : 3 = (x + 2) : 5, (ii) 20 : x = 4 : 5.

2.   The ratio of cost of a pencil to that of a pen is 2 : 3 while that of cost of a pen to a note book is 4 : 5. If the cost of a note book is ₹ 15, find the cost of a pencil.

3.   In 135 litres of milk mixed with water, the ratio of milk to water is 7 : 2. How much water should be added so that the ratio of milk to water becomes 5 : 2.

4.   Monthly incomes of A and B are in the ratio 6 : 7 and those of B and C are in the ratio 7 : 9. If A earns ₹ 36000, find the incomes of B and C.

5.   The ages of two friends are in the ratio 16 : 27 and the difference in their age is 5.5 years. Find their ages.

6. The monthly incomes of A and B are in the ratio 9 : 7 and those of B and C are in the ratio 7 : 5. If 10% of A's income exceeds 16% of C's income by ₹ 120. Find monthly incomes of A, B and C.

7. An ornament of gold weighing 28 gm contains gold and copper in the ratio 13 : 1. How much of pure gold must be added to it, so as to make the ratio of gold to copper 15 : 1 ?

8. Incomes of A, B and C are in the ratio 1 : 2 : 3 while their expenditures are in the ratio 2 : 3 : 4. If A saves one-third of his income, find the ratio of their savings.

9. The total salary bill of a company employing 25 men and 35 women is ₹ 7,80,000 per month. A man earns 20% more than a woman, on an average. What is monthly salary of each man and each woman ?

10. A student declared "Passed" if he secures 40% of the total marks. In an examination a student secured 24 marks and hence scored 4 marks more than that are necessary for passing. Find the maximum marks at the examination.

11. In a constituency of 80500 voters 60% cast their votes and in a straight contest between two candidates, the winner obtained 2600 votes more than his opponent. What is percentage of votes cast in favour of each candidate ?

12. The market share of an organisation in the year 2006 was 50%. After the takeover of another company, it increased by 40% in the year 2007. Due to competition by other organisation it reduced by 10% in the 2007 year 2008 as compared to the year 2007. What is the share in the year 2008 as compared to the year 2006 ?

13. The sales in 2 shopes were in the ratio 4 : 7. After advertising, sales in shop A increased by 10% and in B by 8%. The difference in new sales is 79 articles. Find the original sales.

14. A customer paid ₹ 330 for 220 telephone calls. The telephone charges increased by 10% what should be the percentage reduction in the number of calls in order to keep the expenditure over telephone sanu ?

15. A man spends 30% on house rent, 30% on food, 12% on clothing, 10% on fuel and the remaining on miscellaneous items from his salary. If he spends ₹ 1350 on miscellaneous items, what is his salary ? What is the amount spent under each heading ?

Answers

(1) (i) 3, (ii) 25   (2) ₹ 8   (3) 12 litres   (4) ₹ 4,2000, ₹ 5,4000   (5) 8 years, 13.5 years.   (6) A's ₹ 10800, B's ₹ 8400, C's ₹ 6000   (7) 4 gm   (8) 1 : 3 : 5   (9) ₹ 14,400, ₹ 12,000   (10) 50   (11) loser 47.31%, winner 52.69%   (12) 26% increase in the year 2008   (13) 100, 175   (14) reduction of 9.09% in number of telephone calls   (15) ₹ 2250, ₹ 2250, ₹ 900, ₹ 750.

Chapter **2**...

Profit and Loss

Contents ...

Learning Objectives:

Market price, Selling Price, Trade Discount, Cash Discount, Commission, Brokerage.

Chapter Objectives ...

To understand the concept and application of profit and loss in business.

Although you have studied this topic earlier in school, we give below certain terms and formulae :

2.1 Terms and Formulae

Cost Price (C.P.) (Oct. 2013) : The total amount paid for purchasing an article, transport charges, octroi etc. is called *cost price* of that article.

Marked Price (M.P.) (Oct. 2013, 2014) : The price of an article which is printed in the price list or catalogue so as to ensure that the consumer gets the article at that price is called *marked price* or *list price* or *catalogue price.*

Selling Price (S.P.) (Oct. 2013, 2014) : Total amount realised by selling an article is called *selling price* of that article.

2.2 Trade Discount and Cash Discount   (Oct. 2013, 2014)

Traders who buy goods in large quantities from manufacturers or wholesalers are generally given an allowance on the list price of the goods. This is known as *trade discount.*

The discount given by retailer to a purchaser is called *cash discount.*   **(Oct. 2013)**

Sometimes, a buyer may get benefit of both discounts. In such a case, cash discount should be calculated on the net value of the goods after deducting trade discount.

Thus, net selling price is the amount realised by the seller after giving discount. If no discount is given, then S.P. will be same as the M.P.

If S.P. is more than the C.P. then we say that a profit is realised in the transaction.

$$\boxed{\text{Profit} = \text{S.P.} - \text{C.P.}}$$

If C.P. is more than the S.P. then we say that a loss is incurred the transaction.

$$\boxed{\text{Loss } = \text{ C.P.} - \text{S.P.}}$$

While solving the problems, students are advised to remember the following points :

1. *Percentage profit or loss is always calculated on the C.P.*
2. *Commission or discount is always given on S.P.*
3. *Percentage profit or loss does not depend on number of articles sold (or purchased).*

Note : If an article costing ₹ x is sold at y% profit, its

$$\text{S.P.} = \left(\frac{100 + y}{100}\right) x$$

and if it is sold at y% loss,

$$\text{then its S.P.} = \left(\frac{100 - y}{100}\right) x.$$

Illustrative Examples

Type 1 : To find percent profit / loss when S.P. and C.P. are given.

Example 2.1 : *A scooter costing ₹ 12,000 was sold for ₹ 10,400 after two years. Find the percentage loss.*

Solution : Loss = ₹ 12,000 – 10,400 = ₹ 1,600

On C.P. ₹ 12,000 loss ₹ 1,600	$\dfrac{100}{12,000} \times 1,600$
∴ On C.P. ₹ 100, loss ₹ $\dfrac{40}{3}$	$= \dfrac{40}{3}$
∴ There is $\dfrac{40}{3}$ % loss	

Type 2 : To find S.P. when C.P. and per cent profit / loss is given.

Example 2.2 : *Goods worth ₹ 6,000 are purchased. What should be the S.P. to earn a profit of 12% ?*

Solution : To earn 12% profit, an article costing ₹ 100 should be sold for ₹ 112. Thus,

when C.P. is ₹ 100, S.P. is ₹ 112	$\dfrac{600}{100} \times 112$
∴ when C.P. is ₹ 6,000, S.P. is ₹ 6,720	$= 6,720$
∴ Goods should be sold for ₹ **6,720.**	

Type 3 : To find C.P. when S.P. and percent profit/loss is given

Example 2.3 : *A camera when sold for ₹ 1,674 resulted in a loss of 7%. What was the C.P. of the camera ?*

Solution : A loss of 7% means if the camera was purchased for ₹ 100, it is sold for ₹ 93. Thus,

when S.P. is ₹ 93, C.P. is ₹ 100	$\dfrac{1,674}{93} \times 100$
∴ when S.P. is ₹ 1,674, C.P. is ₹ 1,800	$= 1,800$
∴ C.P. of the camera was ₹ 1,800	

Type 4 : To find per cent profit/loss when some goods are sold at profit and remaining at loss.

Example 2.4 : *A book-seller purchased 800 copies of a book for ₹4,400. He sold 600 at a profit of 20% and remaining copies at a loss of 25%. Find per cent profit/loss in the total transaction.*

Solution : Since C.P. of 800 copies is ₹ 4,400 each copy costs ₹ 5.50.

$$\text{C.P. of 600 copies is } ₹ (600 \times 5.50) = ₹ 3,300$$

$$\text{S.P. of these copies at 20\% profit} = ₹ \left(100 + \frac{20}{100}\right) \times 3,300$$

$$= ₹ \left(\frac{6}{5} \times 3,300\right)$$

$$= ₹ (6 \times 660) = ₹ 3,960$$

$$\text{C.P. of remaining 200 copies} = ₹ (200 \times 5.50)$$

$$= ₹ 1,100$$

These copies are sold at a loss of 25%

$$\therefore \qquad \text{S.P.} = ₹ \left(\frac{100 - 25}{100}\right) 1,100$$

$$= ₹ \frac{3}{4} \times 1,100 = ₹ 825$$

$$\therefore \qquad \text{Total S.P.} = ₹ (3,960 + 825) = ₹ 4,785$$

$$\therefore \qquad \text{Profit} = \text{S.P.} - \text{C.P.}$$

$$= ₹ (4,785 - 4,400) = ₹ 385$$

when C.P. is ₹ 4,400, profit ₹ 385 $\dfrac{100}{4,400} \times 385 = 8.75$

∴   when C.P. is ₹ 100, profit ₹ 8.75

∴   There is 8.75% profit in the total transaction.

Type 5 : To decide the marked price of an article when C.P., per cent profit and per cent commission is known.

Example 2.5 : *A dealer in furniture buys chairs at ₹340 each. At what price should he mark them for sale, so that he may earn a profit of 25% after giving 15% discount ?*

Solution : Let the marked price of a chair be ₹ x.   **(April 2015)**

$$\therefore \qquad \text{Discount at 15\%} = \frac{15\,x}{100}$$

$$\therefore \qquad \text{Net S.P.} = x - \frac{15\,x}{100} = \frac{85\,x}{100} = \frac{17\,x}{20}$$

The chair costs ₹ 340 and 25% profit is to be realised.

∴   Net S.P. $= ₹ \left(\dfrac{100 + 25}{100}\right) \times 340 = ₹ \dfrac{5}{4} \times 340 = ₹ 425$

Thus, $\dfrac{17\,x}{20} = 425$

∴ $x = 425 \times \dfrac{20}{17} = 500$

∴   Marked price of the chair should be ₹ 500.

Note : In this problem, we have seen how to find the M.P. of an article when the following are known :

(a) C.P. of the article.

(b) % profit to be realised.

(c) % discount to be given.

However, we give below an elegant formula to find M.P. at once :

$$\text{M.P.} = \left[\dfrac{100 + (\% \text{ profit})}{100 - (\% \text{ discount})}\right] \times \text{C.P.}$$

Thus in the above problem,

$$\text{M.P.} = \left(\dfrac{100 + 25}{100 - 15}\right) \times 340 = \dfrac{125}{85} \times 340 = 125 \times 4 = 500 \text{ rupees.}$$

Type 6 : Miscellaneous

Example 2.6 : *The profit realised by selling an article at ₹ 49.50 is 7/4 times the profit realised by selling it At ₹ 45. Find the C.P. of the article.*

Solution : Let the C.P. of the article be ₹ x.

∴   Profit when it is sold at ₹ 45. $= ₹ (45 - x)$

∴   Profit when it is sold at ₹ 49.50 $= ₹ (49.50 - x)$

By given information,

$$49.50 - x = \dfrac{7}{4}(45 - x)$$

∴ $198 - 4\,x = 315 - 7\,x$

∴ $3\,x = 315 - 198 = 117$

∴ $x = 39$

∴   C.P. of the article is ₹ 39.

Example 2.7 : $\dfrac{1}{17}$ *th of the cost price is* $\dfrac{1}{22}$ *of S.P. 10% of the C.P. and 5% of the S.P. differ by 12. Find the C.P. and S.P.*

Solution : Let x be the C.P. and y be the S.P. of article.

$$\therefore \qquad \frac{x}{17} = \frac{y}{22}$$

i.e. $\qquad 22\,x = 17\,y$ ... (i)

Also, $\qquad \frac{x}{10} = \frac{y}{20} + 12$ (why ?)

$$\therefore \qquad 2\,x = y + 240$$ ... (ii)

From (i) and (ii)

$$22\,x - 17\,y = 0$$

and $\qquad 22\,x - 11\,y = 240 \times 11$

Subtracting, $\qquad 6\,y = 240 \times 11$

$$\therefore \qquad y = 440$$

Substituting in equation (ii)

$$x = 340$$

Example 2.8 : *A man sold two machines at ₹990 each. On one, he gained 10 % and on the other, he lost 10%. Find percentage profit or loss in the total transaction.* **(Oct. 2014)**

Solution : Let the C.P. of the machine on which he gained 10% be ₹ x.

By formula, $\qquad$ S.P. $= \dfrac{100 + 10}{100}$ (C.P.) $= \dfrac{11\,x}{10}$

$$\therefore \qquad \frac{11\,x}{10} = 990$$

$$\therefore \qquad x = 900$$

Let the C.P. of the machine on which he lost 10 % be ₹ y.

By formula, $\qquad$ S.P. $= \dfrac{100 - 10}{100}$ (C.P.) $= \dfrac{9\,y}{10}$

$$\therefore \qquad \frac{9\,y}{10} = 990$$

$$9y = 9900$$

$$y = \frac{9900}{9} = 1100$$

$\therefore \qquad$ Total C.P. $= ₹\,(900 + 1100) = ₹\,2000$

$\qquad$ Total S.P. $= 2 \times 990 = ₹\,1{,}980$

$\therefore \qquad$ Loss $= ₹\,20$

For C.P. of ₹ 2000, loss ₹ 20

$\therefore \quad$ For C.P. of ₹ 100, loss ₹ 1

Thus there is 1% loss in the total transaction.

Exercise 2.1

1. Fill in the blanks :
    (i)   The C.P. of an article should be .... time S.P. if there is 25% profit.
    (ii)   The S.P. of an article is $\dfrac{6}{5}$ times the C.P.

    ∴ The profit is .... %.

    (iii) An article when sold for ₹ 20, yields 25% profit. If it is sold for ₹ 24, the profit would be .... %
    (iv)   A man sold 12 pens for the C.P. of 15 pens.

    ∴ Profit is .... %.

    (v)   A dealer sells 25 chairs for the cost price of 20 chairs.

    ∴ He losses .... %.

    (vi)   If an article is marked 10% above C.P. and if 10% discount is given, there is ...... (profit, loss, neither profit nor loss).

2. A piano is sold for ₹ 42,500 at a loss of 15%. For how much should it have been sold to earn a profit of 15% ?

3. 60 litres of diesel is bought at ₹ 8 per litre. If 10% is lost in transit, at what rate should the remainder be sold to earn 10% on the whole ?

4. A dealer bought a T.V. set and music system for ₹ 50,000. He sold T.V. set at a gain of 20% and music system at a loss of 10%. He gained 2% on the whole. Find the C.P. of T.V. set.

5. The cost of printing 2000 copies of a book is as follows :
    Paper : ₹ 6,400
    Printing : ₹ 4,000 per thousand copies
    Binding : ₹ 280 per thousand copies.

    If the publisher allows 15% discount to the bookseller and realizes a profit of $27\dfrac{1}{2}$ %, what is the S.P. of each copy ?

6. A trader allows trade discount at 25% off the list price and further 5% for cash. How much an article costing ₹ 100, he should mark, so as to realise net profit of 14% on the cost ?

7. 10 kg tea of quality 'A' costing ₹ 70 per kg and 20 kg tea of quality B at ₹ 65 per kg are mixed. What should be the rate of selling the mixture to earn a profit of 20% ?

8. A manufacturer sells his article at 20% profit to the wholesaler. The wholesaler sells it to the retailer at 25% and the retailer sells it to the customer at 40% for ₹ 175. Find the C.P. to the manufacturer.

9. Material worth ₹ 5,000 was required for making 10 chairs. Labour charges were ₹ 2,500.

    What should be the S.P. of each chair to realise a profit of $33\dfrac{1}{3}$ % ?

10. A, B, C are partners in a business with capitals ₹ 50,000, ₹ 40,000 and ₹ 30,000 respectively gets 20% of the profit for managing the business and rest is divided in the ratio of their capitals. At the end of the year, C gets ₹ 4,000 more than B. Find the to profit and share of each.

11. A dealer purchased two machines for a total of ₹ 22,000. He sold one of them at a gain of 6% and the other at a loss of 5%, but then he finds that he has neither gain nor loss in the total transaction. Find C.P. of the machines.

12. An article when sold for ₹ 875 resulted in a loss of 30% ₹ 150 were paid towards transport and octroi. What was the original C.P. of the article ?

13. A merchant purchased rice worth ₹ 16,500. 1/3 of the rice was partly damaged and had to sold at 10% loss. Find the percentage of profit at which he should sell the remaining stock so that he may make 20% on the whole.

14. A VCR is sold at a profit of 20%. If the C.P. and S.P. would each be less by ₹ 1,000, there would be an increase in profit by $\frac{5}{3}$ %. Find the C.P. of the VCR.

15. A retailer is given 15% trade discount and further 5% cash discount. What is the list price of an article for which retailer pays ₹ 1,615 in cash ?

Answers 2.1

(1) (i) $\frac{4}{5}$ (ii) 20 (iii) 50 (iv) 25 (v) 20 (vi) loss.

(2) ₹ 57,500 (3) ₹ 9.78 (approx.) (4) ₹ 20,000 (5) ₹ 15 (6) ₹ 160

(7) ₹ 80 per kg (8) ₹ 83.33 (9) ₹ 1,000

(10) ₹ 30,000, ₹ 10,000, ₹ 8,000, ₹ 12,000 (11) ₹ 12,000, ₹ 10,000

(12) ₹ 1,100 (13) 35% (14) ₹ 13,000 (15) ₹ 2,000

2.3 Introduction to Commission and Brokerage　　　　　(April 2015)

Sale and purchase of various commodities form an important part of business and commerce. However, it is not possible for the manufacturer of goods to approach customers directly. The goods are generally sold through middlemen called agents or brokers. Our Government encourages industrialization in rural and backward areas. But then how to arrange the markets of such goods ? The middlemen look after this process. They are called wholesale dealers, retailers, agents etc. This arrangement suits the producer also since he can concentrate on the production of his goods.

The remuneration paid by manufacturer to the agent is called *commission*. The rate of commission can be fixed on the entire sale or it may vary after certain amount of sale (as an incentive). Sometimes, apart from commission, a fixed amount is also paid to the agent per month or per year.

In modern times, we come across various types of agents, involved in activities such as selling tea, arranging accommodation, arranging sale and purchase of shares etc.

A *commission agent* involved in selling of goods, normally gets commission from manufacturer only, but commission agents involved in selling shares or vehicles charge commission to both the parties, viz buyer and seller. This type of commission is called *brokerage*.   **(Oct. 2013, 2014)**

Note that commission is always paid on selling price.

Illustrative Examples

Example 2.9 : *A commission agent gets 12 % commission upto a sale of ₹30,000/- and 15 % on the sales exceeding ₹ 30,000/-. In a month, his sales are ₹ 67,000/- find his commission.*

Solution : The amount of commission on ₹ 30,000/- @ 12 % is ₹ 3600.

Since the total sale is ₹ 67,000/- the sale exceeding ₹ 30,000/- is worth ₹ 37,000/-.

The amount of commission on ₹ 37000/- @ 15 % is ₹ 4050.

Hence, the total commission earned by the agent is ₹ (3600 + 4050) = ₹ 7650/-.

Example 2.10 : *The rate of commission is increased from 5 % to 8 %; still the income of an agent remains the same. Find the percentage change in his sales.*

Solution : Suppose that originally the sale of the agent was ₹ 100/-.

∴   His commission, then @ 5 % was ₹ 5.

Let the sale of the agent, now be ₹ x.

∴   His commission, @ 8 % would be $\dfrac{8x}{100}$.

This is same as his earlier commission.

∴ $\dfrac{8x}{100} = 5$

∴ $x = \dfrac{500}{8} = 62.5$

Thus now his sale is ₹ 62.50.

∴   There is a reduction of (100 – 62.50) = 37.5 % in his sales.

Example 2.11 : *A commission agent is paid a fixed monthly income plus commission on the sales at a fixed percent of sales. If in two successive months, his incomes are ₹4406 and ₹ 5555 respectively and the sales in these two months are ₹ 46350 and ₹ 65,500, find his monthly salary and rate of commission.*

Solution : Let the monthly salary of the agent be ₹ x and rate of commission be y %.

∴   On the sale of ₹ 46350, his total income would be

     x + 463.5 y = 4406 (given)   ... (1)

Similarly, his income on sale of ₹ 65,500 would be

$$x + 655\,y = 5555 \qquad \qquad \ldots (2)$$

Subtracting (1) from (2)

$$191.5\,y = 1149$$

$$\therefore \qquad y = \frac{1149}{191.5} = 6$$

Putting this value in equation (2),

$$x + (655)\,(6) = 5555$$

$$\therefore \qquad x + 3930 = 5555$$

$$\therefore \qquad x = 5555 - 3930 = 1625$$

Thus, the monthly salary is 1625 and rate of commission is 6 %.

Another Method : Since monthly salary is fixed, the rise in income has taken place due to the rise in sales only.

$$\text{Rise in income} = ₹ (5555 - 4406) = ₹ 1149$$

$$\text{Rise in sales} = ₹ (65500 - 46350) = ₹ 19150$$

Thus, for a sale of ₹ 19150, the commission is ₹ 1149

∴   for a sale of ₹ 100 the rise is 6.

∴   Rate of commission is 6 %.

∴   On the sale of ₹ 65,500, the commission is ₹ 3930.

$$\therefore \qquad \text{Salary} = \text{Total income} - \text{Commission}$$

$$= 5555 - 3930$$

$$= ₹ 1625$$

Example 2.12 : *The salary of a salesman was reduced from ₹ 3000 to ₹ 2500 but his rate of commission increased from $2\frac{1}{2}$ % to 3 %. Due to this, his income increased by ₹ 100 than in previous month. Find his sales in the month.*

Solution : The salary of the salesman is decreased by ₹ 500/- still his income increases by ₹ 100. This means there is net rise of ₹ 600/- in his income. This has taken place due to rise in rate of commission which is $\frac{1}{2}$ %.

Thus $\frac{1}{2}$ % commission corresponds to sales of ₹ 600.

∴   100 % commission corresponds to sales of ₹ 1,20,000. Thus his sales in the month is ₹ 1,20,000.

Example 2.13 : *Three scooters were sold through an agent for ₹20,000/- ₹16,800 and ₹ 15,000 respectively. The rate of commission were 15 % on the first and 12 % on the second. If, on the whole, the agent received a commission of 14 %, find the commission received by him on the third scooter.* **(Oct. 2013)**

Solution : The commission on first scooter @ 15 % = 3000 and the commission on second scooter @ 12 % = $16800 \times \dfrac{12}{100}$ = 2016.

∴ Total of commission on two scooters = 5016.

The total S.P. of three scooters

$$= ₹ (20000 + 16800 + 15000)$$

$$= ₹ 51800$$

The agent receives a commission on this at 14 %.

∴ Total commission

$$= 51800 \times \dfrac{14}{100} = ₹ 7252$$

∴ Commission on third scooter

$$= ₹ (7252 - 5016) = ₹ 2236.$$

The third scooter is sold for ₹ 15000.

∴ Rate of commission is $100 \times \dfrac{2236}{15000}$

$$= 14.91 \% \text{ (approx.)}$$

Exercise 2.2

1. A merchant asked his agent to sell 350 shirts on 6 % commission and to invest the balance in purchasing sportswear. The agent charged 9 % commission on the purchase and earned ₹ 10,122/- on the two transactions. At what price was each shirt sold ?

2. A car was bought for ₹ 86,000/- and sold for ₹ 92,000/- through a broker who charges commission of 2 % on purchase and 3 % on sales. Find the total gain on the transactions.

3. An agent is paid commission at 8 % on cash sales and 6 % on credit sales made by him. If 35 % of his sales are for cash and rest on the credit, find the average rate of commission earned by him.

4. An agent was paid ₹ 19,440/- as commission on the sale of T.V. sets. If the rate of commission was 12 % and the price of each set, ₹ 10,800/-, how many sets did he sell ?

5. An agent buys 500 pens and sells them at 20 % profit. The agent charges commission of 10 % on the purchase and 20 % on the sales. If his total commission is ₹ 2040/-, find the S.P. of each pen.

6. A salesman is paid a fixed monthly salary plus a commission based as a percentage on the sales made by him. If on the sales of ₹ 64000/- and 72000/-, in two successive months, he receives in all ₹ 10650/- and 11450/- respectively find his monthly salary and rate of commission paid to him.

7. A house is sold at 25 % profit. The amount of brokerage at 3/4 % comes to ₹ 5250/-. Find the cost of the house. **(Oct. 2014)**

8. An insurance agent gets a commission of 25 % on the first years, 20 % on second years and 10 % on each of the subsequent years premia on a life insurance policy. If the rate of premium is ₹ 62.5 per thousand and amount of policy is 20,000/- find his total income for which 5 premia have been paid.

9. By selling a plot of land through an agent, the owner received. ₹ 7,12,500 net. If the agent charged commission at 5 %, what was the cost of the land ?

10. The income of a broker remains unchanged though rate of commission is increased from 8 % to 12 %. Find the percentage reduction in his business.

11. A trader offers 25 % discount on the catalogue price of a bicycle and yet makes 20 % profit. If he gains ₹ 200 per bicycle, what must be the catalogue price of the cycle ?

12. After deducting commission at $7\frac{1}{2}$ % on first ₹ 10,000 and 5 % on the balance of sales made by him, an agent remits ₹ 33950 to his principal. Find the value of goods sold by him.

Answers 2.2

(1) ₹ 200	(2) ₹ 1520	(3) 6.7 %
(4) 15	(5) ₹ 14.40	(6) ₹ 4250 and 10 %
(7) ₹ 5,60,000	(8) ₹ 937.50	(9) ₹ 7,50,000
(10) 33.33	(11) ₹ 1600	(12) ₹ 36,000

Miscellaneous Exercise 2

1. An article was sold at a loss of 3%. Had it been sold for ₹ 35 more, there would be a gain of 4%. Find the cost price of the article.

2. A man sells two plots for ₹ 98,560 each. On one, he gets 12% profit and on the other he loses 12%. Find his gain/loss percent.

3. At what price should an article costing ₹ 510 be sold so that after giving 15% cash discount, a profit of 20% is made ?

4. A man sold his radio-set at a loss of 20%. If he would have sold it for ₹ 90 more, his loss would have been only 10%. Find C.P. of the radio-set.

5. A dealer sells two qualities of washing powders at ₹ 18 and ₹ 14 per kg respectively making a profit of 8% and 5% respectively. How, should he mix the two if he desires to sell the mixture at ₹ 17 per kg to earn a profit of $10\frac{1}{2}$ % ?

6. At what price should goods costing ₹ 48,250 be sold though an agent so that after paying him a commission of $3\frac{1}{2}$ % on sales, a net gain of 20% be made ?

7. An agent is paid a commission of 12% on cash sales and 8% on credit sales. If on the sales of ₹ 1,75,000, the agent receives a total commission of ₹ 16,880, find sales made by him in cash and on credit.

8. The cost price of a book to the book seller is ₹ 75.00. What should be the marked price of the book, so that after allowing a discount of $7\frac{1}{2}$ % to the customer, he realizes a profit of 20%.

9. A salesman gets fixed monthly salary plus commission based on the sales. In two successive months he received ₹ 16000 and ₹ 16500. On the sales of ₹ 3,00,000 and ₹ 3,50,00 respectively. Find his monthly salary and the rate of commission.

10. An agent is paid commission at following rates : 16% on sand, 10% on wood and 8% on cement. If he sold these goods in the ratio 8 : 5 : 7, what is the average rate of commission ?

Answers

(1) ₹ 500   (2) 1.46% loss   (3) ₹ 720   (4) ₹ 900   (5) 8 : 5   (6) ₹ 60,000

(7) ₹ 72,000, ₹ 1,04,000   (8) ₹ 97.30 (approx.)   (9) ₹ 13,000, 1%   (10) 11.7%.

Chapter 3...

Interest

Contents ...

Learning Objectives:

Simple Interest, Compound Interest, Nominal and Effective Rates of Interest, Annuity, EMI.

Chapter Objectives ...

To understand difference between effective and nominal rate of interest. To enable to calculate EMI.

3.1 Simple Interest   (Oct. 2014)

When a person borrows some amount of money from other person or institution, the borrower has to pay some *charge* to the lender for the use of the money. This charge is called *interest*. The interest depends on two things viz., the period for which the money is borrowed and secondly the rate of interest.

The sum borrowed is called *principal*, time for which it is borrowed is called *term*. The total sum returned by the borrower i.e. principal together with interest is called *amount*.

When interest is calculated on the original principal, whatever the term may be, it is called *simple interest.*

If　P denotes the principal,

　　n denotes term in years,

　　r denotes rate of interest % per annum (p.c.p.a.),

　　I denotes simple interest,

then we have a simple formula $\boxed{I = \dfrac{Prn}{100}}$ 　　　　　　　　**(April 2015)**

amount A is found by adding interest to the principal.

Thus,　$A = P + I = P + \dfrac{Prn}{100} = P\left(1 + \dfrac{rn}{100}\right)$ 　　　　**(April 2015)**

Illustrative Examples

Example 3.1 : *Find the simple interest on ₹1,250 for $2\frac{1}{2}$ years at 12% p.a.*

Solution : Here $P = ₹\,1,250\,;\ n = \dfrac{5}{2}\,;\ r = 12$

Now,　　　　　　　$I = \dfrac{Prn}{100} = \dfrac{1250 \times \dfrac{5}{2} \times 12}{100} = 375$

∴　Simple interest is ₹ 375.

Example 3.2 : *A sum of money borrowed on 26ᵗʰ March is repaid on 7ᵗʰ June in the same year. If the simple interest paid is ₹75.75 at 7.5% p.a., find the sum borrowed.*

Solution : Let the sum borrowed be ₹ P.

Given $I = ₹\,75.75,\ r = 7.5$

Let us calculate the period for which interest is charged.

Month	March	April	May	June	Total
Number of days	5	30	31	7	73

∴　Interest is charged for 73 days.

$$n = \dfrac{73}{365} = \dfrac{1}{5} \text{ year} \qquad (\because 1 \text{ year} = 365 \text{ days})$$

Now,　　　　　　$I = \dfrac{Prn}{100}$

∴　　　　　$75.75 = \dfrac{P \times \dfrac{1}{5} \times 7.5}{100}$

∴　　　　　$P = 5050$

i.e.　Sum borrowed is ₹ 5,050.

Example 3.3 : *A sum of ₹4,800 amounted to ₹6,240 in a certain period. If the rate of simple interest is 12% p.a., find the period.*

Solution : Here P = ₹ 4,800; A = ₹ 6,240 ; r = 12% p.a. To find n.

Now,
$$A = P\left(1 + \frac{r\,n}{100}\right)$$

∴
$$6240 = 4800\left(1 + \frac{12\,n}{100}\right)$$

$$\frac{6240}{4800} = 1 + \frac{12\,n}{100}$$

∴
$$\frac{13}{10} = 1 + \frac{12\,n}{100}$$

∴
$$\frac{3}{10} = \frac{12\,n}{100}$$

∴
$$n = \frac{5}{2}$$

Thus, the period is 2.5 year.

Example 3.4 : *A sum of money doubles itself in 6 year. Find the rate of simple interest.*

Solution : Let P be the principal.

∴   Amount A = 2P ; n = 6. To find r.

Now,
$$A = P\left(1 + \frac{r\,n}{100}\right)$$

∴
$$2P = P\left(1 + \frac{6\,r}{100}\right)$$

∴
$$2 = 1 + \frac{6\,r}{100}$$

∴
$$1 = \frac{6\,r}{100}$$

∴
$$r = 16\frac{2}{3}$$

Thus the rate of interest is $16\frac{2}{3}$ % p.a.

Example 3.5 : *What sum will amount to ₹3,296 in 4 months at 9% p.a. simple interest ?*

Solution : Here A = ₹ 3,296 ; r = 9 ; $\left(n = \frac{4}{12} = \frac{1}{3}\right)$. To find P.

∴
$$A = P\left(1 + \frac{r\,n}{100}\right)$$

∴
$$3296 = P\left(1 + \frac{9 \times \frac{1}{3}}{100}\right)$$

$$\therefore \qquad 3296 = P\left(\frac{103}{100}\right)$$

$$\therefore \qquad P = \frac{3296 \times 100}{103} = 3200$$

∴   Principal is ₹ 3,200.

Example 3.6 : *A person borrows ₹15,000, partly at 10% and remaining at 12%. If at the end of $2\frac{1}{2}$ years, he pays a total simple interest ₹4,050, how much did he borrow at each rate ?*

Solution : Suppose he borrows ₹ x at 10%.

∴   He borrows ₹ (15,000 – x) at a 12%

$$\therefore \quad \text{Total S.I. for } 2\tfrac{1}{2} \text{ years} = \frac{x \times \frac{5}{2} \times 10}{100} + \frac{(15000 - x) \times \frac{5}{2} \times 12}{100}$$

$$= \frac{25\,x + 30\,(15000 - x)}{100}$$

$$= \frac{25\,x + 30 \times 15000 - 30\,x}{100} = 4500 - \frac{5\,x}{100}$$

But total S.I. is 4,050.

$$\therefore \qquad 4500 - \frac{5\,x}{100} = 4050$$

$$\therefore \qquad \frac{5\,x}{100} = 450$$

$$\therefore \qquad x = 9,000$$

Thus he has borrowed ₹ 9,000 at 10% and hence ₹ 6,000 at 12%.

Example 3.7 : *S.I. on a sum at 4% p.a. for $1\frac{1}{2}$ years is less than that on the same sum at the rate of $3\frac{1}{4}$ % p.a. for $2\frac{1}{2}$ years by ₹38.25. Find the sum.*

Solution : Let P be the sum. S.I. on P at 4% for $\dfrac{3}{2}$ years is

$$\frac{P\,n\,r}{100} = \frac{P \times \frac{3}{2} \times 4}{100} = \frac{6\,P}{100} = I_1 \text{ (say)}$$

S.I. on P at $3\frac{1}{4}$ % for $\dfrac{5}{2}$ years is

$$\frac{P\,n\,r}{100} = \frac{P \times \frac{5}{2} \times \frac{13}{4}}{100} = \frac{65\,P}{800} = I_2 \text{ (say)}$$

It is given that $I_1 < I_2$.

Moreover, $I_2 - I_1 = 38.25$

$\therefore$ $\dfrac{65\,P}{800} - \dfrac{6\,P}{100} = 38.25$

$\therefore$ $\dfrac{65\,P - 48\,P}{800} = 38.25$

$\therefore$ $17\,P = 38.25 \times 800$

$\therefore$ $P = 1800$

Example 3.8 : *A certain sum of money is deposited in a bank annually for 5 years at 8% p.a. S.I. If at the end of 5 years, the amount standing to the credit of the depositor is ₹49,600, then find the amount deposited each year.*

Solution : Suppose the person deposits ₹ x every year. Then he will get interest on ₹ x deposited in the first year for 5 years, interest on ₹ x deposited in the second year for 4 years and so on. In other words, he will get interest on ₹ x for (5 + 4 + 3 + 2 + 1) years i.e. for 15 years.

$\therefore$ $\text{S.I.} = \dfrac{P\,n\,r}{100} = \dfrac{x \times 15 \times 8}{100} = \dfrac{12\,x}{10}$

Now,   Amount $= P + I$

$\therefore$ $49,600 = 5\,x + \dfrac{12\,x}{10}$

$\therefore$ $49,600 = \dfrac{62\,x}{10}$

$\therefore$ $x = 8,000$

$\therefore$ The person deposits ₹ 8,000 each year.

Exercise 3.1

1. Find the simple interest on ₹ 1,000 at 6% p.a. for 5 months.

2. What sum of money put at simple interest for two years at 8% p.a. will amount to ₹ 1,276 ?

3. In how many years will ₹ 35,000 will amount to ₹ 87,500 at 10% p.a. simple interest ?

4. Suresh borrowed ₹ 1,750 from Dinesh for 5 months. Dinesh charged him ₹ 43.75 as simple interest. At what rate was the interest reckoned ?

5. Mahesh invested ₹ 2,000 for 3 years and ₹ 3,550 for 5 years at the same rate of simple interest. If he received a total simple interest of ₹ 893.75, find the rate of interest.

6. A sum of money amounts to ₹ 10,400 in 6 years and ₹ 11,200 in 8 years. Find the sum and rate of interest.

7. A sum of money doubles itself in 6 years at certain rate of interest. In how many years would it triple if the rate of interest is increased by $3\frac{1}{3}$ p.a. ?

8. How should a sum of ₹ 25,000 be divided between two boys aged 15 years and 10 years now, so that at the age of 25 they would get equal amounts, interest being charged at 8% p.a. ?

9. A certain sum amounted to ₹ 5,750 in $2\frac{1}{2}$ years at 6% p.a. Find after how many more years it will amount to ₹ 6,200.

10. A person deposits ₹ 100 on the 1st day of each month throughout the year. If the bank pays 8% p.a. rate of interest, what amount will he get at the end of year ?

11. A bank increased the rate of interest on saving bank accounts from 3.5% p.a. to 4% p.a. Sumit withdrew ₹ 1570 from his account and as a result, in that half of the year his interest was reduced by ₹ 20.40. How much amount had he in his account at the beginning ?

12. A person borrowed ₹ 20,000 from a bank, part of it was borrowed at 8% p.a. and part of it was borrowed at 12% p.a. simple interest. At the end of 2.5 years he paid an interest of ₹ 4240 on the whole sum. Find the sum borrowed at 12%.

13. The simple interest on ₹ 1900 for 4 years exceeds the simple interest on ₹ 1200 for the same period by ₹ 308. Find the rate of interest.

14. A person brought a shares of ₹ 100 for ₹ 250. Off 20% divided was declared on that share, what is the rate of interest realised on his investment.

Answers 3.1

1.	25	2.	₹ 1,100	3.	5/4 years
4.	6% p.a.	5.	3.76% p.a.	6.	₹ 8,000, 5% p.a.
7.	5/6	8.	₹ 13,750 , ₹ 11,250	9.	$1\frac{1}{2}$
10	₹ 1,252	11.	₹ 3,840	12.	₹ 2,400
13.	11% p.a.	14.	8%		

3.2 Compound Interest

When interest is added to the principal at the end of each period, and the total so obtained is treated as the principal for the next period, then the interest so obtained is called *compound interest.*

For example, suppose Rasiklal starts an industry by taking a loan of ₹ 50,000 from a bank at 16% p.a. Bank charges interest quarterly. However, Rasiklal is not able to pay interest at the end of each quarter. Naturally, the bank will add the interest at the end of each quarter to the principal. Let us find how much Rasiklal has to pay towards interest at the end of 1st year.

$$\text{Interest on ₹ 50,000 for } 1^{st} \text{ quarter } = ₹ 2,000$$

$$\text{Principal for } 2^{nd} \text{ quarter } = 50,000 + 2,000$$

$$= 52,000$$

$\therefore$ $\text{Interest on ₹ 52,000 for } 2^{nd} \text{ quarter } = 2,080$

$\therefore$ $\text{Principal for } 3^{rd} \text{ quarter } = 52,000 + 2,080$

$$= 54,080$$

$\therefore$ $\text{Interest on ₹ 54,080 for } 3^{rd} \text{ quarter } = 2,163.20$

$\therefore$ $\text{Principal for } 4^{th} \text{ quarter } = 54,080 + 2163.20$

$$= 56,243.20$$

$\therefore$ $\text{Interest on ₹ 56,243.20 for } 4^{th} \text{ quarter } = 2249.73$

$\therefore$ $\text{Total interest that Rasiklal has to pay } = ₹ (2,000 + 2,080 + 2,163.20 + 2,249.73)$

$$= ₹ 8,472.93$$

However, it is not necessary to find principal for each period while solving problems.

If P is the principal, r the rate of interest p.a. and n, the period in years then amount A at the end of n years is given by

$$\boxed{A = P\left(1 + \frac{r}{100}\right)^n}$$ **(April 2015)**

Then the compound interest is given by

$$\text{C.I.} = A - P$$

$$= P\left(1 + \frac{r}{100}\right)^n - P$$

$$= P\left[\left(1 + \frac{r}{100}\right)^n - 1\right]$$

Thus, $$\boxed{\text{C.I.} = P\left\{\left(1 + \frac{r}{100}\right)^n - 1\right\}}$$ **(April 2015)**

Note :

1. In general, the compound interest on a given sum will be greater than the simple interest on the same sum for the same period. (rate of interest being same)

2. In case of calculation of compound interest, it is convenient to find amount first and then C.I. is given by subtracting principal from the amount.

3. As we have to find powers of $\left(1+\dfrac{r}{100}\right)^n$, use of log tables/calculators will be helpful.

4. The S.I. and C.I. for 1st year are same when interest is calculated annually.

Compound interest when period is different from a year :

Sometimes the period at the end of which interest is calculated is different from a year. It may be a month, a quarter, half year. In such a case, the same formula for amount viz.

$$A = P\left(1 + \frac{r}{100}\right)^n \text{ is valid.}$$

However, then　　　　　n = Number of periods

　　　　　　　　　　r = Rate of compound interest % *per period.*

For example, if we want to find compound interest on ₹ 1000 at 10 % p.a. for 3 years when interest is compounded half yearly,

$$n = \text{Number of periods} = 6$$

$$r = \frac{10}{2} = 5$$

then,　　　　　$A = P\left(1+\dfrac{r}{100}\right)^n = 1000\left(1+\dfrac{5}{100}\right)^6$

$$= 1341$$

Compound Interest on a given sum in the nth year :

We know that the compound interest for the nth year will be given by

$$I_n = \text{C.I. in n years} - \text{C.I. in (n – 1) years}$$

$$= P\left\{\left(1+\frac{r}{100}\right)^n - 1\right\} - P\left\{\left(1+\frac{r}{100}\right)^{n-1} - 1\right\}$$

$$= P\left\{\left(1+\frac{r}{100}\right)^n - \left(1-\frac{r}{100}\right)^{n-1}\right\}$$

$$= P\left(1+\frac{r}{100}\right)^{n-1}\left\{\left(1+\frac{r}{100}\right) - 1\right\} \qquad \left\{\begin{array}{l} \because x^n - x^{n-1} \\ = x^{n-1}(x-1) \end{array}\right\}$$

$$= P\left(1+\frac{r}{100}\right)^{n-1}\left(\frac{r}{100}\right)$$

Thus,　　　　　$$\boxed{I_n = \frac{Pr}{100}\left(1+\frac{r}{100}\right)^{n-1}}$$

3.3 Problems on Growth and Decay

The formula for C.I. can also be used in the cases of uniform periodical increase or decrease at a constant rate. They are known as problems on growth and decay respectively.

For the problems on growth, the formulae for amount viz.

$A = P\left(1 + \dfrac{r}{100}\right)^n$ gives the total quantity at the end of n periods when the rate of growth is r % per period.

For example, Consider the problem. "The population of a town is 40,000 and increases every year 1.8 % of the population at the beginning of that year. Find the population after 15 years".

Since increase in population in each year is taken as the base for next year, this is an illustration of compounding.

Here, $\qquad P = 40{,}000, \quad r = 1.8, \quad n = 15$

Now, $\qquad A = P\left(1 + \dfrac{r}{100}\right)^n$

$$= 40{,}000\left(1 + \dfrac{1.8}{100}\right)^{15} = 40{,}000\,(1.018)^{15}$$

$$= 40{,}000 \times 1.3 = 52{,}000$$

In the case of problems on decay, we replace $\dfrac{r}{100}$ by $-\dfrac{r}{100}$ in the formula for compound interest.

Thus for depreciated value at the end of n periods, we use the formula

$$V = P\left(1 - \dfrac{r}{100}\right)^n$$

For example, a machine depreciates at rate of 20 % on the reducing balance. The original cost was ₹ 1,00,000, find its cost after $7\dfrac{1}{2}$ years.

Here initial value $\qquad P = 1{,}00{,}000, \quad r = 20, \quad n = \dfrac{15}{2}$

Now, $\qquad V = P\left(1 - \dfrac{r}{100}\right)^n$

$$= 1{,}00{,}000\left(1 - \dfrac{20}{100}\right)^{15/2}$$

$$= 1{,}00{,}000\,(0.8)^{15/2} = 1{,}00{,}000\,(0.1876)$$

$$= ₹\,18{,}760$$

Illustrative Examples

Example 3.9 : *Find the compound interest on ₹10,000 for 4 years at 5 % p.a.*

Solution : Here P = 10,000,　r = 5,　n = 4,　To find C.I.

The amount of the end of 4 years is given by,

$$A = P\left(1+\frac{r}{100}\right)^n = 10,000\left(1+\frac{5}{100}\right)^4$$

$$= 10,000\ (1.05)^4 = ₹\ 12,155$$

∴　　　　C.I. $= A - P = ₹\ 2,155$

Example 3.10 : *What sum will amount to ₹2000 in 3 years at 6 % p.a. compound interest ?*

Solution : Here A = 2,000,　r = 6,　n = 3,　To find P.

Now,　　　　$A = P\left(1+\frac{r}{100}\right)^n$

$$2000 = P\left(1+\frac{6}{100}\right)^3$$

$$2000 = P\ (1.06)^3$$

∴　　　　$P = \dfrac{2000}{(1.06)^3}$

∴　　　　$P = ₹\ 1679.24$

Example 3.11 : *Find in what time a sum of money will double itself at 8 % p.a. compound interest.*

Solution : Let P be the sum which doubles itself in n years at 8 % p.a.

We have,　　　　$A = P\left(1+\frac{r}{100}\right)^n$

∴　　　　$2\,P = P\left(1+\frac{8}{100}\right)^n$

∴　　　　$2 = (1.08)^n$

∴　　　　$\log 2 = n\ \log 1.08$

∴　　　　$\dfrac{0.3010}{0.0334} = n$

i.e.　　　　$n = 9\ \text{(approx.)}$

Example 3.12 : *Find the rate % p.a. at which a sum of money trebles itself in 12 years.*

Solution : Let P be the sum which trebles itself in 12 years, at r % p.a.

We have　　　　$A = P\left(1+\frac{r}{100}\right)^n$

∴　　　　$3\,P = P\left(1+\frac{r}{100}\right)^{12}$

$\therefore \qquad\qquad 3 = \left(1+\dfrac{r}{100}\right)^{12}$

$\therefore \qquad\qquad \log 3 = 12 \log\left(1+\dfrac{r}{100}\right)$

$\therefore \qquad\qquad 0.4771 = 12 \log\left(1+\dfrac{r}{100}\right)$

$\therefore \qquad \log\left(1+\dfrac{r}{100}\right) = \dfrac{0.4771}{12} = 0.0398$

$\therefore \qquad\qquad 1+\dfrac{r}{100} = \text{Antilog } (0.0398) = 1.096$

$\therefore \qquad\qquad \dfrac{r}{100} = 0.096$

$\therefore \qquad\qquad r = 9.6$

$\therefore$ Required rate is 9.6 % p.a.

Example 3.13 : *Find the amount of ₹ 5,000 at 12 % p.a. in 4 years compounded quarterly.*

Solution : As the rate of interest is 12 % p.a. and period is a quarter,

$$r = \text{Rate \% per period} = 3$$
$$n = \text{Number of periods (quarters)} = 16$$

Now, $\qquad\qquad A = P\left(1+\dfrac{r}{100}\right)^{n}$

$$= 5,000 \left(1+\dfrac{3}{100}\right)^{16}$$
$$= 5000 \,(1.03)^{16}$$
$$= 5000 \,(1.6047)$$
$$= ₹ \,8023.53$$

Example 3.14 : *The difference between the simple and compound interest on a certain sum of money for 4 years at 6 % p.a. is ₹168.75. What is the sum ?*

Solution : Let the sum be ₹ 100

$\therefore \qquad\qquad \text{S.I.} = \dfrac{100 \times 6 \times 4}{100} = ₹ \,24$

By compound interest,

$$A = P\left(1+\dfrac{r}{100}\right)^{n}$$

$$= 100\left(1+\dfrac{6}{100}\right)^{4} = 100\,(1.06)^{4} = 126.25$$

∴   Interest = ₹ 26.25

∴ Difference between C.I. and S.I.

$$= ₹ 26.25 - ₹ 24 = ₹ 2.25$$

For difference ₹ 2.25, the sum = ₹ 100

∴ For difference ₹ 168.75, the sum

$$= \left(\frac{100 \times 168.75}{2.25}\right) = ₹ 7{,}500$$

Example 3.15 : *Find the C.I. on ₹5,600 for 4th year when the rate of interest is 8 % p.a.*

Solution : Here P = ₹ 5,600, r = 8,

$$\text{C.I. for 4}^{th}\text{ year} = A_4 - A_3 \quad (A_n = \text{Amount at the end of n years})$$

$$= P\left(1 + \frac{r}{100}\right)^4 - P\left(1 + \frac{r}{100}\right)^3$$

$$= P\left(1 + \frac{r}{100}\right)^3 \left[1 + \frac{r}{100} - 1\right]$$

$$= \frac{Pr}{100}\left(1 + \frac{1}{100}\right)^3$$

$$= \frac{5600 \times 8}{100}\left(1 + \frac{8}{100}\right)^3$$

$$= 448\,(1.2597) = 564.35$$

∴ Interest in the 4th year is ₹ 564.35.

Example 3.16 : *A sum of money amounts to ₹2812.16 in 3 years and to ₹3041.50 in 5 years, find the sum and rate of interest.*

Solution : Given $A_3 = P\left(1 + \frac{r}{100}\right)^3 = 2812.16$ ... (1)

$$A_5 = P\left(1 + \frac{r}{100}\right)^5 = 3041.50 \qquad\qquad ... (2)$$

∴ $\dfrac{A_5}{A_3} = \left(1 + \dfrac{r}{100}\right)^2 = \dfrac{3041.50}{2812.16} = 1.08155$

∴ $1 + \dfrac{r}{100} = \sqrt{1.08155} = 1.04$

∴ $1 + \dfrac{r}{100} = 1.04$

∴ $\dfrac{r}{100} = 0.04$

∴ $r = 4$

Now

$$P\left(1 + \frac{r}{100}\right)^3 = 2812.16 \qquad\qquad \text{[From equation (1)]}$$

∴ $$P\left(1 + \frac{4}{100}\right)^3 = 2812.16$$

∴ $$P = \frac{2812.16}{(1.04)^3} = 2500$$

The principal is ₹ 2500 and rate of interest is 4 % p.a.

Example 3.17 : *The depreciation on a machine is charged at 15 % p.a. on the diminishing balance method. In how many years will the original value of ₹ 1,50,000 be reduced to its scrap value estimated at 10 % of the cost ?*

Solution : Since the original value of the machine is ₹ 1,50,000, scrap value is ₹ 15,000 (10 %).

Suppose that it takes n years for the machine to reduce it to scrap value.

Now, $$V = P\left(1 - \frac{r}{100}\right)^n$$

i.e. $$15,000 = 1,50,000\left(1 - \frac{15}{100}\right)^n$$

∴ $$\frac{1}{10} = (0.85)^n$$

∴ $$\log\left(\frac{1}{10}\right) = n \log (0.85)$$

$$\overline{1}.0000 = n\,(\overline{1}.9294) = n\,(-0.0706)$$

∴ $$-1 = -0.0706\,n$$

∴ $$n = \frac{1000}{706} = 14.16 \approx 14 \text{ years and 2 months.}$$

Exercise 3.2

1. Find the C.I. on ₹ 2750 at $4\frac{1}{2}$ % p.a. for 6 years.

2. A person borrows ₹ 6,000 for $3\frac{1}{2}$ years at $7\frac{1}{2}$ % p.a. C.I. How much does he replay ?

3. What sum will amount to ₹ 12167 in 5 years at 4% p.a. C.I. ?

4. Find the amount at the end of 5 years of a sum of ₹ 2,000 at 6% p.a. payable half yearly.

5. How long would a sum of money take to double itself, if allowed to accumulated at $7\frac{1}{2}$ % p.a. ?

6. Find the rate of C.I. at which a sum of money triples itself in 8 years.

7. If the population of a town increased every year by 2.1% of the population at the beginning of that year, in how many years will the total increase of population be 20% ?

8. The difference between S.I. and C.I. on a sum of money for 2 years is ₹ 15. The S.I. on the same sum for 4 years is ₹ 1,200. Find the sum and rate of interest.

9. A man left for his 2 sons aged 10, 12 years ₹ 15,000 and ₹ 12,000 respectively. The money is invested in 6% and 9% compound interest respectively. The sons will receive the amounts when each of them attains the age of 20 years. Which one will receive larger amount ?

10. A sum of money amounts to ₹ 5681.15 in 5 years and ₹ 6766.33 in 8 years.

11. Find the C.I. on ₹ 6,200 at $4\frac{1}{2}$ % p.a. in the 3rd year.

12. A machine is depreciated at rate of 20% on the reducing balance. The original cost was ₹ 1,00,000 and the ultimate scrap value was ₹ 30,000. Find the effective life of machine.

13. A machine depreciated 10% p.a. for the first two years and then 7% p.a. for the next 3 years, depreciation being calculated on the diminishing value. If the value of the machine be ₹ 10,000 initially, then find the average rate of depreciation and the depreciated value of the machine at the end of the 5th year.

14. A person invested ₹ 4 lac in a business. His money grew at the compound rate of 10% for first 5 years and then there was a decline at the compound rate of 10%. What shall be the amount at the end of 10 years ? Is it same as the invested amount ?

15. A person wants to deposit ₹ 1 lac quarterly rate of interest is 9.10% and annual rate of interest is 9.40%. Which scheme will give him better yield ?

16. A bank payes 6.25% interest on monthly recurring deposit scheme. What is effective rate of interest ?

Answers 3.2

1. ₹ 831.22	2. ₹ 7728.24	3. ₹ 10,000
4. ₹ 2687.83	5. 9.55 years	6. 14.8% p.a.
7. 8.7 years	8. ₹ 6,000, 5% p.a.	

9.   Younger son will receive larger amount

10. ₹ 4245.29, 6% p.a.   11. ₹ 304.68   12. 5.4 years

13. Rate 8.2%, value ₹ 6515

14. ₹ 380396.02 less than the original

15. Quarterly rate of interest gives him ₹ 15 more   16. 6.43%

3.4 Simple Annuities

Introduction : We know that loans are made available by banks as well as other financial companies for the purchase of household items like furniture, T.V. sets, refrigerator to costlier items like flats, luxury cars etc.

In such cases the repayment of loan is made by the borrower in installments.

Suppose that an ownership flat whose cash down price is ₹ 50 lakhs can be purchased by paying ₹ 10 lakh cash down and remaining amount in monthly instalments of ₹ 50000 for 10 years.

Thus here is a series of payments made at equal intervals. Such a series is called an *annuity*.

Common examples of annuity are insurance premia, recurring deposit etc.

Some definitions and terms

We have just learnt that an annuity is a series of payments made at equal intervals. The payments may be equal or different. When payments are equal, the annuity is called "*Simple Annuity*". (We shall study simple annuities only).

The time interval between two successive payments is called *period* of the annuity. The period may be a month, a quarter, six months or even an year.

In the above mentioned example of purchase of flat, the period is one month. The payments are to be made for 10 years. This span is called *status* of the annuity. When this span is fixed, as in the present case, the annuity is called certain annuity. Sometimes this span is uncertain.

For example, pension of a retired employee. Here the paying authority (or institution) does not know how long it will have to pay pension to the employee. Such an annuity is called *annuity contingent.*

The amount of loan ₹ 40 lakhs is called *present value* of the annuity.

Since the purchaser does not have this amount ready with him, he has to take loan. This loan is repaid alongwith compound interest. In the present case this amount is ₹ 60 lakhs (₹ 50000 × 120). This amount is called *amount of the annuity.*

Perpetuity : In some annuities, the payments are made forever.

For example, academic prizes etc. such an annuity is called **perpetuity**.

3.5 Immediate Annuity and Annuity Due

We have already stated that some common examples of annuity are recurring deposits, insurance premia, repayment of loan etc. In some of these cases like insurance premia, recurring deposits the payment is made at the beginning of each period while in case of repayment of loan, instalment is paid at the end of each period.

If payments of an annuity are made at the beginning of each period then the annuity is called *annuity due* and when payments are made at the end of each period, then the annuity is called *immediate annuity*. Thus, recurring deposit is an example of annuity due and house rent is example of immediate annuity if rent is paid at the end of every month.

We shall study problems of immediate annuity only, however formulae for annuity due are also given at the end.

Students are advised to use calculators for solving problems in annuities.

3.6 Formulae for Amount & Present Value of Simple Immediate Annuity

Let,　　　　　　P : Present value of immediate annuity

　　　　　　　　x : Periodic installment

　　　　　　　　n : Number of installments

　　　　　　　　i : Rate of (compound) interest per rupee per period

Then　　　　$$P = \frac{x}{i} \left\{ 1 - (1 + i)^{-n} \right\}$$

If A denotes the amount of an immediate annuity then,

$$A = \frac{x}{i} \left\{ (1 + i)^{n} - 1 \right\}$$

3.7 Relation between Amount and Present Value of Immediate Annuity

$$\frac{1}{P} - \frac{1}{A} = \frac{i}{x}$$

3.8 Present Value of a Perpetuity

$$P = \frac{x}{i}$$

Remark : Since in most cases, amount of loan P, rate of interest i and number of installments through which loan is to be repaid are known the following formula helps us in deciding x, the installment.

$$P = \frac{x}{i} [1 - (1 + i)^{-n}]$$

Illustrative Examples

Example 3.18 : *Find the amount of an immediate annuity of ₹1500 per year payable for 12 years at 10 % p.a.*

Solution : Here

$$x = \text{Periodic installment} = 1500, \ n = 12, \ i = 0.1$$

∴ Amount of the annuity

$$A = \frac{x}{i}\{(1 + i)^n - 1\} = \frac{1500}{0.1}\{(1.1)^{12} - 1\}$$

$$= 15000\{3.1384 - 1\}$$

$$= 32076.42$$

Example 3.19 : *A company wishes to set aside a certain sum at the end of each year to create a sinking fund. If it should amount to 10 lakhs in 10 years at 12 % p.a., find the sum to be set aside each year.*

Solution : Here,

Amount of annuity A= 10,00,000

No. of installments n = 10

Rate of interest per rupee i = 0.12 (per year)

To find x.

Now
$$A = \frac{x}{i}[(1 + i)^n - 1]$$

∴
$$10,00,000 = \frac{x}{0.12}[(1.12)^{10} - 1]$$

∴
$$10,00,000 \times \frac{12}{100} = x[3.1058 - 1]$$

∴
$$1,20,000 = 2.1058 \ x$$

∴
$$x = \frac{1,20,000}{2.1058} = 56985.47$$

Hence the company should set aside ₹ 56985 per year for the requisite sinking fund.

Example 3.20 : *A sewing machine worth ₹5000 is purchased on installment basis under five equal annual installments including compound interest at 10 % p.a. Find the amount of installment.*

Solution : It is clear that ₹ 5000/- is the present value of the annuity under consideration.

Thus
$$P = 5000, \ n = 5, \ i = 0.1$$

To find x.

Now, $\quad P = \frac{X}{i} \{1 - (1 + i)^{-n}\}$

∴ $\quad 5000 = \frac{X}{0.1} \{1 - (1.1)^{-5}\}$

∴ $\quad 500 = x \{1 - 0.6209\}$

∴ $\quad 0.3790\, x = 500$

∴ $\quad x = 1319.26$

∴ Amount of installment is ₹ 1319 / -.

Example 3.21 : *What is the purchase price of a perpetuity of ₹ 1500 per year at 10 %* p.a ?

Solution : The purchase price of a perpetuity means the present value of the perpetuity P.

Here $\quad x = 1500$ and $r = 10\,\%$ p.a.

∴ $\quad i = 0.1$

For a perpetuity, present value

$$P = \frac{X}{i}$$

$$= \frac{1500}{0.1}$$

$$= 15000$$

Example 3.22 : *ULIP is a scheme of Unit Trust of India under which a person can deposit upto ₹ 10,000/- per year. The status of ULIP is 10 years or 15 years. A person takes membership of ULIP by paying ₹ 10,000/- for 10 years. Assuming the rate of compound interest to be 12 %, find the amount he will receive at the end of 10 years.*

Solution : Here $x = 10,000$

$$n = 10$$

$$i = 0.12$$

To find amount A

Now, $\quad A = \frac{X}{i} [(1 + i)^n - 1]$

$$= \frac{10000}{0.12} [(1.12)^{10} - 1]$$

$$= 83333.33 [3.1058 - 1]$$

$$= ₹ 175483$$

Example 3.23 : *The present value of an annuity of ₹3600 per year is ₹12,000 and its amount at the same rate for the same period is ₹15000. Find the rate of interest.*

Solution : Here, we are given that

$$\text{Amount A} = 15,000$$

$$\text{Present value} = 12,000$$

$$\text{Installment x} = 3,600$$

To find r, rate % p.a. we have,

$$\frac{1}{P} - \frac{1}{A} = \frac{i}{x}$$

$$\therefore \quad \frac{1}{12000} - \frac{1}{15000} = \frac{i}{3600}$$

$$\therefore \quad 1000\left[\frac{1}{12000} - \frac{1}{15000}\right] = 1000 \times \frac{i}{3600}$$

$$\therefore \quad \frac{1}{12} - \frac{1}{15} = \frac{10}{36}i$$

$$\therefore \quad \frac{5-4}{60} = \frac{10}{36}i$$

$$\therefore \quad \frac{1}{60} = \frac{10}{36}I$$

$$\therefore \quad i = \frac{36}{600} = \frac{6}{100}$$

This is rate per rupee per period.

$$\therefore \quad \text{Rate \% per period} = \frac{6}{100} \times 6 = 6$$

Example 3.24 : *A person deposits ₹20,000 in a bank at 15 % p.a. to give scholarship to needy students every year. Find the amount of yearly scholarship.*   **(Oct. 2014, April 2015)**

Solution : Since the amount of ₹ 20,000 is deposited forever, to give scholarship perpetually, this is an example of perpetuity in which present value P is ₹ 20,000.

Now, rate % per year = 15.

$\therefore$ Rate per rupee per year $= i = 0.15$

Let x be the amount of annual scholarship.

Now, for a perpetuity,

$$P = \frac{x}{i}$$

$$\therefore \qquad 20{,}000 \;=\; \frac{X}{0.5}$$

$$\therefore \qquad 20{,}000 \times \frac{15}{100} \;=\; X$$

i.e. $\qquad\qquad X \;=\; 3000$

Example 3.25 : *Find the amount of an annuity of ₹ 200 payable quarterly for 3 years at 16 % p.a.* **(Oct. 2014)**

Solution : Here installment x = 200

Period is 1 quarter.

16 % p.a. means 4 % per quarter i.e. 4 paise per rupee.

Thus, i = 0.04

n : no. of installments = 3×4 = 12

To find amount A.

We have

$$A \;=\; \frac{X}{i}\,[(1+i)^n - 1]$$

$$=\; \frac{200}{0.04}\,[(1.04)^{12} - 1]$$

$$=\; 5000\,[1.60103 - 1]$$

$$=\; 5000 \times 0.60103$$

$$=\; ₹\,3005.15 \text{ approx.}$$

Example 3.26 : *A man deposits his provident fund of ₹ 2,00,000 in a charity trust at 5 % p.a. and settles to withdraw at ₹ 15000/- per month for his expenses. If he begins to spend from first year and goes on spending at this rate, show that he will not be able to withdraw same amount in 23rd year.*

Solution : Suppose that the person can withdraw ₹ 15000 for n years, after which his balance will be less than ₹ 15000. Here, present value P = 2,00,000

Annual installment x = 15000

Rate per rupee p.a.i = 0.05

To find n.

We have $\qquad P \;=\; \frac{X}{i}\,[1 - (1+i)^{-n}]$

$$\therefore \qquad 2{,}00{,}000 \;=\; \frac{15000}{0.05}\,[1 - (1.05)^{-n}]$$

$$\therefore \quad \frac{200}{15} \times \frac{5}{100} = 1 - (1.05)^{-n}$$

$$\therefore \quad \frac{2}{3} = 1 - (1.05)^{-n}$$

$$\therefore \quad (1.05)^{-n} = 1 - \frac{2}{3} = \frac{1}{3}$$

$$\therefore \quad -n \log (1.05) = \log \frac{1}{3}$$

$$\therefore \quad -n \ (0.021) = -0.4771$$

$$\therefore \quad n = \frac{0.4771}{0.021} = 22.61$$

i.e. approximately 23 years.

∴ He will be bankrupt before the end of 23rd year.

3.9 Equated Monthly Installments (EMI)

Of late we find more and more people purchasing vehicles and homes by taking loans from the bank. The repayment is generally made in monthly installments over a period of one year, two years, five years etc. This monthly installment of repayment is called **equated monthly installment (EMI)**. There are two ways by which banks or housing finance companies charge interest.

Interest on reducing balance :

Suppose, Mr. Desai takes a loan of ₹ 15 lacs from a bank for a period of 20 years at 7.5% reducing balance. Every month the E.M.I. consists of principal component and interest component. The principal component is deducted from Mr. Desai's outstanding loan amount and interest is charged on the lesser outstanding principal. For remaining months. The equation (composition) between interest and principal keeps changing every month. Since interest is calculated on the outstanding principal, a higher share goes towards interest during the initial part of the term. The composition of interest and principal for first three months is shown in following table. (Calculation of EMI is shown below).

	Loan	EMI	Interest	Principal
1st month	15,00,000	12090	9375	2715
2nd month	14,97,285	12090	9358	2731
3rd month	14,94,554	12090	9341	2749

The EMI is calculated using formula already given.

i.e. $\qquad P = \frac{x}{i} \left\{ 1 - (1 + i)^{-n} \right\}$ $\qquad$ ... (1)

If r is rate of interest % per year then i = rate per rupee per month = $\dfrac{r}{1200}$.

∴ Formula (1) becomes

$$P = \dfrac{x}{r/1200}\left\{1-\left(1+\dfrac{r}{1200}\right)^{-n}\right\}$$

where,   n = Total number of months in the term.

Thus, in Mr. Desai's case

$$1500000 = \dfrac{x}{7.5/1200}\left\{1-\left(1+\dfrac{7.5}{1200}\right)^{-240}\right\}$$

$$= 160\,x\,\{1-(1.00625)^{-240}\}$$

$$\dfrac{1500000}{160} = x\,\{1-0.224175\}$$

$$9375 = x\,(0.77582)\ 58$$

∴ $$x = 12090$$

From this it is clear that, for calculation of EMI, usual formulae for annuity are to be employed.

Flat interest rate :

In this method, the lending agency (banks, housing finance companies etc.) calculates the amount (principal + interest) for the given term at specified rate of interest. Then the EMI is arrived at by dividing this amount by total number of months in the term. Thus, the method consists of

(i) Calculate amount by using formula

$$A = P\left(1+\dfrac{rn}{100}\right)$$

(ii) $$EMI = \dfrac{A}{K}\ ,\quad \text{where, } K = \text{Number of months.}$$

For example, calculate EMI for ₹ 1 lacks at 5% flat rate over 20 years.

Solution : Here, P = 1,00,000

r = 5

n = 20

K = 240

The amount is given by

$$A = P\left(1+\dfrac{rn}{100}\right) = 100000\left(1+\dfrac{5\times20}{100}\right)$$

$$= 2,00,000$$

$$EMI = \dfrac{A}{K} = \dfrac{2,00,000}{240} = ₹\ 833.33$$

Comparison between flat interest rate and rate of interest on reducing balance :

The following example illustrates that flat interest rate is equivalent to a significantly lower reducing balance interest rate for the same period.

Let amount of loan i.e. P be ₹ 1,00,000 and flat rate of interest be 5%.

Let the term be 20 years then EMI turns out to be ₹ 833.33 as seen above.

Let us calculate EMI on reducing balance, at the same rate and for same term.

$$P = \frac{X}{i}\{1-(1+i)^{-n}\}$$

$$\therefore \qquad 1,00,000 = \frac{X}{5/1200}\left\{1-\left(1+\frac{5}{1200}\right)^{-240}\right\}$$

$$416.67 = x(1-0.3686)$$

$$\therefore \qquad X = \frac{416.67}{0.6314} = ₹ \ 660 \ (approximately)$$

Thus borrowing money on reducing balance (at the same rate) is highly beneficial.

Note : In view of the difference between flat interest rate and rate of reducing balance, people prefer reducing balance scheme.

Now-a-days, flat interest scheme is rarely used.

Illustrative Examples

Example 3.27 : *A two/four wheeler manufacturing company sells a motor-cycle costing ₹44,000 on installment basis by charging EMI ₹4500 for 1 year. Find flat rate of interest.*

(Oct. 2013, 2014)

Solution : Here, $A = 4500 \times 12 = 54000$, $P = 44,000$, $r = ?$, $n = 1$.

$$A = P\left(1+\frac{rn}{100}\right)$$

$$\therefore \qquad 54,000 = 44,000\left(1+\frac{r}{100}\right)$$

$$\therefore \qquad \frac{54}{44} = 1+\frac{r}{100}$$

$$\therefore \qquad \frac{r}{100} = \frac{54}{44}-1 = \frac{10}{44}$$

$$\therefore \qquad r = \frac{1000}{44} = 22.7$$

Example 3.28 : *A person borrows ₹5,00,000 from HDFC for purchase of the flat at 8% per annum reducing balance interest rate. Find EMI for a period of 10 years. Calculate corresponding flat interest rate.*

Solution : Here, $P = 5,00,000, \quad r = 8\%$

$\therefore$ $\quad i = \dfrac{8}{1200}, \quad n = \text{number of months} = 120$

$$P = \frac{x}{i}\{1-(1+i)^{-n}\}$$

$\therefore$ $\quad 5,00,000 = \dfrac{x}{8/1200}\left\{1-\left(1+\dfrac{8}{1200}\right)^{-120}\right\}$

$\therefore$ $\quad 5,00,000 \times \dfrac{8}{1200} = x\{1-(0.4503)\}$

$\therefore$ $\quad 3333.33 = x\,(0.5497)$

$\therefore$ $\quad x = 6064 \ (\text{approximately})$

The total amount payed by the person

$$A = 6064 \times 120$$
$$= 727680$$

Now, $A = P\left(1+\dfrac{rn}{100}\right)$

$\therefore$ $\quad 727680 = 5,00,000\left(1+\dfrac{10r}{100}\right)$

$\therefore$ $\quad 1.4554 = \left(1+\dfrac{r}{10}\right)$

$\therefore$ $\quad r = 10 \times 0.4554$

$\quad r = 4.554$

3.10 Formulae for Present Value and Amount of An Annuity Due

Let x : Periodic installment

n : Number of installments

i : Rate of interest per rupee per period

p' : Present value of annuity due

A' : Amount of annuity due

Then $P' = \dfrac{x\,(1+i)}{i}\{1-(1+i)^{-n}\}$

$A' = \dfrac{x\,(1+i)}{i}\{(1+i)^n - 1\}$

$$\frac{1}{P'} - \frac{1}{A'} = \frac{1}{x\,(1+i)}$$

Present value of a perpetuity :

$$P' = \frac{x\,(1+i)}{i}$$

Exercise 3.3

1. Find the present value of an annuity of ₹ 2500 per year for 20 years at 10 % p.a.

2. A loan is repaid in 4 equal quarterly installments of ₹ 4000 including principal and interest at 16 % p.a. what was the amount of the loan ?

3. What is the amount of an immediate annuity of ₹ 2000 per year payable for 12 years at 10 % ?

4. A man deposits ₹ 500 at the end of every month in a bank for 3 years. If the rate of interest is 12 % p.a. find the amount he will get at the end of 3 years.

5. A company sets aside ₹ 75000 at the end of every year to create a sinking fund. What will it amount to at the end of 25 years at 10 % ?

6. The present value and amount of an immediate annuity are ₹ 20,000 and ₹ 30,000 respectively (for the same period). If the installment is ₹ 4500 p.a., find the rate of interest.

7. The cash price of a flat is ₹ 4,80,000. A person paid 25 % of this in cash and borrowed 75 % from HDFC at 15 % p.a. repayable in monthly equal installments spread over 15 years. Find the amount of instalment.

8. A loan of ₹ 1,00,000 is to be repaid in 30 equal annual installments payable at the end of each year to cover principal and compound interest at 12 %. Find the amount of instalment.

9. Find the present value of an annuity of ₹ 500 payable at the end of every half year for 10 years at 10 % p.a. compound interest.

10. Find the amount of an annuity of ₹ 200 payable quarterly for 5 years at 12 % p.a.

11. What sum set aside every year will amount to ₹ 5 lakhs at the end of 10 years at 12 % ?

12. For what period should a man mortgage his property yielding. ₹ 30000 per year to clear a debt of ₹ 2 lakhs at 10 % p.a. ?

13. A sum was borrowed at 10 % compound interest and was repaid in 3 equal annual installments of ₹ 6655 each, at the end of each year. Find the sum borrowed.

14. A man deposits ₹ 3000 at the end of every year in a bank and at the end of 3 years receives a sum of ₹ 10,000. Find the rate of compound interest.

(**Given :** $\sqrt{93} = 9.6436$.)

15. How much amount a person should deposit in a bank to ensure yearly scholarship of ₹ 500 for ever ? Rate of interest is 16 %.

16. A man pays ₹ 1200 as house rent to the owner of the house per month. If he goes abroad for 2 years, how much rent he should pay in advance if the owner is to receive 10 % p.a.

17. A person wants to borrow ₹ 5 lacs for purchase of a house. Bank A lends at the rate of 5% p.a. flat while bank B lends at 8% on monthly reducing balance for the same period of 10 years. Compare the EMI's. Which bank the person should opt for ?

18. A motor-cycle manufacturing company gives partial loan of ₹ 33000 and charges ₹ 3018 per month for one year. The company claims it charges 5% rate of interest. Is it flat or on monthly reducing balance ?

19. Mr. Choudhary wants to take a loan of ₹ 10 lacks on monthly reducing balance. Find the interest paid by for a period of 15 years if rate of interest is 8%.

$$\left[\textbf{Hint :} \text{Find A} = \frac{X}{i} \ [(1+i)^n - 1], \ \text{Interest} = A - P. \right]$$

Answers 3.3

1. ₹ 21284

2. ₹ 14520

3. ₹ 42769

4. ₹ 21538

5. ₹ 73,76,029

6. $7\frac{1}{2}$ % p.a.

7. ₹ 5040

8. ₹ 12414

9. ₹ 6231

10. ₹ 5374

11. ₹ 28492

12. 11.5 years

13. ₹ 16550

14. 10.7 %

15. ₹ 3125

16. ₹ 25065

Miscellaneous Exercise 3

1. What is the simple interest on ₹ 4980 at 12% p.a. for 8 months ? What is the amount ?

2. The simple interest on a certain sum of the end of 4 years is 1/4th the sum itself. Find the rate of interest.

3. Further wanted to gift his son on his 18th birthday a sum of ₹ 6000. If the present age of the son is 12 years and rate of interest is 10% p.a. simple interest, what amount should be invest now ?

4. Madhu invested ₹ 10,000 at 16% p.a., ₹ 8000 at 14% p.a., ₹ 5000 at 10% p.a. simple interest. Find the average rate of return on his investment.

5. The simple interest on a sum at 7% p.a. for $3\frac{1}{3}$ years exceeds that on the same sum at 10% p.a. for 2 years by ₹ 200. Find the sum.

6. The simple interest on a certain sum for 2 years at 12% p.a. exceeds the compound interest on it for the same period at 10% p.a. by ₹ 240. Find the sum.

7. ₹ 16000 invested at 10% p.a. compounded semi-annually amounts to ₹ 18522. Find the time period of investment.

8. Find C.I. on ₹ 5500 for 6 months at 12% p.a. compounded quarterly.

9. Find the rate of interest p.a. if ₹ 2,00,000 amount to ₹ 231525 in $1\frac{1}{2}$ years interest compounded half yearly.

10. ₹ 15000 is invested in a Term Deposit Scheme that hatches interest 6% p.a. compound quarterly. What will be the interest after one year ? What is the effective rate of interest ?

11. Find effective rate of interest corresponding to a nominal rate 3% p.a. payable (i) half yearly, (ii) quarterly.

12. Find EMI if a loan of ₹ 2,00,000 at the rate of 12% p.a. (reducing balance) is to be repaid in equal monthly installments in 10 years.

13. Amol borrows ₹ 8 lacs from a finance company at 10% flat rate of interest for a period of 8 years. Compute EMI.

14. Find the difference between, EMI's by flat rate of interest and reducing balance of interest on ₹ 6 lacks at 9% p.a. for a period of 10 years.

15. Find the EMI on a loan of ₹ 16,00,000 for a period of 20 years at 12% p.a. reducing balance.

Miscellaneous Exercise 3

1. ₹ 398.40, ₹ 5378.4   2. 6.25%   3. ₹ 3750

4. ₹ 6000   5. 14% p.a.   6. ₹ 8000

7. 3   8. ₹ 334.95   9. 0.5%

10. ₹ 920.45, 6.13%   11. 3.0225% p.a., 3.033% 12. ₹ 2869.42

13. ₹ 15000   14. ₹ 1899.45   15. ₹ 17617.38

(Almost all answers are approximate)

Unit 4...

Shares and Dividends

Contents ...

Learning Objectives:

Equaity Share, Preference Share, Debentures, Stock Market.

Chapter Objectives ...

To understand dealings in stock market.

4.1 Introduction

We know that a person or a small group of persons can start a business upto medium size. However, when a big industry is to be launched, several persons come together to raise required capital. These are called *promoters* of the company. The capital is divided into small parts called *shares*. The people who purchase shares are called *shareholders* of the company and in a way they are owners of the company. The company is managed by a body of persons known as *Board of Directors* of the company.

4.2 Share Capital

The total capital of the company is divided into a number of small unit of equal value called *'shares'*. Thus a capital of ₹ 100000 may be divided into 1000 shares of ₹ 100 each, or 2000 shares of ₹ 50 each. The rights of the holders of each class of shares are governed by the companies act and also by the Articles and Association of the company.

4.3 Kinds of Shares

(i) **Preference shares :** The holders of these shares enjoy a preferential rights as regards the payment of dividend, and the repayment of capital in the event of winding-up. The rate of profit or dividend is fixed but it is paid before the profit is distributed on equity shares.

The preference shares are of the following kinds :

(a) **Cumulative preference shares :** The holders of these shares are entitled to a fixed dividend each year. But the amount of the dividend not paid in any year stands as arrears and is payable out of the profits of subsequent years.

(b) **Non-cumulative preference shares :** The holders of these shares have a preferential right for a fixed dividend out of the profits before the same are distributed to other classes of shares, but such dividend is payable only out of the profits of each particular year. Thus each year it lapses and cannot be claimed out of the future profits.

(ii) **Equity shares :** These shares ware formerly called 'ordinary' shares. They have no special rights attached to them. The holders of these shares are paid dividend after the claims of the preference shares holders are satisfied. The rate of the dividend is not fixed; it varies from year to year depending on the profits of the company. In some years they may have to go without dividend while in others they may get a very high rate of dividend. An equaity share is also called a "*scrip*".

4.4 Dividend   (April 2007, 2009)

The net profit made by the company every year is ascertained from its Profit and Loss Account prepared at the end of the year. Out of the net profits, dividend at a specified rate is paid on preference shares. Arrears of dividend, if any, on cumulative preference shares are also paid, if the amount of profit permits. The balance is then utilised for payment of dividend on equity shares. Dividend may be declared as fixed amount per share or as a percentage of the capital of the company.

4.5 Debenture

A company may require additional long-term capital for extension and development schemes. One of the methods of raising such finance is by means of debentures. Debentures are long-term loans taken by the company from the public. The total amount to be borrowed is divided like share capital into small units of equal amounts; and the members of the public are invited to lend such amounts to the company at a specified rate of interest.

4.6 Bonus Shares   (April 2007)

Sometimes a company rewards its share holders by issuing free shares to them in proportion of the shares held by them. These (free) shares are called **bonus shares**. They are entitled for all rights, that an ordinary share has. In this way, the holding of a person increases and the amount corresponding to bonus shares is capitalised. The company can use this amount for capital expenditure. Bonus shares are issued in some ratio. The ratio a : b means **a** free shares for **b** shares held.

4.7 Stock Exchange, Face Value, Market Value of Shares

(April 2011; Oct. 2013, 2014)

Shares and debentures are transferable assets. They are bought and sold in **"Stock Exchanges"**. A stock exchange is a form of exchange, which provides services for stock brokers and traders to trade stocks, bonds and other securities. Stock exchanges also provide facilities for issue and redemption of securities and other financial instruments and capital events including payment of income and dividends.

In India there are two prominent stock exchanges, the Bombay Stock Exchange (BSE) and National Stock Exchange (NSE).

Bombay Stock Exchange, known as BSE limited is the oldest stock exchange in entire Asia. It is located at Jeejee bhoy towers, Dalal street in fort, Mumbai. It has largest number of companies of the world listed on it. As per March 2012 there are more than 5000 Indian companies listed on BSE. The BSE sensex which is also known as BSE-30 (weighed average of 30 leading companies) is most commonly used term while referring to trading volume in India and Asia. The total capital of all shares listed on BSE in 2012 was approximately ₹ 5,00,00 crores. In term of share volume NSE is almost twice that of BSE.

Now-a-days shares in physical form have given way to shares in demat (dematerialize) form. In short, an investor has a list of shares he possesses and not physical share certificates. This has simplified several procedures and reduced lot of paper work.

The price stated on the body of share or debenture is called its **face value** (F.V.) or **nominal value.**

The price at which a debenture or share is actually bought or sold is called **market value** or **cash value** of the share.

If the face value and market value of a share are equal, the share is said to be "**at par**".

Illustrative Examples

Example 4.1 : *A sum of money got by selling shares of ₹ 1,500 in 10% at 135 was deposited in a bank at 8% p.a. which investment gives a better return ?*

Solution : As there is no mention of brokerage, we need not think of it.

By 10% at 135 we mean a share with face - value ₹ 100 is having a market price ₹ 135 and fetches dividend ₹ 10. Let us find the amount realised by selling shares of face-value ₹ 1,500.

When face-value is ₹ 100, market price is 135.

∴ When face-value is ₹ 1,500, market price

$$= \frac{135 \times 1500}{100} = ₹ \, 2,025$$

However, the income by way of dividend on these shares is ₹ 15 × 10 = 150 (since there are 15 shares of face-value ₹ 100 each).

The annual interest received from the bank at 8% p.a.

$$= \frac{Pnr}{100}$$

$$= \frac{2025 \times 1 \times 8}{100}$$

$$= ₹ \, 162$$

∴ Investment in bank is better as it gives ₹ 12 more annually.

Example 4.2 : *A sum of ₹ 1,350 was invested in 6% stock at 87. When it rose to 91 all the shares were sold. In the meanwhile dividend was received. For purchasing the brokerage was 3%, while selling it was 2%. What is the total gain or loss in the total transaction ?*

Solution : Since rate of commission is 3% for purchase, each share costs ₹ (87 + 3) = ₹ 90.

∴ In ₹ 1,350, a person will get $\dfrac{1350}{90}$ = 15 shares.

The dividend received on it will be ₹ (15 × 6) = ₹ 90.

While selling the shares, amount received per share will be ₹ (91 – 2) = ₹ 89.

∴ Amount received by selling all 15 shares = ₹ (15 × 89) = ₹ 1,335.

∴ Total gain = ₹ (1,335 + 90 – 1,350) = ₹ 75.

Example 4.3 : *Two companies have shares of 12% at 124 and 16% at 145. In which of the shares would the investment be more profitable ?*

Solution : Clearly, the face-value of the share must be ₹ 100 in each case.

Let us find percentage return in each case.

For ₹ 124, the return is ₹ 12

For ₹ 100, the return is ₹ 9.677 $\left(\dfrac{100}{124} \times 12 = 9.677\right)$

For the second company.

For ₹ 145, the return is ₹ 16

∴ For ₹ 100, the return is ₹ 11.03 $\left(\dfrac{100}{145} \times 16 = 11.03\right)$

As the percentage return in second case is more, the investment in the second company is more profitable.

Example 4.4 : *The capital of a company consists of ₹ 6,00,000, 10% preference shares and ₹ 24,00,000 equity shares. What percentage dividend can be declared out of a total profit of ₹ 3,75,000 after making a tax provision of 20% on the profit ?*

Solution : Tax @ 20% on 3,75,000 = 75,000, Net profit = ₹ 3,00,000

less 10% dividend on ₹ 6 lacs. (preference shares) = ₹ 60,000.

∴   Profit available for equity dividend = ₹ 2,40,000.

Equity share capital is ₹ 24 lacks.

∴   Rate of dividend on equity shares = 10%.

Example 4.5 : *The capital of a company consists of 1 lac, 8% cumulative preference shares of ₹ 100 each and 5 lack equity shares of ₹ 10 each. In a year there was no profit, in the next year company decided to pay 15% on equity shares. What was the total dividend distribution ?*

Solution : Cumulative preference share capital

$$= ₹\, 1,00,000 \times 100$$

$$= ₹\, 1 \text{ crore}$$

The company has to pay dividend for 2 years at 8% (each year).
i.e. 16% in all.

∴   dividend outgo $= ₹\, 16,00,000$

equity capital $= ₹\, 5,00,000 \times 10$

$$= ₹\, 50,00,000$$

dividend at the rate of 15% $= ₹\, 7,50,000$

∴   Total dividend outgo $= ₹\, 16,00,000 + 7,50,000$

$$= ₹\, 23,50,000$$

Example 4.6 : *A person holds 400, 8% preference shares of ₹100 each, ₹50 paid-up and 300 equity shares of ₹10 each, 5 paid up. If the company declares a dividend of 20% on equity shares, find the total dividend received by him.*

Solution : Since the company declares dividend on equity shares, it has to pay dividend on preference shares.

Preference capital of the person $= 400 \times 100$

$$= 40,000$$

But it is 50% paid-up.

∴   Paid-up preference capital $= 20,000$

Dividend on preference shares $= 20,000 \times \dfrac{8}{100} = ₹\, 1600$

Equity capital $= 300 \times 30 = 3000$

It is also 50% paid up.

∴   Paid-up equity capital $= 1500$

Dividend @ 20% $= 300$

∴   Total dividend received by him $= 3300$.

Example 4.7 : *A persons finds that if he invests his money in 15% stock at 225, his income will be ₹270 greater than if he invest it in 22% stock at 375. Find the sum invested.*

Solution : Suppose that the person invests ₹ x. On ₹ 225, earn ₹ 15.

∴   On ₹ x, he earn $\dfrac{15x}{225}$

In the other case, on ₹ 375, he earns ₹ 22.

∴   On ₹ x, he earns $\dfrac{22x}{375} = 270$

$$\dfrac{15x}{225} - \dfrac{22x}{375} = 270$$

∴ $x = 33750$

∴   His investment is ₹ 33750.

Example 4.8 : *Ashok purchased 10 share of Infosys at ₹ 2000 per share cum-bonus. Bonus was declared at 1 : 1. Ashok sold 15 share ex-bonus at ₹1250. He had to pay 1% brokerage each time on the market value. What is the cost price of remaining 5 shares held by him ?*

Solution : Cost price of 10 shares @ ₹ 2000 = ₹ 20,000.

       Selling price of 15 shares @ ₹ 1250 = ₹ 18,750.

Total brokerage paid on ₹ 38750 @ 1% = ₹ 387.50.

∴   His net outgo = ₹ 20,000 + 387.50 = ₹ 20387.50

     His earning by selling shares = ₹ 18750.

∴   His net cost of 5 shares = ₹ 1637.50.

∴   Cost price per share ₹ 327.50.

Example 4.9 : Mr. A invested ₹3,100 in 6% shares at ₹124. How much divided will be get ? (Face value = ₹100)   **(April 2010)**

Solution :   Market value of the share = ₹ 124

                Amount invested = ₹ 3100

$$\text{Number of shares purchased} = \frac{\text{Rs. } 3100}{124} = 25$$

           Face value of each share = ₹ 100

           Face value of 25 shares = 25 × 100 = ₹ 2500

∵   Mr. A received dividend at 6%

∴   Dividend received by him $= ₹\, 2500 \times \dfrac{6}{100} = ₹\, 150$

Example 4.10 : *A man invested ₹2000 in 10% shares at 125 of company 'A' and ₹2400 in 15% shares at 120 of company 'B'. Which investment is more profitable ? Why ?*

(April 2007)

Solution : The man invested ₹ 2000 in 10% shares at 125 in company 'A'.

$$\text{Number of shares} = \frac{2000}{125} = 16$$

So,   Dividend on 16 shares of company A = 16 × 10 = ₹ 160 ∴ % return is $\dfrac{160}{20} = 8$

The man also invested ₹ 2400 in 15% shares at 120 in company 'B'.

∴   Number of shares $= \dfrac{2400}{120} = 20$

So,   dividend on 20 shares of company B = 20 × 15 = ₹ 300 ∴ % return is $\dfrac{300}{24} = 12.5$

Therefore, the investment in company B is more profitable than company A.

Example 4.11 : *Pragat invested ₹13,568/- in 7% shares at ₹106/-. Find his profit at the end of the year. [F.V. 100].*   **(April 2008)**

Solution : Pragat invested ₹ 13568/- in 7% shares at 106/-.

$$\text{Number of shares} = \frac{13568}{106} = 128$$

          Profit on 128 shares = 128 × ₹ 7 (7% of ₹ 100) = 896

Example 4.12 : *Which of the following is the better investment ?*

(i) 8% at ₹80/-.   **(April 2011)**

(ii) 15% at ₹120/- [F.V. = ₹100]   **(April 2008)**

Solution : Two companies have shares 8% at 80 and 15% at 120. The face value in each case is 100. Let us find percentage return in each case.

For the first company : For ₹ 80 the return is 8 for ₹ 100 the return is

$$\frac{100}{80} \times 8 \ = \ 10$$

For the second company : For ₹ 120 the return is 15 for ₹ 100 the return is

$$\frac{100}{120} \times 15 \ = \ 12.5$$

As the percentage return in second case is more than first case, investment in the second company is more profitable.

Example 4.13 : *Mrs. 'A' buys 100 shares of ₹ 100 each at ₹ 125 of a company. If company pays dividend at 12% what is the percentage return on her investment ?*

(April 2009)

Solution : The dividend is declared on the face value ₹ 100 at the rate of 12%. Mrs. A will get $100 \times \frac{12}{100}$ = ₹ 12 divided on an investment of ₹ 125 on each share.

    On ₹ 125, return is ₹ 12.

∴   On ₹ 100, return is ₹ 9.6

$$\left(\frac{1200}{125} = 9.6\right)$$

∴   % return is 9.6.

Example 4.14 : *Ramesh sold 2000 shares of a company 'X' of face value ₹ 100 each paying a dividend of 12% at ₹126. He invested the proceeds in another company (Y) shares of face value ₹25 at ₹30 each, giving a dividend of 20%.*

Find : (i) The number of shares of the company 'Y' purchased by Ramesh.

(ii) Change in the dividend income.

Solution : Dividend at ₹ 12 on 2000 shares = ₹ 24000.

S.P. of 2000 shares of company X = 200 × 126 = 252000.

(i) Number of shares of company Y = $\frac{252000}{30}$ = 8400.

(ii) Company Y pays dividend at 20%.

∴   On a share of face value ₹ 25, dividend is ₹ 4.

∴   On 8400 shares, total dividend = 8400 × 4 = ₹ 9600.

∴   Change in dividend = ₹ 33600 – 24000 = ₹ 9600.

Example 4.15 : *A man invested ₹6200 in 6% shares at ₹124. How much dividend will be get ? What percent of dividend does he get on his investment ?*   **(Oct. 2011)**

Solution : For ₹ 124, he gets one share.

∴   For ₹ 6200, he gets $\dfrac{6200}{124}$ = 60 shares.

Dividend at 6% = 60 × 6 = ₹ 360.

He gets ₹ 360 on investment of ₹ 6200.

∴   % dividend $= \dfrac{360}{6200} \times 100 = 5.806$ (approximately)

Example 4.16 : *Arvind purchased a share of ₹100 for ₹2000. The company declared a dividend of 40%. After receiving the dividend, Arvind sells the share for ₹2200. Find the average returns on his investment.*   **(April 2013)**

Solution : Arvind receives divided of ₹ 40 on his investment.

∴   His outgo from packet = 2000 – 40 = ₹ 1960.

By selling the share at ₹ 2200, his profit = 2200 – 1960 = 240.

Thus he gets ₹ 240 on investment of ₹ 2000.

∴   % return $= \dfrac{1000 \times 240}{2000} = 12$

Exercise 4.1

1.   Explain the term 'shares'.   **(Nov. 2010)**

2.   Explain the term dividend. State its types.   **(April 2007, 2009, Nov. 2010)**

3.   Explain the term "Bonus Shares".   **(April 2007)**

4.   Define the following terms :

(i) Share, (ii) Dividend, (iii) Bonus shares.

Exercise 4.2

1.   A man purchased shares of face-value ₹ 3,200 by investing ₹ 4,000. What was the market price of a share ? If the shares fetched 6% dividend, what percentage of dividend did he get on his investment ?

2.   Suresh invested ₹ 1,080 in shares of face value ₹ 50 at ₹ 54. After receiving dividend on them at 8% he sold them at 52. In each of the transactions he paid 2% brokerage. How much did he gain or lose in the overall transaction ?   **(Oct. 2011)**

3.   A man invested ₹ 6,200 in 6% shares at 124. How much dividend will he get ? How much per cent of dividend does he get on his investment ?

4. Shah spent ₹ 7,560 in purchasing 5% shares at 126. After getting the dividend on them, he sold them at the same price. In each transaction he had to pay 2% brokerage. Did he gain or lose in the total transaction ? By how much ?

5. A man invested ₹ 13,568 in 7% shares at 106 and ₹ 12,648 in 11% shares at 124. How much income would he get in all ?

6. Hussen and Altaf each invested ₹ 4,550 in $5\frac{1}{2}$ at 91 and $7\frac{1}{2}$ at 130 respectively. Whose investment is more profitable and by how much ?

7. A man purchased shares worth ₹ 18,900 when the market price was ₹ 94.50. Out of those shares he sold shares of face value ₹ 12,600 when the market rate was 104, and sold the remaining shares at 98. He had to pay 1.5% brokerage each time. What was his gain or loss on the whole ?

8. The amount realised by selling 8% shares at 144 of the face value of ₹ 2,400 was invested in 6% shares at 96. What would be the difference in annual income ?

9. Two companies have shares of 13% at 122 and 17% at 150 respectively. In which of the shares would the investment be more profitable ?   **(April 2013)**

10. The capital of a company consists of 10 lac., 8% cumulative preference shares and of ₹ 10 each and 50 lac equity shares of ₹ 10 each. The company could not declared dividend on preference shares. In the third year company decided to pay 12% dividend on equity shares. Find the total amount paid by the company, by way of dividend.

11. The ordinary share capital of a company is thrice preference capital. Preference shares carry 8% dividend. When the distributable profit amounted to ₹ 22 lacs, equity holders received dividend at 12%. Find amount of each kind of capital.

12. Mahesh purchased 400 shares of a company of ₹ 10 at ₹ 80 each through a broker. Mahesh paid 1.5% brokerage and 0.5% of the market price towards transfer charges. The company declared a dividend of 25% and declared bonus in the ratio 1 : 4. Mahesh sold all the shares at ₹ 60 each. Find his net gain/loss.

13. Explain the terms :

    (a) Equity shares, (b) Preference shares, (c) Bonus shares, (d) Stock exchange.

14. Salil has following investment in shares :

    (i)   300 shares of ₹ 90 each paying 20% dividend.

    (ii) 500 shares of ₹ 80 each paying 10% dividend.

    (iii) 600 shares of ₹ 100 each paying 15% dividend.

    What is average rate of return (%) on his investment.

15. Swati purchased 900 shares of a company at par (f.v. = 100 ₹) company issued right shares at a premium of ₹ 5 in the ratio 5 : 4. How many right shares did she get ? If the company declared 25% dividend next year, what was her dividend income ?

Answers 4.2

1. ₹ 125, 4.8%,　　　　　　2. No gain, no loss,　　　3. ₹ 300, 4.84%,

4. Gain of ₹ 60,　　　　　　5. ₹ 2,108,

6. Hussen's investment is profitable by ₹ 12.50,

7. Gain of ₹ 856,　　　　　　8. Gain ₹ 24,　　　　　9. 17% at 150

10. ₹ 84 lacs.

11. Preference capital ₹ 50 lacs. 12. Loss : ₹ 1640

14. 14.4%　　　　　　　　　15. 720 shares, dividend ₹ 40000.

Unit **5**...

Matrices and Determinants

Contents ...

Learning Objectives:

➤ Determinant, matrix, minors and cofactors, adjoint and inverse of a square matrix, system of equations, homogeneous and non-homogeneous system.

Chapter Objectives ...

➤ To understand applications of matrices in business.

5.1 Introduction

Although the title of this chapter is "Matrices and Determinants", we begin with Determinants for two reasons. Firstly you are already familiar with 2×2 determinants in your school and secondly, the knowledge of determinant is a pre-requisite for learning definitions of some special matrices like singular and non-singular.

5.2 Determinants

In standard X, you have studied the use of determinants of order 2 in the solution of two linear equations in two unknowns. A determinant D of order 2 may be written as

$$D = \begin{vmatrix} a & b \\ c & d \end{vmatrix}$$, where a, b, c, d are certain numbers. They are called the *elements of the determinant*. The expression ad – bc is the expansion or the value of the determinant and we write D = ad – bc.

For example, $$\begin{vmatrix} 2 & -1 \\ 3 & 4 \end{vmatrix} = (2 \times 4) - (-1 \times 3) = 11,$$

$$\begin{vmatrix} 1 & 2 \\ 3 & 6 \end{vmatrix} = (1 \times 6) - (3 \times 2) = 0,$$

$$\begin{vmatrix} \cos\theta & -\sin\theta \\ \sin\theta & \cos\theta \end{vmatrix} = \cos^2\theta + \sin^2\theta = 1 \text{ etc.}$$

5.3 Determinant of Order 3

A determinant of order 3 contains $3 \times 3 = 9$ elements in all. It is convenient to take nine elements as $a_1, b_1, c_1, a_2, b_2, c_2, a_3, b_3, c_3$. These are arranged below in the form of a square array and enclosed between two vertical lines.

$$\begin{vmatrix} a_1 & b_1 & c_1 \\ a_2 & b_2 & c_2 \\ a_3 & b_3 & c_3 \end{vmatrix}$$

This is a determinant of order 3. Here a_1, b_1, c_1 form the first row, a_2, b_2, c_2 form the second row and a_3, b_3, c_3 form the third row. These rows may be denoted by R_1, R_2, R_3 respectively. Similarly, a_1, a_2, a_3 form the first column b_1, b_2, b_3 form the second column and c_1, c_2, c_3 form the third column. These three column may be denoted by C_1, C_2, C_3 respectively. The determinant may be denoted by D.

The value of the expansion of this determinant is given by the following expression :

$$a_1 \begin{vmatrix} b_2 & c_2 \\ b_3 & c_3 \end{vmatrix} - b_1 \begin{vmatrix} a_2 & c_2 \\ a_3 & c_3 \end{vmatrix} + c_1 \begin{vmatrix} a_2 & b_2 \\ a_3 & b_3 \end{vmatrix} \qquad \dots (5.1)$$

$$= a_1 (b_2 c_3 - c_2 b_3) - b_1 (a_2 c_3 - c_2 a_3) + c_1 (a_2 b_3 - b_2 a_3)$$

$$= a_1 b_2 c_3 - a_1 c_2 b_3 - b_1 a_2 c_3 + b_1 c_2 a_3 + c_1 a_2 b_3 - c_1 b_2 a_3 \qquad \dots (5.2)$$

Expression (5.1) is written down as follows. Elements a_1, b_1, c_1 of R_1 appear in this expression with alternately positive and negative signs and each is multiplied by a certain determinant of order 2. The element a_1 is in the first row and the first column. If we imagine all the elements in this row and column as deleted, there remains the array b_2 c_2, a_1 is multiplied by the determinant of b_3 c_3 order 2 formed by this array. Similarly b_1 and c_1 are

multiplied by the determinants of order 2 formed by the arrays $\begin{vmatrix} a_2 & c_2 \\ a_3 & c_3 \end{vmatrix}$ and $\begin{vmatrix} a_2 & b_2 \\ a_3 & b_3 \end{vmatrix}$.

The determinants of order 2 are then expanded and finally expression (5.2) results after simplification. This expansion is called the expansion by the first row.

Illustrative Examples

Example 5.1 : *Let* $D = \begin{vmatrix} 4 & -3 & 2 \\ 1 & 2 & 1 \\ 3 & 1 & -2 \end{vmatrix}$

Solution : Following the procedure explained above, we get

$$D = 4\begin{vmatrix} 2 & 1 \\ 1 & -2 \end{vmatrix} - (-3)\begin{vmatrix} 1 & 1 \\ 3 & -2 \end{vmatrix} + 2\begin{vmatrix} 1 & 2 \\ 3 & 1 \end{vmatrix}$$

$$= 4(-4-1) + 3(-2-3) + 2(1-6)$$

$$= -20 - 15 - 10 = -45$$

Example 5.2 : *Let* $D = \begin{vmatrix} a & b & c \\ c & a & b \\ b & c & a \end{vmatrix} = a\begin{vmatrix} a & b \\ c & a \end{vmatrix} - b\begin{vmatrix} c & b \\ b & a \end{vmatrix} + c\begin{vmatrix} c & a \\ b & c \end{vmatrix}$

Solution :
$$= a(a^2 - bc) - b(ac - b^2) + c(c^2 - ab)$$

$$= a^3 + b^3 + c^3 - 3abc$$

Example 5.3 : *Expand the determinant* $D = \begin{vmatrix} a & h & g \\ h & b & f \\ g & f & c \end{vmatrix}$

Solution : We have

$$D = a\begin{vmatrix} b & f \\ f & c \end{vmatrix} - h\begin{vmatrix} h & f \\ g & c \end{vmatrix} + g\begin{vmatrix} h & b \\ g & f \end{vmatrix} = a(bc - f^2) - h(ch - fg) + g(hf - bg)$$

$$= abc - af^2 - ch^2 + fgh + fgh - bg^2 = abc + 2fgh - af^2 - bg^2 - ch^2$$

Example 5.4 : *Find the value of x if* $\begin{vmatrix} 3+x & 4+x & 5+x \\ 1 & -1 & 2 \\ 1 & 4 & 2 \end{vmatrix} = 0$

Solution : Expanding the determinant on the L.H.S, we get

$$(3+x)(-2-8) - (4+x)(2-2) + (5+x)(4+1) = 0$$
$$-30 - 10x - 0 + 25 + 5x = 0 \therefore -5x - 5 = 0 \therefore x = -1$$

Example 5.5 : *Find the value of x if* $\begin{vmatrix} 5 & 5 & x \\ x & 5 & 5 \\ 5 & 5 & 4 \end{vmatrix} = 0$

Solution : Expanding the determinant on the L.H.S. we get

$$5(20-25) - 5(4x-25) + x(5x-25) = 0$$
$$\therefore -5 - 4x + 25 + x^2 - 5x = 0 \qquad\qquad \therefore x^2 - 9x + 20 = 0$$
$$\therefore (x-4)(x-5) = 0 \qquad\qquad \therefore \quad x = 4 \text{ or } x = 5.$$

Example 5.6 : *Evaluate :* $\begin{vmatrix} a & h & g \\ h & b & f \\ g & f & c \end{vmatrix}$. 　　　　　　　　　　　　　(Oct. 2008)

Solution : $\begin{vmatrix} a & h & g \\ h & b & f \\ g & f & c \end{vmatrix} = a \begin{vmatrix} b & f \\ f & c \end{vmatrix} - h \begin{vmatrix} h & f \\ g & c \end{vmatrix} + g \begin{vmatrix} h & b \\ g & f \end{vmatrix}$

$$= a(bc - f^2) - h(hc - gf) + g(hf - gb)$$
$$= abc - af^2 - h^2c - hgf + hgf + g^2b$$
$$= abc - af^2 - bg^2 - ch^2$$

Exercise 5.1

Evaluate the following determinants. (Problem 1 to 6)

1. $\begin{vmatrix} 1 & 1 & 2 \\ 2 & 1 & 2 \\ 3 & 2 & 1 \end{vmatrix}$ 　　2. $\begin{vmatrix} 1 & 4 & 3 \\ -10 & -2 & 4 \\ 0 & 1 & 2 \end{vmatrix}$ 　　3. $\begin{vmatrix} 10 & 20 & 30 \\ 30 & 40 & 50 \\ 50 & 60 & 70 \end{vmatrix}$

4. $\begin{vmatrix} -b & c & 1 \\ a & 1 & -c \\ -1 & a & -b \end{vmatrix}$ 　　5. $\begin{vmatrix} a & -b & 1 \\ 1 & c & -a \\ -c & 1 & b \end{vmatrix}$ 　　6. $\begin{vmatrix} a & b & c \\ b+c & c+a & a+b \\ 1 & 1 & 1 \end{vmatrix}$

Solve the following equations. (Problem 7, 8)

7. $\begin{vmatrix} x-1 & x+1 & 1 \\ 1 & 2 & 1 \\ 1 & 2 & 3 \end{vmatrix} = 0$

8. $\begin{vmatrix} 2 & x+1 & 4 \\ 4 & x+2 & x+1 \\ x+2 & 1 & x+1 \end{vmatrix} = 0$

9. Prove that $\begin{vmatrix} a & a & a \\ a & b & b \\ a & b & c \end{vmatrix} = a\,(b-c)\,(a-b)$

Hence find the value of $\begin{vmatrix} 5 & 5 & 5 \\ 5 & 4 & 4 \\ 5 & 4 & 2 \end{vmatrix}$

Answers 5.1

1. 3
2. 423.
3. 0
4. $a^2 + b^2 + c^2 + 1$
5. $a^2 + b^2 + c^2 + 1$
6. 0
7. $x = 3$
8. $x = 0$ or $x = -3$ or $x = 5$
9. 10

5.4 Properties of Determinants

1. *The value of a determinant remains unchanged if its rows and columns are interchanged.*

i.e. $\begin{vmatrix} a_1 & b_1 & c_1 \\ a_2 & b_2 & c_2 \\ a_3 & b_3 & c_3 \end{vmatrix} = \begin{vmatrix} a_1 & a_2 & a_3 \\ b_1 & b_2 & b_3 \\ c_1 & c_2 & c_3 \end{vmatrix}$

Note that first row becomes first column, second row becomes second column and third row becomes third column.

Remark : In view of this property, any result applicable to rows is also applicable to columns of a determinant.

2. *The value of determinant is changed in sign only, if any two rows (or columns) in it are interchanged.*

e.g. $\begin{vmatrix} a_1 & b_1 & c_1 \\ a_2 & b_2 & c_2 \\ a_3 & b_3 & c_3 \end{vmatrix} = - \begin{vmatrix} c_1 & b_1 & a_1 \\ c_2 & b_2 & a_2 \\ c_3 & b_3 & a_3 \end{vmatrix}$

Column 1 is interchanged with column 3. This is denoted by C_{13}.

3.　*The value of a determinant is zero if any two rows (or columns) in it are identical.*

e.g.　$\begin{vmatrix} a_1 & b_1 & c_1 \\ a_2 & b_2 & c_2 \\ a_1 & b_1 & c_1 \end{vmatrix} = 0$　　　$(\because R_1 \equiv R_3)$

4.　*If all the elements of a row (or column) are multiplied by a constant, then it is equivalent to multiplying the determinant by that constant.*

i.e.　$\begin{vmatrix} ka_1 & kb_1 & kc_1 \\ a_2 & b_2 & c_2 \\ a_3 & b_3 & c_3 \end{vmatrix} = k \begin{vmatrix} a_1 & b_1 & c_1 \\ a_2 & b_2 & c_2 \\ a_3 & b_3 & c_3 \end{vmatrix}$

Note : The property, in other words, states that if all elements of a row (or column) has a factor k it can be taken out as coefficient of determinant.

e.g.　$\begin{vmatrix} 2 & 3 & 10 \\ -1 & 4 & -15 \\ 7 & 2 & 25 \end{vmatrix} = 5 \begin{vmatrix} 2 & 3 & 2 \\ -1 & 4 & -3 \\ 7 & 2 & 5 \end{vmatrix}$

(5 is taken common from C_3)

5.　*Two determinants can be added if they have two identical rows (or columns).*

e.g.　$\begin{vmatrix} a_1 & b_1 & c_1 \\ a_2 & b_2 & c_2 \\ a_3 & b_3 & c_3 \end{vmatrix} + \begin{vmatrix} a_1 & b_1 & c_1 \\ l & m & n \\ a_3 & b_3 & c_3 \end{vmatrix} = \begin{vmatrix} a_1 & b_1 & c_1 \\ a_2+l & b_2+m & c_2+n \\ a_3 & b_3 & c_3 \end{vmatrix}$

Note that identical rows (columns) remain as they are after addition. Only the unequal elements get added.

e.g.　$\begin{vmatrix} 2 & -3 & 4 \\ 10 & 8 & 5 \\ 5 & 6 & -7 \end{vmatrix} + \begin{vmatrix} 5 & 1 & -10 \\ 10 & 8 & 5 \\ 5 & 6 & -7 \end{vmatrix} = \begin{vmatrix} 7 & -2 & -6 \\ 10 & 8 & 5 \\ 5 & 6 & -7 \end{vmatrix}$

(Corresponding elements of first row are added. R_2 and R_3 remain the same.)

6.　*The value of a determinant remains the same if k multiples of any row (or column) are added to corresponding elements of any other row (or column).*

i.e.　Consider the determinant.

$\begin{vmatrix} a_1 & b_1 & c_1 \\ a_2 & b_2 & c_2 \\ a_3 & b_3 & c_3 \end{vmatrix} = D$ (say) if we add k multiples of first row and m multiples of third row to second row then we get the determinant.

$$\begin{vmatrix} a_1 & b_1 & c_1 \\ a_1 + ka_1 + ma_3 & b_2 + kb_1 + mb_3 & c_2 + kc_1 + mc_3 \\ a_3 & b_3 & c_3 \end{vmatrix} = D' \text{ (say)}$$

Then   D = D'

As a simple case, consider the determinant

$$D = \begin{vmatrix} 5 & 4 \\ +1 & 6 \end{vmatrix} = 6 \times 5 - (1)(4) = 30 - 4 = 26$$

Suppose elements of second row are multiplied by 100 and added to first row, then

$$\begin{vmatrix} 5 + 100 & 4 + 600 \\ 1 & 6 \end{vmatrix} = \begin{vmatrix} 105 & 604 \\ 1 & 6 \end{vmatrix}$$

$$= (105 \times 6) - (604 \times 1)$$

$$= 630 - 604$$

$$= 26$$

Note : By "without expanding the determinant" we mean by using properties of determinant mentioned above.

Notation : We know that R_1, R_2, R_3 denote first, second and third row. Also C_1, C_2, C_3 denote first, second, third column. For different operations on rows/columns following notations are used.

(1) kR_i : Multiplying every element of ith row by k.

(2) R_{ij} : Interchange of ith and j^{th} row.

(3) $R_i + kR_j$: Adding k multiples of jth row to corresponding elements of ith row.

Similarly, kC_i, C_{ij}, $C_i + kC_j$ are used for column operations.

Illustrative Examples

Example 5.7 : *Find the value of x if* $\begin{vmatrix} 2 + x & 3 + x & 4 + x \\ 1 & 2 & -1 \\ 2 & 1 & 3 \end{vmatrix} = 0.$ **(April 2011)**

Solution : $\begin{vmatrix} 2 + x & 3 + x & 4 + x \\ 1 & 2 & -1 \\ 2 & 1 & 3 \end{vmatrix} = 0.$

$\therefore$ $(2 + x) [(2 \times 3) - (- |x|)] - (3 + x) [1 \times 3 - (2x - 1)] + (4 + x) [|x| - 2 \times 2] = 0.$

$\therefore$ $(2 + x) (6 + 1) - (3 + x) (3 + 2) + (4 + x) (1 - x) = 0$

$\therefore$ $7 (2 + x) - 5 (3 + x) - 3 (4 + x) = 0$

$\therefore$ $14 + 7x - 15 - 5x - 12 - 3x = 0$

$\therefore$ $- x - 13 = 0$

$\therefore$ $x + 13 = 0$

$\therefore$ $x = - 13$

Example 5.8 : Evaluate $\begin{vmatrix} 47 & 78 & 25 \\ 111 & 173 & 58 \\ 64 & 95 & 33 \end{vmatrix}$.

Solution : $\begin{vmatrix} 47 & 78 & 25 \\ 111 & 173 & 58 \\ 64 & 95 & 33 \end{vmatrix} = \begin{vmatrix} 47 & 78 & 25 \\ 0 & 0 & 0 \\ 64 & 95 & 33 \end{vmatrix}$ $[(by\ R_2 - (R_1 + R_3)]$

$= 0$

Example 5.9 : Evaluate $D = \begin{vmatrix} 28 & 45 & 63 \\ 20 & 34 & 48 \\ 21 & 36 & 51 \end{vmatrix}$.   **(April 2015)**

Solution : $D = \begin{vmatrix} 28 & 45 & 63 \\ 20 & 34 & 48 \\ 21 & 36 & 51 \end{vmatrix} = \begin{vmatrix} 8 & 11 & 15 \\ 20 & 34 & 48 \\ 1 & 2 & 3 \end{vmatrix}$ (by $R_1 - R_2, R_3 - R_2$)

$= \begin{vmatrix} 3 & 1 & 0 \\ 4 & 2 & 0 \\ 1 & 2 & 3 \end{vmatrix}$ (by $R_2 - 16R_3, R_1 - 5R_3$)

$= 3 (6 - 0) - 1 (12 - 0) + 0$

$= 18 - 12$

$= 6$

Example 5.10 : Without expanding prove that

$$\begin{vmatrix} a & b & c \\ x & y & z \\ p & q & r \end{vmatrix} = \begin{vmatrix} y & b & q \\ x & a & p \\ z & c & r \end{vmatrix}$$

Solution : $\quad \begin{vmatrix} a & b & c \\ x & y & z \\ p & q & r \end{vmatrix} = \begin{vmatrix} a & x & p \\ b & y & q \\ c & z & r \end{vmatrix}$ $\qquad$ (Interchanging rows and columns)

$$= - \begin{vmatrix} b & y & q \\ a & x & p \\ c & z & r \end{vmatrix} \qquad \text{(by } R_{12})$$

$$= \begin{vmatrix} y & b & q \\ x & a & p \\ z & c & r \end{vmatrix} \qquad \text{(by } C_{12})$$

$$= \text{R.H.S.}$$

Exercise 5.2

1. Without expanding the determinants, show that

(i) $\begin{vmatrix} 7 & 2 & 5 \\ -a & -3 & 1 \\ 15 & 4 & 8 \end{vmatrix} + \begin{vmatrix} -1 & 2 & 5 \\ 5 & -3 & 1 \\ -3 & 4 & 8 \end{vmatrix} = 2 \begin{vmatrix} 3 & 2 & 5 \\ -2 & -3 & 1 \\ 6 & 4 & 8 \end{vmatrix}$.

(ii) $\begin{vmatrix} 1 & bc & bc\,(b+c) \\ 1 & ca & ca\,(c+a) \\ 1 & ab & ab\,(a+b) \end{vmatrix} = 0$

2. Show that : $\begin{vmatrix} 1+x & 1 & 1 \\ 1 & 1+y & 1 \\ 1 & 1 & 1+z \end{vmatrix} = xyz \left(1 + \dfrac{1}{x} + \dfrac{1}{y} + \dfrac{1}{z} \right)$

3. Show that : $\begin{vmatrix} a & b-c & b+c \\ c+a & b & c-a \\ a-b & a+b & c \end{vmatrix} = (a+b+c)\,(a^2+b^2+c^2)$

4. Prove that : $\begin{vmatrix} x^2 & x & 1 \\ y^2 & y & 1 \\ z^2 & z & 1 \end{vmatrix} = (x-y)\,(y-z)\,(z-x).$

5. Show that : $\begin{vmatrix} a & b & c \\ b & c & a \\ b+c & c+a & a+b \end{vmatrix} = 3\,abc - a^3 - b^3 - c^3.$

6. Prove that : $\begin{vmatrix} b+c & a & a \\ b & c+a & b \\ c & c & a+b \end{vmatrix} = 4\,abc.$

7. Show that : $\begin{vmatrix} a^2+2a & 2a+1 & 1 \\ 2a+1 & a+2 & 1 \\ 3 & 3 & 1 \end{vmatrix} = (a-1)^3.$

5.5 Matrices

Introduction : Early development of matrix theory is due to European mathematicians Sylvester, Cayley and Hamilton. This branch of mathematics has applications in many other subjects such as Statistics, Physics, Economics, Psychology etc.

Many a times, it is convenient to present numerical data in the form of rectangular array of rows and columns. Example, (i) At recently concluded IPL matches various teams fared as follows :

Team	P	W	L	Points
Chennai Superkings	16	11	5	22
Mumbai Indian	16	11	5	22
Rajasthan Royals	16	10	6	20
Sunrisers Hydrabad	16	10	6	20
Royal Challengers Bangalore	16	9	7	18
Kings XI Punjab	16	8	8	16
Kolkata Knight Riders	16	6	10	12
Pune Warriers India	16	4	12	08
Delhi Daredevils	16	3	13	06

P : Played, W : Won, L : Lost

(ii) The daily sales of hot drinks from a shop for 5 days of a week are as follows :

$$\begin{array}{c c c c} & \text{Tea} & \text{Coffee} & \text{Milk} \\ \text{Mon.} & 37 & 56 & 49 \\ \text{Tue.} & 50 & 58 & 70 \\ \text{Wed.} & 80 & 45 & 79 \\ \text{Thu.} & 85 & 79 & 43 \\ \text{Fri.} & 30 & 24 & 13 \end{array}$$

Such a system is called a **matrix**.

Definition of matrix, Notation for writing a matrix :　　　(Oct. 2014)

Definition : An arrangement of mn numbers in the form of a rectangular block of m rows and n columns, enclosed in rectangular brackets is called a *matrix of the order m* $\times$ *n.*

For example,　　$A = \begin{bmatrix} 2 & 3 \\ 1 & -1 \end{bmatrix}$, $B = \begin{bmatrix} 2 & 3 & 7 \\ 1 & -1 & 1 \end{bmatrix}$

Any element in a matrix may be located by stating the number of row and number of column in which the element occurs. Thus in matrix A above, element 2 is in place (1, 1), 3 is in place (1, 2), 1 is in place (2, 1) etc.

A useful notation for writing matrices in theoretical work is as follows :

We use letters such as a, b, c, d, ... with proper suffixes to denote the elements of a matrix. For example, we may denote the elements in the places (1, 1), (1, 2), (1, 3), (2, 1), ... etc. by $a_{11}, a_{12}, a_{13}, a_{21}$ ... etc. With this notation a matrix of the order 2×2 may be written as $\begin{bmatrix} a_{11} & a_{12} \\ a_{21} & a_{22} \end{bmatrix}$. This matrix is then denoted by the corresponding capital letter A. Thus we write

$A = \begin{bmatrix} a_{11} & a_{12} \\ a_{21} & a_{22} \end{bmatrix}$ or just $A = [a_{ij}]$ i = 1, 2; j = 1, 2.

Similarly, a matrix of the order 3×2 may be written as

$$B = \begin{bmatrix} b_{11} & b_{12} \\ b_{21} & b_{22} \\ b_{31} & b_{32} \end{bmatrix} \text{ or } B = [b_{ij}] \text{ i = 1, 2, 3; j = 1, 2}$$

Note :　(1) There should be no confusion between the ideas of a determinant and a matrix. Unlike a determinant, (a) the number of rows and the number of columns in a matrix need not be equal and (b) there is no such thing as the value or expansion of matrix.

(2) A matrix of the order 1×1 is regarded as a scalar. (i.e. just a real number).

Illustrative Examples

Example 5.11 : *Write down the matrices of the coefficients of the following sets of equations. State their orders.*

(i)　$x + 2y - z = 2$　　(ii) $x + z = 4$

　　$2x - 5y + 6z = 3$　$x + y + z = 6$

　　　　　　　　$2y + z = 5$

Solution : (i) There are 3 unknowns x, y, z and 2 equations. The required matrix is $\begin{bmatrix} 1 & 2 & -1 \\ 2 & -5 & 6 \end{bmatrix}$. It is of the order 2×3.

(ii) There are 3 unknowns x, y, z and 3 equations. In the first equation, y is absent. We can say that coefficient of y is zero. Thus this equation may be written as $x + 0y + z = 6$. Similarly, taking the coefficient of x in the third equation as zero, it can be written as $0x + 2y + z = 5$. Therefore the required matrix is $\begin{bmatrix} 1 & 0 & 1 \\ 1 & 1 & 1 \\ 0 & 2 & 1 \end{bmatrix}$. It is of the order 3×3.

Example 5.12 : *Find the elements a_{12}, a_{21}, a_{23} in the matrix.*

$$A = \begin{bmatrix} 5 & 4 & -3 \\ 2 & 1 & 6 \\ 7 & -2 & -1 \end{bmatrix}$$

Solution : a_{12} is the element in the first row and second column. It is 4. Thus $a_{12} = 4$. Similarly $a_{21} = 2$, $a_{23} = 6$.

Exercises 5.3

1. Write down two matrices of each of the following orders :

    (i) 2×2 (ii) 2×3 (iii) 3×2 (iv) 1×3 (v) 3×1

2. Write down the matrices of the coefficients of the following sets of equations. State their orders.

    (i) $x + 2y = 5$ (ii) $x + y = 3$ (iii) $x + y + z = 12$

    $\quad\;\; 5x - 3y = -1$ $\quad\;\; y + z = 5$ $\quad\;\;\; x + z = 8$

    $\quad\quad\quad\quad\quad\quad\quad\;\; 2z + x = 7$ $\quad\;\;\; y - z = -1$

3. Find the elements a_{22}, a_{32}, a_{33} in the following matrix :

    $$A = \begin{bmatrix} 2 & 3 & 4 \\ 4 & -5 & 6 \\ -1 & 1 & -4 \end{bmatrix}$$

4. State the orders of the following matrices :

    (i) $[1, 0, 0]$ (ii) $\begin{bmatrix} 3 \\ 4 \end{bmatrix}$ (iii) $\begin{bmatrix} 2 & 3 & 0 \\ 0 & 3 & 2 \end{bmatrix}$ (iv) $\begin{bmatrix} 1 \\ 2 \\ 3 \end{bmatrix}$ (v) $\begin{bmatrix} 1 & 2 \\ 3 & 4 \\ 5 & 6 \end{bmatrix}$

    (vi) $\begin{bmatrix} 5 & 0 & 1 \\ 4 & 0 & 2 \\ 3 & 0 & 3 \end{bmatrix}$

5. Write down the matrix A given that $a_{11} = a_{22} = a_{33} = 0$,

    $a_{12} = -a_{21} = 2$, $a_{13} = -a_{31} = -4$, $a_{23} = -a_{32} = -1$.

Answers 5.3

2. (i) $\begin{bmatrix} 1 & 2 \\ 5 & -3 \end{bmatrix}$ (ii) $\begin{bmatrix} 1 & 1 & 0 \\ 0 & 1 & 1 \\ 1 & 0 & 2 \end{bmatrix}$ (iii) $\begin{bmatrix} 1 & 1 & 1 \\ 1 & 0 & 1 \\ 0 & 1 & -1 \end{bmatrix}$

3. $a_{22} = -5, a_{32} = 1, a_{33} = -4$

4. (i) 1×3 (ii) 2×1 (iii) 2×3 (iv) 3×1 (v) 3×2 (vi) 3×3

5. $A = \begin{bmatrix} 0 & 2 & -4 \\ -2 & 0 & -1 \\ 4 & 1 & 0 \end{bmatrix}$

5.6 Types of Matrices   (Oct. 2013, 14; April 2015)

Depending on the order and the nature of the elements, matrices are classified into various categories.

(1) Zero matrix : A matrix whose all elements are zero is called a *zero matrix* (or a null matrix).

For example, $[0, 0]$, $\begin{bmatrix} 0 \\ 0 \\ 0 \end{bmatrix}$, $\begin{bmatrix} 0 & 0 \\ 0 & 0 \end{bmatrix}$, $\begin{bmatrix} 0 & 0 & 0 \\ 0 & 0 & 0 \\ 0 & 0 & 0 \end{bmatrix}$

are all zero matrices. They are of the orders $1 \times 2, 3 \times 1, 2 \times 2$ and 3×3 respectively. A zero matrix is denoted by O. (capital letter O).

(2) Row matrix : A matrix having only one row is called a *row matrix*. A row matrix containing n elements is a matrix of the order $1 \times n$. For example,

$[1 \ 2], [2 \ 3 \ 4], [0 \ 1 \ 2], [p \ q \ r]$

are all row matrices. They are of the orders $1 \times 2, 1 \times 3, 1 \times 3, 1 \times 3$ respectively.

(3) Column matrix : A matrix having only one column is called a *column matrix*. A column matrix containing n elements is a matrix of the order $n \times 1$.

For example, $\begin{bmatrix} 0 \\ 1 \end{bmatrix}$, $\begin{bmatrix} -1 \\ 1 \\ 1 \end{bmatrix}$, $\begin{bmatrix} 4 \\ 5 \\ 6 \end{bmatrix}$, $\begin{bmatrix} k \\ l \\ m \end{bmatrix}$

are all column matrices. They are of the orders $2 \times 1, 3 \times 1, 3 \times 1, 3 \times 1$ respectively.

(4) Square matrix : A matrix in which the number of rows is equal to the number of columns is called a square matrix. A square matrix having n rows and n columns is a matrix of the order $n \times n$. It is usually called a *square matrix of order n* (instead of order $n \times n$).

For example, $\begin{bmatrix} 1 & 2 \\ 3 & 4 \end{bmatrix}$, $\begin{bmatrix} 1 & 0 \\ 0 & 1 \end{bmatrix}$, $\begin{bmatrix} 0 & -2 & 3 \\ 2 & 0 & -5 \\ -3 & 5 & 0 \end{bmatrix}$, $\begin{bmatrix} a & h & g \\ h & b & f \\ g & f & c \end{bmatrix}$

are all square matrices. The first two are of order 2 and the next two are of order 3.

In a square matrix, the elements in the places (1, 1), (2, 2), (3, 3), ... are called the diagonal elements. (In the four matrices above, the diagonal elements are 1, 4; 1, 1; 0, 0, 0; a, b, c respectively.) They are said to form the principal diagonal or the leading diagonal of the matrix. In a square matrix, the elements other than the diagonal elements are called the *non-diagonal elements*. Thus in the square matrix $\begin{bmatrix} a & b \\ c & d \end{bmatrix}$ b, c are the non-diagonal elements.

(5) Diagonal matrix : A square matrix in which all the non-diagonal elements are zero is called *a diagonal matrix*. For example,

$$\begin{bmatrix} 2 & 0 \\ 0 & 4 \end{bmatrix}, \quad \begin{bmatrix} 1 & 0 & 0 \\ 0 & -1 & 0 \\ 0 & 0 & 1 \end{bmatrix}, \quad \begin{bmatrix} 4 & 0 & 0 \\ 0 & 0 & 0 \\ 0 & 0 & 3 \end{bmatrix}, \quad \begin{bmatrix} p & 0 & 0 \\ 0 & q & 0 \\ 0 & 0 & r \end{bmatrix}$$

are diagonal matrices. Note that in a diagonal matrix, one or more of the diagonal elements may be zero while all the non-diagonal elements must be zero.

(6) Scalar matrix : A diagonal matrix in which all the diagonal elements are equal, is called a *scalar matrix*. For example,

$$\begin{bmatrix} 3 & 0 \\ 0 & 3 \end{bmatrix}, \quad \begin{bmatrix} 5 & 0 & 0 \\ 0 & 5 & 0 \\ 0 & 0 & 5 \end{bmatrix}, \quad \begin{bmatrix} -2 & 0 & 0 \\ 0 & -2 & 0 \\ 0 & 0 & -2 \end{bmatrix}, \quad \begin{bmatrix} a & 0 & 0 \\ 0 & a & 0 \\ 0 & 0 & a \end{bmatrix}$$

are scalar matrices.

(7) Unit matrix : A scalar matrix in which all the diagonal elements are 1 is called a *unit matrix* (or an identity matrix). For example,

$$\begin{bmatrix} 1 & 0 \\ 0 & 1 \end{bmatrix}, \quad \begin{bmatrix} 1 & 0 & 0 \\ 0 & 1 & 0 \\ 0 & 0 & 1 \end{bmatrix}$$

are unit matrices of order 2 and 3 respectively. A unit matrix is denoted by I. If we want to mention the order of a unit matrix, we write I_2, for unit matrix of order 2, I_3 for unit matrix of order 3 etc.

(8) Upper triangular matrix (Oct. 2008) : A square matrix in which all the elements below the principal diagonal are zero is called an *upper triangular matrix*. For example,

$$\begin{bmatrix} 2 & 3 \\ 0 & 4 \end{bmatrix}, \quad \begin{bmatrix} 1 & 2 & 3 \\ 0 & 4 & -2 \\ 0 & 0 & -1 \end{bmatrix}, \quad \begin{vmatrix} p & q & r \\ 0 & 0 & m \\ 0 & 0 & k \end{vmatrix}$$

are upper triangular matrices.

(9) Lower triangular matrix (Oct. 2008) : A square matrix in which all the elements above the principal diagonal are zero is called a *lower triangular matrix* For example,

$$\begin{bmatrix} 1 & 0 \\ 2 & 3 \end{bmatrix}, \quad \begin{bmatrix} 2 & 0 & 0 \\ -1 & 1 & 0 \\ 3 & 2 & 0 \end{bmatrix}, \quad \begin{bmatrix} a & 0 & 0 \\ b & d & 0 \\ c & e & f \end{bmatrix}$$

are lower triangular matrices.

A matrix which is both, upper triangular and lower triangular is clearly a diagonal matrix.

(10) Symmetric matrix : A square matrix

$$A = \begin{bmatrix} a_{11} & a_{12} & a_{13} \\ a_{21} & a_{22} & a_{23} \\ a_{31} & a_{32} & a_{33} \end{bmatrix} \text{ is called } symmetric \ matrix.$$

if $a_{12} = a_{21}$, $a_{13} = a_{31}$ and $a_{23} = a_{32}$. This means the elements which are symmetrically situated w.r.t. the principal diagonal are equal. For example,

$$\begin{bmatrix} 1 & 4 \\ 4 & 2 \end{bmatrix}, \quad \begin{bmatrix} 1 & 3 & -2 \\ 3 & 4 & 0 \\ -2 & 0 & 5 \end{bmatrix}, \quad \begin{bmatrix} a & h & g \\ h & b & f \\ g & f & c \end{bmatrix}$$

are symmetric matrices.

(11) Skew-symmetric matrix : A square matrix $A = [a_{ij}]$ is called a skew-symmetric matrix. if $a_{ij} = -a_{ji}$ for all i and j. This means that the $(ij)^{th}$ element and the $(ji)^{th}$ element are equal in magnitude but have opposite signs. Further, all its diagonal elements are zero.

$$\begin{bmatrix} 0 & 1 \\ -1 & 0 \end{bmatrix}, \quad \begin{bmatrix} 0 & 2 & -1 \\ -2 & 0 & -4 \\ 1 & 4 & 0 \end{bmatrix}, \quad \begin{bmatrix} 0 & p & q \\ -p & 0 & -r \\ -q & r & 0 \end{bmatrix}$$

are all skew-symmetric matrices.

5.7 Transpose of a Matrix

Consider the matrix $A = \begin{bmatrix} 2 & 3 & 4 \\ 1 & -1 & 3 \end{bmatrix}$. It is of the order 2×3. Let us write another matrix B from A by writing the rows of A as columns of B. We have

$$B = \begin{bmatrix} 2 & 1 \\ 3 & -1 \\ 4 & 3 \end{bmatrix}$$

The matrix B is called the *transpose* of A and it is denoted by A' (read A prime).

Definition : The matrix obtained from a given matrix A by interchanging its rows and columns is called the *transpose of A*. Transpose of A is denoted by A'.

If A is of the order m × n, then A' is of the order n × m.

Clearly, the transpose of the transpose of A is the matrix A itself. i.e. (A')' = A.

Determinant of a square matrix

With any square matrix A we can associate a determinant which is formed by the same array of elements as the matrix A. This determinant is called the *determinant of the matrix A* and it is denoted by |A| (or det A).

e.g. if (i) $A = \begin{bmatrix} 10 & 3 \\ 2 & 1 \end{bmatrix}$, then $|A| = \begin{vmatrix} 10 & 3 \\ 2 & 1 \end{vmatrix} = 4$

(ii) $A = \begin{bmatrix} a & h \\ h & b \end{bmatrix}$, then $|A| = \begin{vmatrix} a & h \\ h & b \end{vmatrix} = ab - h^2$

(iii) $A = \begin{bmatrix} 1 & 2 & 3 \\ 0 & 2 & 5 \\ 0 & 0 & 4 \end{bmatrix}$, then $|A| = \begin{vmatrix} 1 & 2 & 3 \\ 0 & 2 & 5 \\ 0 & 0 & 4 \end{vmatrix} = 8$ etc.

5.8 Singular and Non-singular Matrices   (April 2010)

A square matrix A is called a singular matrix if |A| = 0 and a non-singular matrix if |A| ≠ 0. For example,

let $A = \begin{bmatrix} 1 & 0 & 1 \\ 2 & 1 & 2 \\ 1 & 2 & 6 \end{bmatrix}$. Then $|A| = \begin{vmatrix} 1 & 0 & 1 \\ 2 & 1 & 2 \\ 1 & 2 & 6 \end{vmatrix} = 2 + 3 = 5$

∴ |A| ≠ 0 ∴ the matrix A is a non-singular matrix.

Let $A = \begin{bmatrix} 1 & 2 & 1 \\ 2 & 3 & 1 \\ 3 & 5 & 2 \end{bmatrix}$. Then $|A| = \begin{vmatrix} 1 & 2 & 1 \\ 2 & 3 & 1 \\ 3 & 5 & 2 \end{vmatrix} = 1 - 2 + 1 = 0$

∴ the matrix A is a singular matrix.

Exercise 5.4

1. State the types of the following matrices :

(i) [1, 2, 3]   (ii) $\begin{bmatrix} 0 & 0 & 0 \\ 0 & 0 & 0 \end{bmatrix}$ (iii) $\begin{bmatrix} 2 \\ 3 \end{bmatrix}$ (iv) $\begin{bmatrix} p & 0 & 0 \\ 0 & q & 0 \\ 0 & 0 & r \end{bmatrix}$

(v) $\begin{bmatrix} p & s & t \\ 0 & 0 & 0 \\ 0 & 0 & r \end{bmatrix}$ (vii) $\begin{bmatrix} 1 & 0 \\ 0 & 1 \end{bmatrix}$ (viii) $\begin{bmatrix} 2 & 0 & 0 \\ 0 & 2 & 0 \\ 0 & 0 & 2 \end{bmatrix}$ (ix) $\begin{bmatrix} 0 & 1 \\ 1 & 0 \end{bmatrix}$

$$\text{(x)} \begin{bmatrix} 2 & 0 & 0 \\ 0 & 3 & 0 \\ 0 & 0 & 0 \end{bmatrix} \quad \text{(xi)} \begin{bmatrix} -1 & 0 & 0 \\ 0 & -1 & 0 \\ 0 & 0 & -1 \end{bmatrix} \quad \text{(xii)} \begin{bmatrix} 1 & 0 & 0 \\ 0 & 1 & 0 \\ 0 & 0 & 1 \end{bmatrix}$$

$$\text{(xiii)} \begin{bmatrix} 1 & 3 & 5 \\ 3 & 0 & -2 \\ 5 & -2 & 4 \end{bmatrix} \quad \text{(xiv)} \begin{bmatrix} 0 & 2 & -3 \\ -2 & 0 & 4 \\ 3 & -4 & 0 \end{bmatrix} \quad \text{(xv)} \begin{bmatrix} 1 & -2 & 5 \\ 2 & 4 & 3 \\ -5 & -3 & 2 \end{bmatrix}$$

2. Write down the transposes of the following matrices :

$$\text{(i) } [1\ 3\ 5] \quad \text{(ii) } \begin{bmatrix} 2 & 1 & 3 \\ 5 & 6 & 7 \end{bmatrix} \quad \text{(iii) } \begin{bmatrix} 1 & 2 \\ 2 & 1 \\ 4 & 2 \end{bmatrix} \quad \text{(iv) } \begin{bmatrix} 1 & 0 & 0 \\ 0 & 2 & 0 \\ 0 & 0 & 3 \end{bmatrix}$$

3. Consider the symmetric matrix $A = \begin{bmatrix} 2 & 1 & 3 \\ 1 & 1 & -4 \\ 2 & -4 & 5 \end{bmatrix}$

Write down A'. What do you observe ?

4. Determine whether the following matrices are singular or non-singular :

$$\text{(i) } \begin{bmatrix} 2 & 3 \\ -2 & -3 \end{bmatrix} \quad \text{(ii) } \begin{bmatrix} 1 & 3 & 4 \\ 0 & 5 & 6 \\ 0 & 0 & 2 \end{bmatrix} \quad \text{(iii) } \begin{bmatrix} 4 & 0 & 0 \\ 0 & 4 & 0 \\ 0 & 0 & 4 \end{bmatrix} \quad \text{(iv) } \begin{bmatrix} 0 & 0 & 1 \\ 0 & 1 & 0 \\ 1 & 0 & 0 \end{bmatrix}$$

$$\text{(v) } \begin{bmatrix} 1 & 0 & 0 \\ 0 & 2 & 0 \\ 0 & 0 & 0 \end{bmatrix} \quad \text{(vi) } \begin{bmatrix} 1 & 1 & 1 \\ 1 & 1 & 1 \\ 1 & 1 & 1 \end{bmatrix} \quad \text{(vii) } \begin{bmatrix} 1 & 2 & 3 \\ 4 & 5 & 6 \\ 1 & 2 & 3 \end{bmatrix}$$

$$\text{(vii) } \begin{bmatrix} 50 & 51 & 52 \\ 52 & 51 & 50 \\ 102 & 102 & 102 \end{bmatrix}$$

Answers 5.4

1. (i)　row matrix　　　　　(ii)　zero matrix　　　　　(iii)　column matrix
　 (iv)　square matrix　　　　(v)　diagonal matrix　　　 (vi)　upper triangular matrix
　 (vii)　unit matrix　　　　 (viii)　scalar matrix　　　　(ix)　symmetric matrix
　　(x)　diagonal matrix　　 (xi)　scalar matrix　　　　 (xii)　unit matrix
(xiii)　symmetric matrix (xiv)　skew-symmetric matrix
　 (xv)　square matrix

$$\text{2. (i) } \begin{bmatrix} 1 \\ 3 \\ 5 \end{bmatrix} \quad \text{(ii) } \begin{bmatrix} 2 & 5 \\ 1 & 6 \\ 3 & 7 \end{bmatrix} \quad \text{(iii) } \begin{bmatrix} 1 & 2 & 4 \\ 2 & 1 & 2 \end{bmatrix} \quad \text{(iv) } \begin{bmatrix} 1 & 0 & 0 \\ 0 & 2 & 0 \\ 0 & 0 & 3 \end{bmatrix}$$

4. (i) singular matrix   (ii) non-singular matrix   (iii) non-singular matrix

   (iv) non-singular matrix   (v) singular matrix   (vi) singular matrix

(vii) singular matrix

(viii) singular matrix

5.9 Algebra of Matrices

Equality of matrices

Definition : Two matrices A and B are said to be equal if (i) they are of the same order and (ii) each element of one is equal to the element in the corresponding place of the other. If A and B are equal, we write A = B. If A and B are not equal, we write A ≠ B.

(1) Consider the matrices $A = \begin{bmatrix} 2 & 3 \\ 1 & 2 \end{bmatrix}$, $B = \begin{bmatrix} 1 & 2 & 3 \\ 2 & 3 & 4 \end{bmatrix}$

A is of the order 2 × 2 and B is the of the order 2 × 3. Since the orders of A and B are not the same, A and B are not equal. (i.e. A ≠ B).

(2) Consider the matrices $A = \begin{bmatrix} 3 & 2 \\ 2 & 4 \\ 1 & 0 \end{bmatrix}$ $B = \begin{bmatrix} 3 & 2 \\ 2 & 4 \\ 1 & 0 \end{bmatrix}$

They are of the same order viz. 3 × 2 and their corresponding elements are equal. Therefore A and B are equal. (i.e. A = B)

We now proceed to define some basic operations on matrices. These are (i) Scalar multiplication (ii) Addition (iii) Subtraction (iv) Multiplication. You will see how these operations on given matrices gives rise to new matrices.

(1) Scalar multiplication

Let A be any matrix and c a scalar (i.e. a real number). Then the matrix obtained by multiplying every element of A by c is called the scalar multiple of A by c. It is denoted by cA. Clearly, cA is a matrix of same order as A.

Let $\quad A = \begin{bmatrix} 2 & 3 & -1 \\ 1 & 0 & 4 \end{bmatrix}$ and let c = 2. Then

$$cA = 2 \begin{bmatrix} 2 & 3 & -1 \\ 1 & 0 & 4 \end{bmatrix} = \begin{bmatrix} 2\times2 & 2\times3 & 2\times(-1) \\ 2\times1 & 2\times0 & 2\times4 \end{bmatrix} = \begin{bmatrix} 4 & 6 & -2 \\ 2 & 0 & 8 \end{bmatrix}$$

Similarly, $-3A = \begin{bmatrix} -6 & -9 & 3 \\ -3 & 0 & -12 \end{bmatrix}$, $\frac{1}{2}A = \begin{bmatrix} 1 & 3/2 & -1/2 \\ 1/2 & 0 & 2 \end{bmatrix}$

(Note that c need not be a positive integer.)

In particular, if we take c = – 1, then cA = – 1A. We write – A for – 1A. The matrix – A is called the *negative of the matrix A* and it is obtained by changing the sign of every element of A.

For example, if $A = \begin{bmatrix} 1 & 2 \\ -3 & 4 \\ 0 & -1 \end{bmatrix}$, then $-A = \begin{bmatrix} -1 & -2 \\ 3 & -4 \\ 0 & 1 \end{bmatrix}$

(2) Addition of matrices

Consider the matrices

$$A = \begin{bmatrix} 1 & 2 & 2 \\ -2 & -1 & 4 \end{bmatrix} \text{ and } B = \begin{bmatrix} 2 & -1 & 1 \\ 3 & -2 & -3 \end{bmatrix}$$

Matrices A and B are of the same order (viz. 2 × 3). The sum of A and B written as A + B is a matrix C (say), which is of the same order as A and B and whose elements are obtained by a adding the corresponding elements of A and B. Thus

$$C = A + B = \begin{bmatrix} 1+2 & 2+(-1) & 2+1 \\ -2+3 & -1+(-2) & 4+(-3) \end{bmatrix} = \begin{bmatrix} 3 & 1 & 3 \\ 1 & -3 & 1 \end{bmatrix}$$

Similarly, (i) if $A = \begin{bmatrix} 2 & 3 \\ 1 & 0 \end{bmatrix}$ $B = \begin{bmatrix} 1 & 2 \\ 3 & 1 \end{bmatrix}$ then $A + B = \begin{bmatrix} 3 & 5 \\ 4 & 1 \end{bmatrix}$

(ii) if A = [3 2 – 1],   B = [– 1 1 1] then A + B = [2 3 0]

We now state the following definition.

Definition : Let A = [a_{ij}] and B = [b_{ij}] be two matrices of the same order m × n (say). Then their sum, denoted by A + B, is a matrix C = [c_{ij}] of the order m × n and such that $c_{ij} = a_{ij} + b_{ij}$ for i = 1 to m, j = 1 to n.

Two matrices which are of the same order are said to be conformable for addition. If two matrices are not of the same order then their sum is not defined.

Commutative and Associative laws of addition of matrices

(i) A + B = B + A. This is known as the *commutative law of addition of matrices*.

(ii) (A + B) + C = A + (B + C). This is known as the *associative law of addition of matrices*.

Let us verify these laws for three particular matrices A, B, C.

Let $A = \begin{bmatrix} 1 & 2 \\ 2 & -1 \end{bmatrix}$, $B = \begin{bmatrix} 3 & 1 \\ -1 & -2 \end{bmatrix}$, $C = \begin{bmatrix} -1 & 1 \\ 3 & -2 \end{bmatrix}$

Then $A + B = \begin{bmatrix} 4 & 3 \\ 1 & -3 \end{bmatrix}$, $B + A = \begin{bmatrix} 4 & 3 \\ 1 & -3 \end{bmatrix}$ showing that A + B = B + A.

Further, $(A + B) + C = \begin{bmatrix} 4 & 3 \\ 1 & -3 \end{bmatrix} + \begin{bmatrix} -1 & 1 \\ 3 & -2 \end{bmatrix} = \begin{bmatrix} 3 & 4 \\ 4 & -5 \end{bmatrix}$

and $A + (B + C) = \begin{bmatrix} 1 & 2 \\ 2 & -1 \end{bmatrix} + \begin{bmatrix} 2 & 2 \\ 2 & -4 \end{bmatrix} = \begin{bmatrix} 3 & 4 \\ 4 & -5 \end{bmatrix}$

showing that $(A + B) + C = A + (B + C)$

In view of the associative law, we may just write $A + B + C$ to mean $(A + B) + C$ or $A + (B + C)$. (i.e. the parentheses may be dropped)

Also $A + A = [a_{ij} + a_{ij}] = [2a_{ij}]$ and $2A = [2a_{ij}]$

Therefore we can write $A + A = 2A$. Similarly, we can write $A + A + A = 3A$ etc.

Illustrative Examples

Example 5.13 : Find the matrix X if $\begin{bmatrix} 2 & 3 \\ -1 & 5 \end{bmatrix} + X = \begin{bmatrix} 5 & 2 \\ 3 & 3 \end{bmatrix}$

Solution : Clearly X is a square matrix of order 2. Let

$$X = \begin{bmatrix} a & b \\ c & d \end{bmatrix}. \text{ Then } \begin{bmatrix} 2 & 3 \\ -1 & 5 \end{bmatrix} + \begin{bmatrix} a & b \\ c & d \end{bmatrix} = \begin{bmatrix} 5 & 2 \\ 3 & 3 \end{bmatrix}$$

$\therefore \quad \begin{bmatrix} 2+a & 3+b \\ -1+c & 5+d \end{bmatrix} = \begin{bmatrix} 5 & 2 \\ 3 & 3 \end{bmatrix}$

$\therefore$ by the definition of equality of matrices,

$\therefore \quad 2 + a = 5, 3 + b = 2, -1 + c = 3, 5 + d = 3 \quad \therefore \quad a = 3, b = -1, c = 4, d = -2$

$\therefore \quad X = \begin{bmatrix} 3 & -1 \\ 4 & -2 \end{bmatrix}$

Example 5.14 : If $A = \begin{bmatrix} 2 & 1 & 2 \\ -3 & 4 & 0 \end{bmatrix}$, $B = \begin{bmatrix} 1 & -2 & 3 \\ 2 & -1 & 1 \end{bmatrix}$

find the matrix C such that $A + B + C$ is a zero matrix.

Solution : Clearly C is a matrix of the order 2×3. Let

$$C = \begin{bmatrix} a & b & c \\ d & e & f \end{bmatrix}. \text{ Then }$$

$$A + B + C = \begin{bmatrix} 2 & 1 & 2 \\ -3 & 4 & 0 \end{bmatrix} + \begin{bmatrix} 1 & -2 & 3 \\ 2 & -1 & 1 \end{bmatrix} + \begin{bmatrix} a & b & c \\ d & e & f \end{bmatrix}$$

$$= \begin{bmatrix} 3+a & -1+b & 5+c \\ -1+d & 3+e & 1+f \end{bmatrix}$$

A + B + C = O gives $3 + a = 0, -1 + b = 0, 5 + c = 0, -1 + d = 0,$

$3 + e = 0, 1 + f = 0$ $\therefore$ $a = -3, b = 1, c = -5, d = 1, e = -3, f = -1$

$\therefore \qquad C = \begin{bmatrix} -3 & 1 & -5 \\ 1 & -3 & -1 \end{bmatrix}$

(3) Subtraction of matrices

Let A and B be two matrices of the same order (m × n, say). Let $A = [a_{ij}]$, $B = [b_{ij}]$. Then A – B is a matrix of the same order as A and B and its elements are obtained by subtracting the elements of B from the corresponding elements of A. Thus if $C = [c_{ij}] = A - B$, then $c_{ij} = a_{ij} - b_{ij}$ for i = 1 to m, j = 1 to n.

e.g. let $\quad A = \begin{bmatrix} 2 & 3 \\ -1 & 4 \\ 1 & 2 \end{bmatrix}$ $B = \begin{bmatrix} 1 & 4 \\ 2 & 1 \\ -1 & -2 \end{bmatrix}$. Then

$A - B = \begin{bmatrix} 2-1 & 3-4 \\ -1-2 & 4-1 \\ 1-(-1) & 2-(-2) \end{bmatrix} = \begin{bmatrix} 1 & -1 \\ -3 & 3 \\ 2 & 4 \end{bmatrix}$

Similarly, $B - A = \begin{bmatrix} 1-2 & 4-3 \\ 2-(-1) & 1-4 \\ -1-1 & 2-2 \end{bmatrix} = \begin{bmatrix} -1 & 1 \\ 3 & -3 \\ -2 & -4 \end{bmatrix}$

In view of our definition of the negative of a matrix, we can say that A – B = A + (– B). Also, for any matrix A, A – A = O (zero matrix). If two matrices are not of the same order, then subtraction is not defined.

Note : If A, B, C are matrices of the same order and if A + B = C, then we have A = C – B, B = C – A. In particular, if A + B = O, then A = – B, B = – A.

Ex. 5.13 may now be worked out alternatively, as follows :

$\begin{bmatrix} 2 & 3 \\ -1 & 5 \end{bmatrix} + X = \begin{bmatrix} 5 & 2 \\ 3 & 3 \end{bmatrix}$ $\therefore$ $X = \begin{bmatrix} 5 & 2 \\ 3 & 3 \end{bmatrix} - \begin{bmatrix} 2 & 3 \\ -1 & 5 \end{bmatrix} = \begin{bmatrix} 3 & -1 \\ 4 & -2 \end{bmatrix}$

Illustrative Examples

Example 5.15 : If $A = \begin{bmatrix} 1 & 2 \\ 3 & 4 \end{bmatrix}$, $B = \begin{bmatrix} 2 & 3 \\ -4 & 2 \end{bmatrix}$, $C = \begin{bmatrix} 8 & 6 \\ 4 & 4 \end{bmatrix}$

Find $2A + 3B - \dfrac{1}{2} C$.

Solution : We have $2A + 3B - \dfrac{1}{2} C = \begin{bmatrix} 2 & 4 \\ 6 & 8 \end{bmatrix} + \begin{bmatrix} 6 & 9 \\ -12 & 6 \end{bmatrix} - \begin{bmatrix} 4 & 3 \\ 2 & 2 \end{bmatrix}$

$$= \begin{bmatrix} 8 & 13 \\ -6 & 14 \end{bmatrix} - \begin{bmatrix} 4 & 3 \\ 2 & 2 \end{bmatrix} = \begin{bmatrix} 4 & 10 \\ -8 & 12 \end{bmatrix}$$

Example 5.16 : If $A = \begin{bmatrix} 2 & 4 & 3 \\ -3 & -1 & 0 \end{bmatrix}$ and $B = \begin{bmatrix} 1 & -2 & 3 \\ 2 & 4 & 5 \end{bmatrix}$, find a matrix X such that $2X + A - 2B = O$.

Solution : $2X + A - 2B = O$ ∴ $2X = O + 2B - A = 2B - A$

∴ $\qquad 2X = 2 \begin{bmatrix} 1 & -2 & 3 \\ 2 & 4 & 5 \end{bmatrix} - \begin{bmatrix} 2 & 4 & 3 \\ -3 & -1 & 0 \end{bmatrix}$

$$= \begin{bmatrix} 2 & -4 & 6 \\ 4 & 8 & 10 \end{bmatrix} - \begin{bmatrix} 2 & 4 & 3 \\ -3 & -1 & 0 \end{bmatrix} = \begin{bmatrix} 0 & -8 & 3 \\ 7 & 9 & 10 \end{bmatrix}$$

∴ $\qquad X = \dfrac{1}{2} \begin{bmatrix} 0 & -8 & 3 \\ 7 & 9 & 10 \end{bmatrix} = \begin{bmatrix} 0 & -4 & 3/2 \\ 7/2 & 9/2 & 5 \end{bmatrix}$

Example 5.17 : Find the values of x, y, z if

$$\begin{bmatrix} 2x - 1 & 3 \\ 4 & 2 \\ 3z - 1 & 5 \end{bmatrix} + \begin{bmatrix} 7 & 2 \\ 1 & y + 3 \\ z & -4 \end{bmatrix} = \begin{bmatrix} 10 & 5 \\ 5 & 9 \\ 11 & 1 \end{bmatrix}$$

Solution : Adding the two matrices on the L.H.S. we get

$$\begin{bmatrix} 2x + 6 & 5 \\ 5 & y + 5 \\ 4z - 1 & 1 \end{bmatrix} = \begin{bmatrix} 10 & 5 \\ 5 & 9 \\ 11 & 1 \end{bmatrix}$$

∴ by the definition of equality of matrices,

$2x + 6 = 10$, $y + 5 = 9$, $4z - 1 = 11$. ∴ $x = 2$, $y = 4$, $z = 3$.

Exercise 5.5

1. Let $A = \begin{bmatrix} 2 & 1 \\ 1 & 2 \\ 3 & 1 \end{bmatrix}$. Write down 3A and A + A + A. Are they equal ?

2. If $A = \begin{bmatrix} 2 & 3 \\ 4 & 1 \end{bmatrix}$, $B = \begin{bmatrix} 1 & 1 \\ 3 & 2 \end{bmatrix}$

   (i) write down A + B, A – B, B – A, 2A + 3B, 3A – 2B,

   (ii) find a matrix X such that A – 2B + X = O (iii) find a matrix X such that 2A – B + X = 1

3. If $A = \begin{bmatrix} 1 & 2 \\ 2 & 1 \\ 0 & 3 \end{bmatrix}$, $B = \begin{bmatrix} -2 & -4 \\ 1 & 0 \\ 3 & -1 \end{bmatrix}$, find a matrix C such that A + B + C is a zero matrix.

4. If $A = \begin{bmatrix} 2 & 3 & -1 \\ -1 & 2 & 0 \end{bmatrix}$, $B = \begin{bmatrix} 1 & -1 & 4 \\ 2 & 1 & 2 \end{bmatrix}$, $C = \begin{bmatrix} -1 & 2 & 1 \\ 3 & -1 & 0 \end{bmatrix}$

   find (i) 2A + B – C, A – B + C, A + 2B + 3C (ii) a matrix X such that A – 2B + C + X = O (iii) Verify that A – (B – C) = A – B + C

5. If $A = \begin{bmatrix} 4 & 5 \\ 3 & 7 \end{bmatrix}$, find a matrix X such that $A - 2X = \begin{bmatrix} 2 & 3 \\ 7 & 5 \end{bmatrix}$

Answers 5.5

1. $3A = \begin{bmatrix} 6 & 3 \\ 3 & 6 \\ 9 & 3 \end{bmatrix} = A + A + A$

2. (i) $A + B = \begin{bmatrix} 3 & 4 \\ 7 & 3 \end{bmatrix}$, $A - B = \begin{bmatrix} 1 & 2 \\ 1 & -1 \end{bmatrix}$, $B - A = \begin{bmatrix} -1 & -2 \\ -1 & 1 \end{bmatrix}$,

   $2A + 3B = \begin{bmatrix} 7 & 9 \\ 17 & 8 \end{bmatrix}$, $3A - 2B = \begin{bmatrix} 4 & 7 \\ 6 & -1 \end{bmatrix}$ (ii) $X = 2B - A = \begin{bmatrix} 0 & -1 \\ 2 & 3 \end{bmatrix}$

   (iii) $X = 1 + B - 2A = \begin{bmatrix} -2 & -5 \\ -5 & 1 \end{bmatrix}$

3. $C = \begin{bmatrix} 1 & 2 \\ -3 & -1 \\ 3 & -2 \end{bmatrix}$

4. (i) $2A + B - C = \begin{bmatrix} 6 & 3 & 1 \\ -3 & 6 & 2 \end{bmatrix}$, $A - B + C = \begin{bmatrix} 0 & 6 & -4 \\ 0 & 0 & -2 \end{bmatrix}$,

   $A + 2B + 3C = \begin{bmatrix} 1 & 7 & 10 \\ 12 & 1 & 4 \end{bmatrix}$

   (ii) $X = 2B - A - C = \begin{bmatrix} 1 & -7 & 8 \\ 2 & 1 & 4 \end{bmatrix}$

   (iii) $A - (B - C) = A - B + C = \begin{bmatrix} 0 & 6 & -4 \\ 0 & 0 & -2 \end{bmatrix}$

5. $X = \begin{bmatrix} 1 & 1 \\ -2 & 1 \end{bmatrix}$

(4) Multiplication of matrices

Let $\quad A = \begin{bmatrix} 2 & 1 \\ 2 & 3 \end{bmatrix}$, $B = \begin{bmatrix} 1 & 2 & -1 \\ 4 & -2 & 5 \end{bmatrix}$

A is of the order 2×2 and B is of the order 2×3. We have taken the number of columns of A and the number of rows of B equal. The product of the matrices A and B, taken in this order, is defined. It is denoted by AB. It is a matrix which has the same number of rows as A and the same number of columns as B. Thus, here AB is of the order 2×3. Let us denote AB by $C = [c_{ij}]$. Then $i = 1, 2$ and $j = 1, 2, 3$.

The elements c_{ij} are obtained as follows :

To find c_{11}, we take the first row of A viz. [2 1], and the first column of B viz. $\begin{bmatrix} 1 \\ 4 \end{bmatrix}$ and form the sum of the products of the corresponding elements. This sum gives c_{11}. Thus $c_{11} = (2 \times 1) + (1 \times 4) = 2 + 4 = 6$

To find c_{12}, we take the first row of A viz. [2 1] and the second cloumn of B viz. $\begin{bmatrix} 2 \\ -2 \end{bmatrix}$ and form the sum of the products of the corresponding elements. This sum gives c_{12}.

Thus $c_{12} = (2 \times 2) + [1 \times (-2))] = 2$

Similarly, $\quad c_{13} = [2 \times (-1)] + (1 \times 5) = 3 \qquad\qquad c_{21} = (2 \times 1) + (3 \times 4) = 14$

$c_{22} = (2 \times 2) + [3 \times (-2)] = -2 \qquad\qquad c_{23} = [2 \times (-1)] + (3 \times 5) = 13$

$\therefore \qquad\qquad AB = C = \begin{bmatrix} c_{11} & c_{12} & c_{13} \\ c_{21} & c_{22} & c_{23} \end{bmatrix} = \begin{bmatrix} 6 & 2 & 3 \\ 14 & -2 & 13 \end{bmatrix}$

You will observe that in forming the product AB, the rows of A and the columns of B come in the picture. In the above illustration, A has two rows.

Let us denote them by R_1 and R_2 and write $A = \begin{bmatrix} R_1 \\ R_2 \end{bmatrix}$. B has three columns.

Let us denote them by C_1, C_2, C_3 and write $B = [C_1 \ C_2 \ C_3]$. Then AB may be written symbolically as

$$AB = \begin{bmatrix} R_1C_1 & R_1C_2 & R_1C_3 \\ R_2C_1 & R_2C_2 & R_2C_3 \end{bmatrix}$$

Note :

(1) Two matrices A and B such that the number of columns of A is equal to the number of rows of B are said to be *comformable for the product* AB. For example, if A is of the order $m \times n$ and B is of the order $n \times p$ then A and B are conformable for the product AB which is of the order $m \times p$. In the product AB, A is called the *prefactor* and B is called the *postfactor*. A is said to be postmultiplied by B and B is said to be premultiplied by A.

(2) Two matrices A and B which are conformable for the product AB may not be conformable for the product BA. For example, if A is a 3×3 matrix and B is a 3×2 matrix then we can form the product AB but not the product BA.

(3) Even if the products AB and BA are both defined, they may not be equal. For example, if A is a 2×3 matrix and B is a 3×2 matrix then AB is a square matrix of order 2 and BA is a square matrix of order 3. Thus the orders of AB and BA are not the same. Hence the two products are not equal. In general, if A is matrix of the order $m \times n$ and B is a matrix of the order $n \times m$, then AB and BA are both defined and are square matrices of order m and n respectively. If $m \neq n$ then they are of different orders and hence cannot be equal. If A and B are both square matrices of the same order n, then AB and BA are also square matrices of order n. Even in this case, they are, in general, not equal, because their elements are formed in different ways. Thus matrix multiplication is not commutative.

We explain this point by following examples.

(1) Let

$$A = \begin{bmatrix} 2 & 1 & 1 \\ -1 & 3 & 2 \end{bmatrix}, \quad B = \begin{bmatrix} 1 & 2 \\ 2 & 1 \\ -1 & 3 \end{bmatrix}$$

Then

$$AB = \begin{bmatrix} 3 & 6 \\ 3 & 7 \end{bmatrix}, \quad BA = \begin{bmatrix} 0 & 7 & 5 \\ 3 & 5 & 4 \\ -5 & 8 & 5 \end{bmatrix}$$

AB is a square matrix of order 2 while BA is a square matrix of order 3. They are of course not equal.

(2) Let

$$A = \begin{bmatrix} 2 & 3 \\ 1 & 2 \end{bmatrix}, \quad B = \begin{bmatrix} 1 & 1 \\ 2 & 0 \end{bmatrix}.$$

Then $AB = \begin{bmatrix} 8 & 2 \\ 5 & 1 \end{bmatrix}, BA = \begin{bmatrix} 3 & 5 \\ 4 & 6 \end{bmatrix}$

Here AB and BA are of the same order but their corresponding elements are not equal. Hence $AB \neq BA$.

(3) If A and B are square matrices of the same order, then, in some special cases, we may have AB = BA. e.g.

Let $\quad A = \begin{bmatrix} 2 & 3 \\ 4 & 5 \end{bmatrix}, B = \begin{bmatrix} 1 & 0 \\ 0 & 1 \end{bmatrix}.$ Then $AB = \begin{bmatrix} 2 & 3 \\ 4 & 5 \end{bmatrix}, BA = \begin{bmatrix} 2 & 3 \\ 4 & 5 \end{bmatrix}$

$\therefore \quad AB = BA$ (Observe that here $B = I_2$.)

Let $\quad A = \begin{bmatrix} -1 & 1 \\ 2 & 3 \end{bmatrix} B = \begin{bmatrix} 3 & 2 \\ 4 & 11 \end{bmatrix}$ Then $AB = \begin{bmatrix} 1 & 9 \\ 18 & 37 \end{bmatrix}, BA = \begin{bmatrix} 1 & 9 \\ 18 & 37 \end{bmatrix}$

$\therefore \quad AB = BA$

(**Note :** Two matrices A and B such that AB = BA then they are said *to commute.*)

Associative law of matrix multiplication

Let A, B, C be three matrices of the orders m × n, n × p, p × q respectively. Then the product AB is defined and it is of the order m × p. The product (AB) C is also defined and it is of the order m × q. Similarly the product BC is defined and it is of the order n × q. The product A (BC) is also defined and it is of the order m × q. Thus (AB) C and A(BC) are matrices of the same order viz. m × q. Will these products be always equal ? We state (without proof) that the answers is yes. The two products are always equal. We do have

$$(AB)\, C \;=\; A\,(BC)$$

This result is known as the *associative law of matrix multiplication.*

Let us verify this result by an example.

Let $A_{3 \times 2} \begin{bmatrix} 2 & -1 \\ 1 & 2 \\ 1 & 1 \end{bmatrix}$, $B_{2 \times 2} = \begin{bmatrix} 1 & -1 \\ 0 & 1 \end{bmatrix}$, $C_{2 \times 2} = \begin{bmatrix} 2 & 1 \\ 1 & 0 \end{bmatrix}$

Then $\qquad AB = \begin{bmatrix} 2 & 1 \\ 1 & 1 \\ 1 & 0 \end{bmatrix}$, $(AB)\,C = \begin{bmatrix} 3 & 2 \\ 3 & 1 \\ 2 & 1 \end{bmatrix}$

$\qquad\qquad BC = \begin{bmatrix} 1 & 1 \\ 1 & 0 \end{bmatrix}$, $A(BC) = \begin{bmatrix} 3 & 2 \\ 3 & 1 \\ 2 & 1 \end{bmatrix}$ Thus $(AB)\, C = A\,(BC)$

In view of this law, each of the products (AB) C and A (BC) is denoted by ABC i.e. brackets are removed. One may find ABC as (AB) C or A (BC).

(5) Positive integral powers of a square matrix

Let A be a square matrix. Then the product AA is defined. We write $AA = A^2$. Then $A^2 A$ and AA^2 are defined.

We write $A^2\, A = AA^2 = A^3$.

Similarly, $A^3\, A = AA^3 = A^4$ and so on. In this way we can find A^n where n is any positive integer.

e.g. (1) $\qquad$ if $A = \begin{bmatrix} 1 & 1 \\ 2 & 1 \end{bmatrix}$, then $A^2 = \begin{bmatrix} 1 & 1 \\ 2 & 1 \end{bmatrix}\begin{bmatrix} 1 & 1 \\ 2 & 1 \end{bmatrix} = \begin{bmatrix} 3 & 2 \\ 4 & 3 \end{bmatrix}$

$\qquad\qquad A^3 = \begin{bmatrix} 3 & 2 \\ 4 & 3 \end{bmatrix}\begin{bmatrix} 1 & 1 \\ 2 & 1 \end{bmatrix} = \begin{bmatrix} 7 & 5 \\ 10 & 7 \end{bmatrix}$ etc.

(2) $\qquad$ if $I = \begin{bmatrix} 1 & 0 \\ 0 & 1 \end{bmatrix}$, then $I^2 = \begin{bmatrix} 1 & 0 \\ 0 & 1 \end{bmatrix}\begin{bmatrix} 1 & 0 \\ 0 & 1 \end{bmatrix} = \begin{bmatrix} 1 & 0 \\ 0 & 1 \end{bmatrix} = I$

$\qquad\qquad I^3 = \begin{bmatrix} 1 & 0 \\ 0 & 1 \end{bmatrix}\begin{bmatrix} 1 & 0 \\ 0 & 1 \end{bmatrix}\begin{bmatrix} 1 & 0 \\ 0 & 1 \end{bmatrix} = I$ etc.

We can show that $I^n = I$ where n is any positive integer and I is unit matrix of any order.

Illustrative Examples

Example 5.18 : $A = \begin{bmatrix} -1 & 2 \\ 5 & 1 \end{bmatrix}$, find matrix X such that $2A + 3X = \begin{bmatrix} 4 & 16 \\ -5 & 17 \end{bmatrix}$.

(April 2013)

Solution : Since A is of order 2×2, X must be of the order 2×2.

Let $\qquad\qquad\qquad\qquad X = \begin{bmatrix} x & y \\ z & u \end{bmatrix}$

$\therefore \qquad 2\begin{bmatrix} -1 & 2 \\ 5 & 1 \end{bmatrix} + 3\begin{bmatrix} x & y \\ z & u \end{bmatrix} = \begin{bmatrix} 4 & 16 \\ -5 & 17 \end{bmatrix}$

$\therefore \qquad \begin{bmatrix} -2 & 4 \\ 10 & 2 \end{bmatrix} + \begin{bmatrix} 3x & 3y \\ 3z & 3u \end{bmatrix} = \begin{bmatrix} 4 & 16 \\ -5 & 17 \end{bmatrix}$

$\therefore \qquad \begin{bmatrix} -2+3x & 4+3y \\ 10+3z & 2+3u \end{bmatrix} = \begin{bmatrix} 4 & 16 \\ -5 & 17 \end{bmatrix}$

By equality of matrices,

$\qquad -2 + 3x = 4, \quad 4 + 3y = 16, \quad 10 + 3z = -5, \quad 2 + 3u = 17$

$\therefore \quad 3x = 6, \quad 3y = 12, \quad 3z = -15, \quad 3u = 15$

$\therefore \quad x = 2, y = 4, z = -3, u = 5.$

$\therefore \qquad\qquad\qquad\qquad X = \begin{bmatrix} 2 & 4 \\ -3 & 5 \end{bmatrix}$

Example 5.19 : If $A = \begin{bmatrix} 2 & 3 & 4 \\ 1 & 5 & 7 \end{bmatrix}$, $B = \begin{bmatrix} -1 & 2 & 5 \\ 4 & -3 & 7 \\ 3 & 6 & 0 \end{bmatrix}$, find matrix X such that

$AB + X = \begin{bmatrix} 5 & 10 & 15 \\ 0 & -17 & 30 \end{bmatrix}$. **(Oct. 2008)**

Solution : Since A is 2×3 matrix and B is 3×3 matrix AB is a matrix of order 2×3.

$\therefore \quad$ X must be matrix of order 2×3.

Let $\quad X = \begin{bmatrix} a & b & c \\ d & e & f \end{bmatrix}$

Now, $AB = \begin{bmatrix} 2 & 3 & 4 \\ 1 & 5 & 7 \end{bmatrix} \begin{bmatrix} -1 & 2 & 5 \\ 4 & -3 & 7 \\ 3 & 6 & 0 \end{bmatrix}$

$= \begin{bmatrix} 2\times-1+3\times4+4\times3 & 2\times2+3\times-3+4\times6 & 2\times5+3\times7+4\times0 \\ 1\times-1+5\times4+7\times3 & 1\times2+5\times-3+7\times6 & 1\times5+5\times7+7\times0 \end{bmatrix}$

$$= \begin{bmatrix} -2+12+12 & 4-9+24 & 10+21+0 \\ -1+20+21 & 2-15+42 & 5+35+0 \end{bmatrix}$$

$$= \begin{bmatrix} 22 & 19 & 31 \\ 40 & 29 & 40 \end{bmatrix}$$

$$AB + X = \begin{bmatrix} 5 & 10 & 15 \\ 0 & -17 & 30 \end{bmatrix}$$

$$\therefore \quad \begin{bmatrix} 22 & 19 & 31 \\ 40 & 29 & 40 \end{bmatrix} + \begin{bmatrix} a & b & c \\ d & e & f \end{bmatrix} = \begin{bmatrix} 5 & 10 & 15 \\ 0 & -17 & 30 \end{bmatrix}$$

$$\therefore \quad \begin{bmatrix} 22+a & 19+b & 31+c \\ 40+d & 29+e & 40+f \end{bmatrix} = \begin{bmatrix} 5 & 10 & 15 \\ 0 & -17 & 30 \end{bmatrix}$$

By equality of matrices

$$22 + a = 5, \quad 19 + b = 10, \quad 31 + c = 15$$
$$40 + d = 0, \quad 29 + e = -17, \quad 40 + f = 30$$

$$\therefore \quad a = -17, \ b = -9, \ c = -16, \ d = -40, \ e = -46, \ f = -10$$

$$\therefore \qquad X = \begin{bmatrix} -17 & -9 & -16 \\ -40 & -46 & -10 \end{bmatrix}$$

Example 5.20 : If $A = \begin{bmatrix} 2 & 1 \\ 3 & 2 \end{bmatrix}$, show that $A^2 = 4A - I$ **(Oct. 2014)**

Solution : $\quad A^2 = \begin{bmatrix} 2 & 1 \\ 3 & 2 \end{bmatrix}\begin{bmatrix} 2 & 1 \\ 3 & 2 \end{bmatrix} = \begin{bmatrix} 7 & 4 \\ 12 & 7 \end{bmatrix}$ ... (1)

$$4A - I = \begin{bmatrix} 8 & 4 \\ 12 & 8 \end{bmatrix} - \begin{bmatrix} 1 & 0 \\ 0 & 1 \end{bmatrix} = \begin{bmatrix} 7 & 4 \\ 12 & 7 \end{bmatrix} \qquad \text{... (2)}$$

From (1) and (2), $A^2 = 4A - I$

Example 5.21 : If $A = \begin{bmatrix} 2 & 1 \\ -1 & 3 \\ 1 & 2 \end{bmatrix}$, $B = \begin{bmatrix} -1 & 2 \\ 3 & -1 \\ 1 & -1 \end{bmatrix}$, $C = \begin{bmatrix} 2 \\ 1 \end{bmatrix}$, $X = \begin{bmatrix} x \\ y \\ z \end{bmatrix}$

find x, y, z if $(2A + B) C = X$

Solution : $2A + B = \begin{bmatrix} 3 & 4 \\ 1 & 5 \\ 3 & 3 \end{bmatrix}$ $\therefore$ $(2A + B)C = \begin{bmatrix} 3 & 4 \\ 1 & 5 \\ 3 & 3 \end{bmatrix}\begin{bmatrix} 2 \\ -1 \end{bmatrix} = \begin{bmatrix} 2 \\ -3 \\ 3 \end{bmatrix}$

$(2A + B) C = X$ gives $\begin{bmatrix} 2 \\ -3 \\ 3 \end{bmatrix} = \begin{bmatrix} x \\ y \\ z \end{bmatrix}$ $\therefore$ $x = 2, \ y = -3, \ z = 3$

Example 5.22 : If $A = \begin{bmatrix} 3 & 1 \\ 5 & 2 \end{bmatrix}$, find a matrix B such that $AB = I_2$.

Verify that $BA = I_2$.

Solution : Clearly, B must be a square matrix of order 2. Let

$$B = \begin{bmatrix} a & b \\ c & d \end{bmatrix}. \text{ Then } AB = \begin{bmatrix} 3 & 1 \\ 5 & 2 \end{bmatrix}\begin{bmatrix} a & b \\ c & d \end{bmatrix} = \begin{bmatrix} 3a+c & 3b+d \\ 5a+2c & 5b+2d \end{bmatrix}$$

$$AB = I_2 \text{ gives } \begin{bmatrix} 3a+c & 3b+d \\ 5a+2c & 5b+2d \end{bmatrix} = \begin{bmatrix} 1 & 0 \\ 0 & 1 \end{bmatrix}$$

$\therefore$ $3a + c = 1$, $5a + 2c = 0$, $3b + d = 0$, $5b + 2d = 1$. First two equations gives $a = 2$, $c = -5$. Next two equations gives $b = -1$, $d = 3$.

$\therefore$ $$B = \begin{bmatrix} 2 & -1 \\ -5 & 3 \end{bmatrix}. \text{ Also } BA = \begin{bmatrix} 2 & -1 \\ -5 & 3 \end{bmatrix}\begin{bmatrix} 3 & 1 \\ 5 & 2 \end{bmatrix} = \begin{bmatrix} 1 & 0 \\ 0 & 1 \end{bmatrix} = I_2.$$

Example 5.23 : Determine x, y, z if

$$\left\{ 5\begin{bmatrix} 1 & 0 \\ 0 & 1 \\ 1 & 1 \end{bmatrix} - 3\begin{bmatrix} 1 & 2 \\ -2 & 3 \\ 3 & 1 \end{bmatrix} \right\}\begin{bmatrix} 2 \\ 1 \end{bmatrix} = \begin{bmatrix} x \\ y \\ z \end{bmatrix}$$

Solution : $\text{L.H.S} = \left\{ \begin{bmatrix} 5 & 0 \\ 0 & 5 \\ 5 & 5 \end{bmatrix} - \begin{bmatrix} 3 & 6 \\ -6 & 9 \\ 9 & 3 \end{bmatrix} \right\}\begin{bmatrix} 2 \\ 1 \end{bmatrix}$

$$= \begin{bmatrix} 2 & -6 \\ 6 & -4 \\ -4 & 2 \end{bmatrix}\begin{bmatrix} 2 \\ 1 \end{bmatrix} = \begin{bmatrix} -2 \\ 8 \\ -6 \end{bmatrix}$$

$\therefore$ $$\begin{bmatrix} -2 \\ 8 \\ -6 \end{bmatrix} = \begin{bmatrix} x \\ y \\ z \end{bmatrix}$$

$\therefore$ $x = -2$, $y = 8$, $z = -6$

Example 5.24 : Find the values of a and b if $\begin{bmatrix} 3 & 2 \\ 1 & 5 \end{bmatrix}\begin{bmatrix} a & 1 \\ b & 2 \end{bmatrix} = \begin{bmatrix} 8 & 7 \\ 7 & 11 \end{bmatrix}$

Solution : We have, forming the product of the matrices on the L.H.S.

$\begin{bmatrix} 3a+2b & 7 \\ a+5b & 11 \end{bmatrix} = \begin{bmatrix} 8 & 7 \\ 7 & 11 \end{bmatrix}$ $\therefore$ $3a + 2b = 8$, $a + 5b = 7$

Solving these equations we get $a = 2$, $b = 1$.

Example 5.25 : If $A = \begin{bmatrix} 1 & 2 & 3 \\ 2 & -1 & 0 \end{bmatrix}$, $B = \begin{bmatrix} 4 \\ -5 \\ 7 \end{bmatrix}$ then show that $(AB)' = B'A'$.

Solution : $AB = \begin{bmatrix} 1 & 2 & 3 \\ 2 & -1 & 0 \end{bmatrix} \begin{bmatrix} 4 \\ -5 \\ 7 \end{bmatrix}$

$= \begin{bmatrix} 1 \times 4 + 2 \times -5 + 3 \times 7 \\ 2 \times 4 + (-1)(-5) + 0 \times 7 \end{bmatrix}$

$= \begin{bmatrix} 4 - 10 + 21 \\ 8 + 5 + 0 \end{bmatrix}$

$= \begin{bmatrix} 15 \\ 13 \end{bmatrix}$

$\therefore$ $(AB)' = [15 \quad 13]$ ... (1)

$B' = \begin{bmatrix} 4 \\ -5 \\ 7 \end{bmatrix}' = [4 \ -5 \ 7]$

$A' = \begin{bmatrix} 1 & 2 \\ 2 & -1 \\ 3 & 0 \end{bmatrix}$

$\therefore$ $B'A' = [4 \ -5 \ 7] \begin{bmatrix} 1 & 2 \\ 2 & -1 \\ 3 & 0 \end{bmatrix}$

$= [4 \times 1 + (-5)(2) + 7 \times 3 \quad 4 \times 2 + (-5)(-1) + 7 \times 0]$

$= [4 - 10 + 21 \quad 8 + 5 + 0]$

$= [15 \quad 13]$ ... (2)

From equation (1) and (2),

$(AB)' = B'A'$

Example 5.26 : Show that the matrix $A = \begin{bmatrix} 1 & 2 \\ 1 & 3 \end{bmatrix}$ satisfies the equation

$A^2 - 4A + I = 0$ **(April 2011)**

Solution : $A = \begin{bmatrix} 1 & 2 \\ 1 & 3 \end{bmatrix}$

$$A^2 = AA = \begin{bmatrix} 1 & 2 \\ 1 & 3 \end{bmatrix}\begin{bmatrix} 1 & 2 \\ 1 & 3 \end{bmatrix}$$

$$= \begin{bmatrix} 1\times1+2\times1 & 1\times2+2\times3 \\ 1\times1+3\times1 & 1\times2+3\times3 \end{bmatrix}$$

$$= \begin{bmatrix} 3 & 8 \\ 4 & 11 \end{bmatrix}$$

$$A^2 - 4A + I = \begin{bmatrix} 3 & 8 \\ 4 & 11 \end{bmatrix} - 4\begin{bmatrix} 1 & 2 \\ 1 & 3 \end{bmatrix} + \begin{bmatrix} 1 & 0 \\ 0 & 1 \end{bmatrix}$$

$$= \begin{bmatrix} 3 & 8 \\ 4 & 11 \end{bmatrix} - \begin{bmatrix} 4 & 8 \\ 4 & 12 \end{bmatrix} + \begin{bmatrix} 1 & 0 \\ 0 & 1 \end{bmatrix}$$

$$= \begin{bmatrix} 3-4+1 & 8-8+0 \\ 4-4+0 & 11-12+1 \end{bmatrix}$$

$$= 0$$

Exercise 5.6

1. Given the following pairs of matrices, form the products whichever are defined :

   (i) $A = [1 \ 2]$ $B = \begin{bmatrix} 2 & 1 \\ 1 & 1 \end{bmatrix}$

   (ii) $A = [2 \ 1 \ 1]$ $B = \begin{bmatrix} 1 \\ 2 \\ 3 \end{bmatrix}$

   (iii) $A = \begin{bmatrix} 3 & 1 & -1 \\ 1 & 2 & 1 \end{bmatrix}$ $B = \begin{bmatrix} -1 \\ 2 \\ 3 \end{bmatrix}$

   (iv) $A = [p \ q \ r]$ $B = \begin{bmatrix} a & b & c \\ 1 & m & n \\ u & u & w \end{bmatrix}$

2. If $A = \begin{bmatrix} 2 & 3 \\ -3 & 2 \end{bmatrix}$ $B = \begin{bmatrix} 1 & 2 \\ -2 & 1 \end{bmatrix}$, find AB and BA. What do you observe ?

3. If $A = \begin{bmatrix} 2 & 0 & 0 \\ 0 & 3 & 0 \\ 0 & 0 & 4 \end{bmatrix}$, find a matrix X such that AX $= I_3$.

4. If $A = \begin{bmatrix} 5 & 2 \\ 7 & 3 \end{bmatrix}$, find a matrix X such that AX $= I_2$.

5. If $A = \begin{bmatrix} 2 & 1 \\ 1 & 3 \end{bmatrix}$, $B = \begin{bmatrix} 1 & 2 & -1 \\ 2 & -1 & 0 \end{bmatrix}$. Show that (AB)' = B'A'

(April 2011, Oct. 2013)

6. Let $A = \begin{bmatrix} a & 0 & 0 \\ 0 & b & 0 \\ 0 & 0 & c \end{bmatrix}$, $B = \begin{bmatrix} 1 & 0 & 0 \\ 0 & m & 0 \\ 0 & 0 & n \end{bmatrix}$. Form the products AB and BA. Comment on the result.

7. Let $A = \begin{bmatrix} 1 & 2 \\ 2 & 3 \end{bmatrix}$, $B = \begin{bmatrix} 2 & 3 & -1 \\ 1 & 0 & 1 \end{bmatrix}$, $C = \begin{bmatrix} -1 & -2 & 3 \\ 1 & -2 & 2 \end{bmatrix}$

Show that (i) $A(B+C) = AB + AC$ (ii) $A(B-C) = AB - AC$

8. Let $A = \begin{bmatrix} 1 & 1 \\ 0 & 0 \end{bmatrix}$, $B = \begin{bmatrix} 1 & 0 \\ -1 & 0 \end{bmatrix}$. Find AB and BA. What do you observe ?

9. Let $A\ h = \begin{bmatrix} 1 & 1 \\ 2 & 2 \end{bmatrix}$, $B = \begin{bmatrix} 1 & 2 \\ 3 & 4 \end{bmatrix}$, $C = \begin{bmatrix} 3 & 4 \\ 1 & 2 \end{bmatrix}$. Find AB and AC. What do you observe ?

10. If $A = \begin{bmatrix} 2 & 1 \\ 1 & 2 \\ 1 & -1 \end{bmatrix}$, $B = \begin{bmatrix} 1 & 2 \\ -1 & 0 \end{bmatrix}$, $C = \begin{bmatrix} 1 & -1 \\ 2 & 1 \end{bmatrix}$, verify that $(AB)C = A(BC)$.

11. Compute $\left\{ 3\begin{bmatrix} 1 & 2 & 0 \\ 0 & -1 & 3 \end{bmatrix} - \begin{bmatrix} 1 & 5 & -2 \\ -3 & -4 & 4 \end{bmatrix} \right\} \begin{bmatrix} 1 \\ 2 \\ 1 \end{bmatrix}$

12. If $A = \begin{bmatrix} 1 & 0 \\ -1 & 1 \end{bmatrix}$, $B = \begin{bmatrix} 1 & 2 & 3 \\ 4 & 5 & 6 \end{bmatrix}$, determine a matrix X such that AX = B.

13. If $A = \begin{bmatrix} 1 & -1 \\ -1 & 1 \end{bmatrix}$, show that $A^2 = 2A$

14. If $A = \begin{bmatrix} 1 & 2 & 2 \\ 2 & 1 & 2 \\ 2 & 2 & 1 \end{bmatrix}$, show that $A^2 - 4A$ is a scalar matrix.

15. If $A = \begin{bmatrix} 1 & 1 \\ 1 & 2 \end{bmatrix}$, show that A satisfied $A^2 - 3A + I_2 = O$

Answers 5.6

1. (i) AB = [4 3] (ii) AB = 7, BA = $\begin{bmatrix} 2 & 1 & 1 \\ 4 & 2 & 2 \\ 6 & 3 & 3 \end{bmatrix}$ (iii) AB = $\begin{bmatrix} -4 \\ 6 \end{bmatrix}$

(iv) BA = [pa + ql + ru   pb + qm + rv   pc + qn + rw]

2. $AB = \begin{bmatrix} -4 & 7 \\ -7 & -4 \end{bmatrix}$, $BA = \begin{bmatrix} -4 & 7 \\ -7 & 4 \end{bmatrix}$ $AB = BA$.   3. $X = \begin{bmatrix} 1/2 & 0 & 0 \\ 0 & 1/3 & 0 \\ 0 & 0 & 1/4 \end{bmatrix}$

4. $X = \begin{bmatrix} 3 & -2 \\ -7 & 5 \end{bmatrix}$ 5. $(AB)' = B'A' = \begin{bmatrix} 4 & 7 \\ 3 & -1 \\ -2 & -1 \end{bmatrix}$ 6. $AB = BA = \begin{bmatrix} al & 0 & 0 \\ 0 & bm & 0 \\ 0 & 0 & cn \end{bmatrix}$

We observe that two diagonal matrices of the same order commute and that the product is again a diagonal matrix.

7. (i) $A(B + C) = AB + AC = \begin{bmatrix} 5 & -3 & 8 \\ 8 & -4 & 13 \end{bmatrix}$,

$A(B - C) = AB - AC = \begin{bmatrix} 3 & 9 & -6 \\ 6 & 16 & -11 \end{bmatrix}$

8. $AB = \begin{bmatrix} 0 & 0 \\ 0 & 0 \end{bmatrix}$, $BA = \begin{bmatrix} 1 & 1 \\ -1 & -1 \end{bmatrix}$ Neither A nor B is a zero matrix but AB is a zero matrix.

At the same time, BA is not a zero matrix.

9. $AB = AC = \begin{bmatrix} 4 & 6 \\ 8 & 12 \end{bmatrix}$. A is not a zero matrix and AB = AC but B ≠ C. Note that A is a singular matrix.

10. $(AB)C = A(BC) = \begin{bmatrix} 9 & 3 \\ 3 & 3 \\ 6 & 0 \end{bmatrix}$ 11. $\begin{bmatrix} 6 \\ 10 \end{bmatrix}$ 12. Let $X = \begin{bmatrix} p & q & r \\ s & t & u \end{bmatrix}$.

Then AX = B gives

∴ $\begin{bmatrix} p & q & r \\ s-p & t-q & u-r \end{bmatrix} = \begin{bmatrix} 1 & 2 & 3 \\ 4 & 5 & 6 \end{bmatrix}$ ∴ p = 1, q = 2, r = 3, s = 5, t = 7, u = 9.

∴ $X = \begin{bmatrix} 1 & 2 & 3 \\ 5 & 7 & 9 \end{bmatrix}$

13. $A^2 = 2A = \begin{bmatrix} 2 & -2 \\ -2 & 2 \end{bmatrix}$

14. $A^2 - 4A = \begin{bmatrix} 5 & 0 & 0 \\ 0 & 5 & 0 \\ 0 & 0 & 5 \end{bmatrix}$

5.10 Minors and Co-factors

Given a square matrix A, by minor of an element a_{ij} we mean the value of the determinant obtained by deleting i^{th} row and j^{th} column of A. It is denoted by M_{ij}.

Consider the square matrix

$$A = \begin{bmatrix} 2 & -1 & 3 \\ 0 & 4 & 2 \\ 1 & -1 & -2 \end{bmatrix}$$

We first calculate minor of element 2. Since it is (1, 1) element of A, we delete first row and first column, so that determinant of remaining array is

$$\begin{vmatrix} 4 & 2 \\ -1 & -2 \end{vmatrix} = (4 \times -2) - (2 \times -1) = -8 + 2 = -6 = M_{11}$$

Since –1 is (1, 2) element, we delete first row and second column. The determinant of remaining array is

$$\begin{vmatrix} 0 & 2 \\ 1 & -2 \end{vmatrix} = 0 \times -2 - (2 \times 1)$$

$$= -2 = M_{12}$$

The minor of 3 is $\begin{vmatrix} 0 & 4 \\ 1 & -1 \end{vmatrix} = 0 - 4 = -4 = M_{13}$

The minor of 0 is $\begin{vmatrix} -1 & 3 \\ -1 & -2 \end{vmatrix} = (-1)(-2) - (3)(-1) = 2 + 3 = 5 = M_{21}$

The minor of 4 is $\begin{vmatrix} 2 & 3 \\ 1 & -2 \end{vmatrix} = (2)(-2) - (3)(1) = -4 - 3 = -7 = M_{22}$

The minor of 2 (in (2, 3) place is $\begin{vmatrix} 2 & -1 \\ 1 & -1 \end{vmatrix}$

$$= (2)(-1) - (-1)(1)$$
$$= -2 + 1$$
$$= -1 = M_{23}$$

The minor of 1 is $\begin{vmatrix} -1 & 3 \\ 4 & 2 \end{vmatrix} = (-1)(2) - (3)(4)$

$$= -2 - 12$$
$$= -14 = M_{31}$$

The minor of (–1) is $\begin{vmatrix} 2 & 3 \\ 0 & 2 \end{vmatrix}$ = (4) – 0 = 4 = M_{32}

The minor of (–2) is $\begin{vmatrix} 2 & -1 \\ 0 & 4 \end{vmatrix}$ = (2) (4) – 0 = 8 = M_{33}

For a 2 × 2 matrix, calculation of minors is very simple.

consider the matrix $P = \begin{bmatrix} 2 & 6 \\ -4 & 7 \end{bmatrix}$

For finding minor of 2 we delete first row and first column.

i.e. $\begin{bmatrix} -2 & 6 \\ -4 & 7 \end{bmatrix}$

So that remaining array is |7| = 7 = M_{11}.

Similarly, minors of 6, – 4 and 7 will be –4, 6, 2 respectively.

Co-factor : Let A be a square matrix. By cofactor C_{ij} of an element a_{ij} of A, we mean minor of a_{ij} with a positive or negative sign depending on i and j. For a 2 × 2 matrix, negative sign is to be given the minors of elements a_{12} and a_{21}.

$$\begin{bmatrix} + & - \\ - & + \end{bmatrix}$$

∴ $C_{11} = M_{11}, \quad C_{12} = -M_{12}$
$C_{21} = -M_{21}, \quad C_{22} = M_{22}$

e.g. Consider the matrix $A = \begin{bmatrix} 5 & -3 \\ -2 & 0 \end{bmatrix}$.

The minor of 5 is 0 i.e. $M_{11} = 0$.

∴ Cofactor of 5 is 0 (no change in sign)

The minor of – 3 is – 2 i.e. $M_{12} = -2$.

∴ Cofactor of – 3 is + 2 (change in sign)

The minor of – 2 is – 3 i.e. $M_{21} = -3$.

∴ Cofactor of – 2 is + 3 (change in sign)

The minor of 0 is 5 i.e. $M_{22} = 5$.

∴ cofactor of 0 is 5 (no change in sign).

For a 3 × 3 matrix, negative sign is to be given to minors of elements encircled below :

$$\begin{bmatrix} + & - & + \\ - & + & - \\ + & - & + \end{bmatrix}$$

Thus for five positions, co-factor is same as minor while for four positions (encircled) cofactor is obtained by changing sign of the minor.

i.e.
$$C_{11} = M_{11}, \qquad C_{12} = -M_{12}, \qquad\qquad C_{13} = M_{13}$$
$$C_{21} = -M_{21}, \qquad C_{22} = M_{22}, \qquad\qquad C_{23} = -M_{23}$$
$$C_{31} = M_{31}, \qquad C_{32} = -M_{32}, \qquad\qquad C_{33} = M_{33}$$

Note : For a 3×3 matrix, cofactors are minors with alternate positive and negative signs, starting from positive sign for C_{11}.

Consider the third order matrix $M = \begin{bmatrix} 2 & -3 & -1 \\ 6 & 4 & 1 \\ 0 & 5 & 3 \end{bmatrix}$.

Minor of 2 is $\begin{vmatrix} 4 & 1 \\ 5 & 3 \end{vmatrix} = 12 - 5 = 7.$

∴   Cofactor of 2 is 7.

Minor of -3 is $\begin{vmatrix} 6 & 1 \\ 0 & 3 \end{vmatrix} = 18 - 0 = 18.$

∴   Cofactor of -3 is -18 (change in sign)

Minor of -1 is $\begin{vmatrix} 6 & 4 \\ 0 & 5 \end{vmatrix} = 30 - 0 = 30$

∴   Cofactor of -1 is 30

Minor of 6 is $\begin{vmatrix} -3 & -1 \\ 4 & 1 \end{vmatrix} = -3 - (4)(-1) = -3 + 4 = 1$

∴   Cofactor of 6 is -1 (change in sign)

Minor of 4 is $\begin{vmatrix} 2 & -1 \\ 0 & 3 \end{vmatrix} = 2 \times 3 - 0 = 6$

∴   Cofactor of 4 is 6

Minor of 1 is $\begin{vmatrix} 2 & -3 \\ 0 & 5 \end{vmatrix} = 10 - 0 = 10.$

∴   Cofactor of 1 is -10 (change in sign)

Minor of 0 is $\begin{vmatrix} -3 & -1 \\ 4 & 1 \end{vmatrix} = (-3)(1) - (4)(-1) = -3 + 4 = 1$

∴   Cofactor 0 is 1.

Minor of 6 is $\begin{vmatrix} 2 & -1 \\ 6 & 1 \end{vmatrix}$ = (2) (1) – (6) (–1) = 2 + 6 = 8.

∴   Cofactor of 5 is –8 (change in sign)

Minor of 3 is $\begin{vmatrix} 2 & -3 \\ 6 & 4 \end{vmatrix}$ = (2) (4) – (6) (–3) = 8 + 18 = 26.

∴   Cofactor of 3 is 26.

5.11 Adjoint of a Square Matrix   (Oct. 2008)

Definition : Given a square matrix A, the transpose of matrix of cofactors of A is called *adjoint of A* and is denoted by adj A.

e.g. Consider the matrix A = $\begin{bmatrix} 5 & -1 \\ 2 & 2 \end{bmatrix}$.

$M_{11} = 2$, $M_{12} = 2$, $M_{21} = -1$, $M_{22} = 5$

∴ $C_{11} = 2$, $C_{12} = -2$, $C_{21} = +1$, $C_{22} = 5$.

∴   Cofactor matrix = $\begin{bmatrix} 2 & -2 \\ 1 & 5 \end{bmatrix}$

∴   adj A = $\begin{bmatrix} 2 & 1 \\ -2 & 5 \end{bmatrix}$ (transpose of above matrix)

(2)   Find adj A, where A = $\begin{bmatrix} 13 & -9 \\ 0 & 8 \end{bmatrix}$

$M_{11} = 8$, $M_{12} = 0$, $M_{21} = -9$, $M_{22} = 13$

∴ $C_{11} = 8$, $C_{12} = 0$, $C_{21} = 9$, $C_{22} = 13$.

∴   Cofactor matrix = $\begin{bmatrix} 8 & 0 \\ 9 & 13 \end{bmatrix}$

∴   adj A = $\begin{bmatrix} 8 & 9 \\ 0 & 13 \end{bmatrix}$

(3)   Consider the matrix

$$P = \begin{bmatrix} 3 & -2 & -1 \\ 2 & 1 & 5 \\ 0 & 6 & 4 \end{bmatrix}$$

$$M_{11} = \begin{vmatrix} 1 & 5 \\ 6 & 4 \end{vmatrix} = 4 - 30 = -26 \qquad \therefore\ C_{11} = -26$$

$$M_{12} = \begin{vmatrix} 2 & 5 \\ 0 & 4 \end{vmatrix} = 8 - 0 = 18 \qquad \therefore\ C_{12} = -8$$

$$M_{13} = \begin{vmatrix} 2 & 1 \\ 0 & 6 \end{vmatrix} = 12 - 0 = 12 \qquad \therefore\ C_{13} = 12$$

$$M_{21} = \begin{vmatrix} -2 & -1 \\ 6 & 4 \end{vmatrix} = (-2)(4) - (6)(-1) = -8 + 6 = -2 \quad \therefore\ C_{21} = 2$$

$$M_{22} = \begin{vmatrix} 3 & -1 \\ 0 & 4 \end{vmatrix} = 12 - 0 = 12 \qquad \therefore\ C_{22} = 12$$

$$M_{23} = \begin{vmatrix} 3 & -2 \\ 0 & 6 \end{vmatrix} = 18 - 0 = 18 \qquad \therefore\ C_{23} = -18$$

$$M_{31} = \begin{vmatrix} -2 & -1 \\ 1 & 5 \end{vmatrix} = (-2)(5) - (1)(-1) = -10 + 1 = -9 \quad \therefore\ C_{31} = -9$$

$$M_{32} = \begin{vmatrix} 3 & -1 \\ 2 & 5 \end{vmatrix} = (3)(5) - (2)(-1) = 15 + 2 = 17 \quad \therefore\ C_{32} = -17$$

$$M_{33} = \begin{vmatrix} 3 & -2 \\ 2 & 1 \end{vmatrix} = (3)(1) - (2)(-2) = 3 + 4 = 7 \quad \therefore\ C_{33} = 7$$

$$\therefore \qquad \text{Cofactor matrix of P} = \begin{bmatrix} -26 & -8 & 12 \\ 2 & 12 & -18 \\ -9 & -17 & 7 \end{bmatrix}$$

$$\therefore \qquad \text{adj A} = \begin{bmatrix} -26 & 2 & -9 \\ -8 & 12 & -17 \\ 12 & -18 & 7 \end{bmatrix}$$

(4)　Show that adjoint of the following matrix is itself.

$$A = \begin{bmatrix} -4 & -3 & -3 \\ 1 & 0 & 1 \\ 4 & 4 & 3 \end{bmatrix}$$

$$M_{11} = \begin{vmatrix} 0 & 1 \\ 4 & 3 \end{vmatrix} = 0 - 4 = -4 \qquad \therefore C_{11} = -4$$

$$M_{12} = \begin{vmatrix} 1 & 1 \\ 4 & 3 \end{vmatrix} = 3 - 4 = -1 \qquad \therefore C_{12} = +1$$

$$M_{13} = \begin{vmatrix} 1 & 0 \\ 4 & 4 \end{vmatrix} \quad 4 - 0 = 4 \qquad \therefore C_{13} = 4$$

$$M_{21} = \begin{vmatrix} -3 & -3 \\ 4 & 3 \end{vmatrix} = (-3)(3) - (4)(-3) = -9 + 12 = 3 \therefore C_{21} = -3$$

$$M_{22} = \begin{vmatrix} -4 & -3 \\ 4 & 3 \end{vmatrix} = (-4)(3) - (4)(-3) = 0 \qquad \therefore C_{22} = 0$$

$$M_{23} = \begin{vmatrix} -4 & -3 \\ 4 & 4 \end{vmatrix} = (-4)(4) - (4)(-3) = -16 + 12 = -4 \therefore C_{23} = +4$$

$$M_{31} = \begin{vmatrix} -3 & -3 \\ 0 & 1 \end{vmatrix} = (-3)(1) - 0 = -3 \qquad \therefore C_{31} = -3$$

$$M_{32} = \begin{vmatrix} -4 & -3 \\ 1 & 1 \end{vmatrix} = (-4)(1) - (-3)(1) = -4 + 3 = -1 \therefore C_{32} = +1$$

$$M_{33} = \begin{vmatrix} -4 & -3 \\ 1 & 0 \end{vmatrix} = 0 - (-3)(1) = +3 \qquad \therefore C_{33} = 3$$

$$\therefore \qquad \text{Cofactor matrix} = \begin{bmatrix} -4 & 1 & 4 \\ -3 & 0 & 4 \\ -3 & 1 & 3 \end{bmatrix}$$

$$\therefore \qquad \text{adj A} = \begin{bmatrix} -4 & -3 & -3 \\ 1 & 0 & 1 \\ 4 & 4 & 3 \end{bmatrix} = \text{A.}$$

5.12 Inverse of a Matrix

In school algebra you have studied the concept of multiplicative inverse. Given a non-zero real number a, we know that its multiplicative inverse is $\frac{1}{a}$. Can we extend the same idea to Matrices ? The multiplicative inverse of a is $\frac{1}{a}$ since $a \times \frac{1}{a} = 1$, which is multiplicative identity in the set of reals. In case of matrices, identity matrix is the multiplicative identity. Hence, given a matrix A, if there exists a matrix B such that AB = I, then B should be taken as inverse of A.

This is precisely taken as definition of inverse.

Definition : Given a matrix A, if there exists a matrix B such that AB = BA = I, then B is called inverse of A.

Inverse of A is denoted by A^{-1}.

The following results are extremely important.

(1) Only a non-singular matrix can possess inverse i.e. a square matrix A possesses inverse if and only if $|A| \neq 0$. Then A is said to be *invertible*.

(2) Inverse of a matrix, when exists, is unique.

i.e. a non-singular matrix A cannot possess different inverses, say B and C.

Result : If A is a non-singular matrix, then

$$A^{-1} = \frac{1}{|A|} \text{ adj A.}$$

Algorithm of finding inverse : Suppose a square matrix A is given whose inverse is to be obtained.

(1) Find $|A|$. If $|A| = 0$, write "inverse does not exist". If $|A| \neq 0$ write "inverse exists" and proceed to step 2.

(2) Find cofactors of all elements of A.

(3) Write matrix of cofactors of A.

(4) Write adj A.

(5) $A^{-1} = \frac{1}{|A|}$ adj A.

(6) We advise the students to check whether the inverse is correct by verifying $AA^{-1} = I$.

Illustrative Examples

Example 5.27 : If $A = \begin{bmatrix} 3 & -2 \\ 4 & -2 \end{bmatrix}$ satisfy the matrix equation $A^2 - kA + 2I = 0$, find k.

(April 2013, 2015)

Solution :

$$A = \begin{bmatrix} 3 & -2 \\ 4 & -2 \end{bmatrix}$$

$$\therefore \quad A^2 = AA = \begin{bmatrix} 3 & -2 \\ 4 & -2 \end{bmatrix}\begin{bmatrix} 3 & -2 \\ 4 & -2 \end{bmatrix}$$

$$= \begin{bmatrix} 3\times 3 + (-2)\times 4 & 3\times -2 + (-2)(-2) \\ 4\times 3 + (-2)\times 4 & 4\times -2 + (-2)(-2) \end{bmatrix} = \begin{bmatrix} 1 & -2 \\ 4 & -4 \end{bmatrix}$$

$A^2 - kA + 2I = 0$ (given)

$\therefore$ $\begin{bmatrix} 1 & -2 \\ 4 & -4 \end{bmatrix} - k \begin{bmatrix} 3 & -2 \\ 4 & -2 \end{bmatrix} + 2 \begin{bmatrix} 1 & 0 \\ 0 & 1 \end{bmatrix} = 0$

$\therefore$ $\begin{bmatrix} 1 & -2 \\ 4 & -4 \end{bmatrix} + \begin{bmatrix} -3k & 2k \\ -4k & 2k \end{bmatrix} + \begin{bmatrix} 2 & 0 \\ 0 & 2 \end{bmatrix} = 0$

$\therefore$ $\begin{bmatrix} 1 - 3k + 2 & -2 + 2k + 0 \\ 4 - 4k + 0 & -4 + 2k + 2 \end{bmatrix} = \begin{bmatrix} 0 & 0 \\ 0 & 0 \end{bmatrix}$

$\therefore$ $\begin{bmatrix} 3 - 3k & 2k - 2 \\ 4 - 4k & 2k - 2 \end{bmatrix} = \begin{bmatrix} 0 & 0 \\ 0 & 0 \end{bmatrix}$

$3 - 3k = 0 \Rightarrow k = 1.$

Example 5.28 : *Find the inverse of the matrix.*

$$A = \begin{bmatrix} 2 & -3 \\ 1 & -2 \end{bmatrix}$$

Solution : $|A| = \begin{vmatrix} 2 & -3 \\ 1 & -2 \end{vmatrix} = -4 - (-3) = -1$

$\therefore$ $|A| \neq 0$

$\therefore$ A^{-1} exists.

The minors of elements are given by

$M_{11} = -2, \quad M_{12} = 1, \quad M_{21} = -3, \quad M_{22} = 2$

$\therefore$ $C_{11} = -2, \quad C_{12} = 1, \quad C_{21} = +3, \quad C_{22} = 2$

$\therefore$ Cofactor matrix $= \begin{bmatrix} -2 & -1 \\ 3 & 2 \end{bmatrix}$

$\therefore$ adj $A = \begin{bmatrix} -2 & 3 \\ -1 & 2 \end{bmatrix}$

Now, $A^{-1} = \dfrac{1}{|A|}$ adj A

$= \dfrac{1}{-1} \begin{bmatrix} -2 & 3 \\ -1 & 2 \end{bmatrix}$

$= \begin{bmatrix} 2 & -3 \\ 1 & -2 \end{bmatrix}$

Verification : $AA^{-1} = \begin{bmatrix} 2 & -3 \\ 1 & -2 \end{bmatrix} \begin{bmatrix} 2 & -3 \\ 1 & -2 \end{bmatrix}$

$$= \begin{bmatrix} 2 \times 2 + (-3)(1) & 2 \times (-3) + (-3)(-2) \\ 1 \times 2 + (-2)(1) & 1 \times (-3) + (-2)(-2) \end{bmatrix}$$

$$= \begin{bmatrix} 4-3 & -6+6 \\ 2-2 & -3+4 \end{bmatrix}$$

$$= \begin{bmatrix} 1 & 0 \\ 0 & 1 \end{bmatrix}$$

$$= I_2$$

Example 5.29 : *Find the inverse of the following matrix :*   **(Oct. 2013, 2014)**

$$P = \begin{bmatrix} 5 & -8 \\ -10 & 16 \end{bmatrix}$$

Solution : $|P| = \begin{bmatrix} 5 & -8 \\ -10 & 16 \end{bmatrix}$

$$= 16 \times 5 - (-10)(-8)$$

$$= 80 - 80$$

$$= 0$$

∴ P^{-1} does not exist.

Example 5.30 : *Find inverse of the matrix*

$$A = \begin{bmatrix} 1 & 3 & 3 \\ 1 & 4 & 3 \\ 1 & 3 & 4 \end{bmatrix}$$

Solution : $|A| = 1(16-9) - 3(4-3) + 3(3-4)$

$$= 7 - 3(1) + 3(-1)$$

$$= 7 - 3 - 3$$

$$= 1$$

∴ $|A| \neq 0, \quad A^{-1}$ exists.

The minors of various elements are

$$M_{11} = \begin{vmatrix} 4 & 3 \\ 3 & 4 \end{vmatrix} = 16 - 9 = 7 \qquad \therefore \quad C_{11} = 7$$

$$M_{12} = \begin{vmatrix} 1 & 3 \\ 1 & 4 \end{vmatrix} = 4 - 3 = 1 \qquad \therefore \quad C_{12} = -1$$

$$M_{13} = \begin{vmatrix} 1 & 4 \\ 1 & 3 \end{vmatrix} = 3 - 4 = -1 \qquad \therefore \quad C_{13} = -1$$

$$M_{21} = \begin{vmatrix} 3 & 3 \\ 3 & 4 \end{vmatrix} = 12 - 9 = 3 \qquad \therefore \quad C_{21} = -3$$

$$M_{22} = \begin{vmatrix} 1 & 3 \\ 1 & 4 \end{vmatrix} = 4 - 3 = 1 \qquad \therefore \quad C_{22} = 1$$

$$M_{23} = \begin{vmatrix} 1 & 3 \\ 1 & 3 \end{vmatrix} = 3 - 3 = 0 \qquad \therefore \quad C_{23} = 0$$

$$M_{31} = \begin{vmatrix} 3 & 3 \\ 4 & 3 \end{vmatrix} = 9 - 12 = -3 \qquad \therefore \quad C_{31} = -3$$

$$M_{32} = \begin{vmatrix} 1 & 3 \\ 1 & 3 \end{vmatrix} = 3 - 3 = 0 \qquad \therefore \quad C_{32} = 0$$

$$M_{33} = \begin{vmatrix} 1 & 3 \\ 1 & 4 \end{vmatrix} = 4 - 3 = 1 \qquad \therefore \quad C_{33} = 1$$

$\therefore$ Cofactor matrix of A $= \begin{bmatrix} 7 & -1 & -1 \\ -3 & 1 & 0 \\ -3 & 0 & 1 \end{bmatrix}$

$\therefore$ adj. A $= \begin{bmatrix} 7 & -3 & -3 \\ -1 & 1 & 0 \\ -1 & 0 & 1 \end{bmatrix}$

Now, $A^{-1} = \dfrac{1}{|A|}$ adj A $=$ adj A ($\because |A| = 1$)

$$= \begin{bmatrix} 7 & -3 & -3 \\ -1 & 1 & 0 \\ -1 & 0 & 1 \end{bmatrix}$$

Verification : $AA^{-1} = \begin{bmatrix} 1 & 3 & 3 \\ 1 & 4 & 3 \\ 1 & 3 & 4 \end{bmatrix} \begin{bmatrix} 7 & -3 & -3 \\ -1 & 1 & 0 \\ -1 & 0 & 1 \end{bmatrix}$

$$= \begin{bmatrix} 7-3-3 & -3+3+0 & -3+0+3 \\ 7-4-3 & -3+4+0 & -3+0+3 \\ 7-3-4 & -3+3+0 & -3+0+4 \end{bmatrix}$$

$$= \begin{bmatrix} 1 & 0 & 0 \\ 0 & 1 & 0 \\ 0 & 0 & 1 \end{bmatrix} = I_3$$

Example 5.31 : Computer $\left\{(-2)\begin{bmatrix} 1 & -3 \\ 7 & 9 \\ 8 & 0 \end{bmatrix} + (3)\begin{bmatrix} 6 & 0 \\ 9 & 5 \\ 1 & 2 \end{bmatrix}\right\}\begin{bmatrix} 3 \\ -2 \end{bmatrix}$ **(April 2013)**

Solution : $\left\{(-2)\begin{bmatrix} 1 & -3 \\ 7 & 9 \\ 8 & 0 \end{bmatrix} + (3)\begin{bmatrix} 6 & 0 \\ 9 & 5 \\ 1 & 2 \end{bmatrix}\right\}\begin{bmatrix} 3 \\ -2 \end{bmatrix}$

$$= \left\{\begin{bmatrix} -2 & 6 \\ -14 & 18 \\ -16 & 0 \end{bmatrix} + \begin{bmatrix} 18 & 0 \\ 27 & 15 \\ 3 & 6 \end{bmatrix}\right\}\begin{bmatrix} 3 \\ -2 \end{bmatrix}$$

$$= \begin{bmatrix} -2+18 & 6+0 \\ -14+27 & 18+15 \\ -16+3 & 0+6 \end{bmatrix}\begin{bmatrix} 3 \\ -2 \end{bmatrix}$$

$$= \begin{bmatrix} 16 & 6 \\ 13 & 33 \\ -13 & 6 \end{bmatrix}\begin{bmatrix} 3 \\ -2 \end{bmatrix}$$

$$= \begin{bmatrix} 16 \times 3 + 6 \times -2 \\ 13 \times 3 + 33 \times -2 \\ -13 \times 3 + 6 \times -2 \end{bmatrix}$$

$$= \begin{bmatrix} 48 - 12 \\ 39 - 66 \\ -39 - 12 \end{bmatrix} = \begin{bmatrix} 36 \\ -27 \\ -51 \end{bmatrix}$$

Example 5.32 : Find adjoint of the matrix A, where $A = \begin{bmatrix} 2 & 5 \\ 3 & 7 \end{bmatrix}$ and show that

$$A \,(adj\ A) \;=\; |A|\ I \qquad\qquad\qquad \textbf{(April 2011)}$$

Solution : $\qquad\qquad A \;=\; \begin{bmatrix} 2 & 5 \\ 3 & 7 \end{bmatrix}$

∴ $\qquad\qquad |A| \;=\; 2 \times 7 - 5 \times 3 = 14 - 15 = -1$

Minor of 2 $=$ 7

∴ Cofactor of 2 $=$ 7 $\qquad$ (no change in sign)

Minor of 5 $=$ 3

∴ Cofactor of 5 $= -3$ $\qquad$ (change in sign)

Minor of 3 $=$ 5

∴ Cofactor of 3 $= -5$ $\qquad$ (change in sign)

Minor of 7 $=$ 2

∴ Cofactor of 7 $=$ 2 $\qquad$ (no change in sign)

∴   Matrix of cofactor of A $= \begin{bmatrix} 7 & -3 \\ -5 & 2 \end{bmatrix}$

∴   adj A $= \begin{bmatrix} 7 & -5 \\ -3 & 2 \end{bmatrix}$

$$A \text{ (adj A)} = \begin{bmatrix} 2 & 5 \\ 3 & 7 \end{bmatrix} \begin{bmatrix} 7 & -5 \\ -3 & 2 \end{bmatrix}$$

$$= \begin{bmatrix} 2 \times 7 + 5 \times -3 & 2 \times -5 + 5 \times 2 \\ 3 \times 7 + 7 \times -3 & 3 \times -5 + 7 \times 2 \end{bmatrix}$$

$$= \begin{bmatrix} 14 - 15 & -10 + 10 \\ 21 - 21 & -15 + 14 \end{bmatrix}$$

$$= \begin{bmatrix} -1 & 0 \\ 0 & -1 \end{bmatrix}$$

$$= (-1) \begin{bmatrix} 1 & 0 \\ 0 & 1 \end{bmatrix}$$

$$= |A| \, I$$

Exercise 5.7

1. Find adjoint of each of following matrices :

   (i) $\begin{bmatrix} 2 & 5 \\ -1 & 4 \end{bmatrix}$ (ii) $\begin{bmatrix} 1 & 0 \\ 0 & 1 \end{bmatrix}$

2. Find adjoint of each of following matrices :

   (i) A $= \begin{bmatrix} -1 & -2 & -2 \\ 2 & 1 & -2 \\ 2 & -2 & 1 \end{bmatrix}$ (ii) P $= \begin{bmatrix} 3 & -4 & 1 \\ -3 & 6 & -1 \\ 4 & -8 & 2 \end{bmatrix}$

3. Find the inverse of the following matrices :

   (i) A $= \begin{bmatrix} 1 & -4 \\ -2 & 3 \end{bmatrix}$ (ii) B $= \begin{bmatrix} 4 & -5 \\ 2 & 1 \end{bmatrix}$ (iii) C $= \begin{bmatrix} -20 & -43 \\ 40 & 36 \end{bmatrix}$

4. Find the inverse of the following matrices :

   (i) P $= \begin{bmatrix} 1 & 2 & 1 \\ 0 & 2 & 3 \\ 0 & 0 & 1 \end{bmatrix}$, (ii) Q $= \begin{bmatrix} 1 & 2 & -2 \\ -1 & 3 & 0 \\ 0 & -2 & 1 \end{bmatrix}$ (Oct. 08) , (iii) R $= \begin{bmatrix} 3 & 3 & 4 \\ 2 & -3 & 4 \\ 0 & -1 & 1 \end{bmatrix}$

   (iv) S $= \begin{bmatrix} 4 & 2 & 3 \\ 4 & 0 & 1 \\ 1 & 1 & 0 \end{bmatrix}$

Answers 5.7

1. (i) $\begin{bmatrix} 4 & -5 \\ 1 & 2 \end{bmatrix}$ (ii) $\begin{bmatrix} 1 & 0 \\ 0 & 1 \end{bmatrix}$

2. (i) $\begin{bmatrix} -3 & 6 & 6 \\ -6 & 3 & -6 \\ -6 & -6 & 3 \end{bmatrix}$ (ii) $\begin{bmatrix} 4 & 0 & -2 \\ 2 & 2 & 0 \\ 0 & 8 & 6 \end{bmatrix}$.

3. (i) $-\dfrac{1}{5}\begin{bmatrix} 3 & 4 \\ 2 & 1 \end{bmatrix}$, (ii) $\dfrac{1}{14}\begin{bmatrix} 1 & 5 \\ -2 & 4 \end{bmatrix}$, (iii) $\dfrac{1}{1000}\begin{bmatrix} 36 & 43 \\ -40 & -20 \end{bmatrix}$.

4. (i) $\begin{bmatrix} 2 & -2 & 4 \\ 0 & 1 & -3 \\ 0 & 0 & 2 \end{bmatrix}$, (ii) $\begin{bmatrix} 3 & 2 & 6 \\ 1 & 1 & 2 \\ 2 & 2 & 5 \end{bmatrix}$

    (iii) $\dfrac{1}{11}\begin{bmatrix} -1 & 7 & -24 \\ 2 & -3 & 4 \\ 2 & -3 & 15 \end{bmatrix}$, (iv) $\dfrac{1}{10}\begin{bmatrix} -1 & 3 & 2 \\ 1 & -3 & 8 \\ 4 & -2 & -8 \end{bmatrix}$

5.13 System of Linear Equations

You are familiar with equations of the type $2x - y = 1$, $3x + 2y = 12$

This is called a system of two linear equation in two unknowns x and y.

Let us generalize this idea and then extend it to three equations in three unknowns.

A system of two linear equations in two unknowns x and y is as follows :

$$\left.\begin{aligned} a_{11}\,x + a_{12}\,y &= b_1 \\ a_{21}\,x + a_{22}\,y &= b_2 \end{aligned}\right\} \qquad \dots (5.3)$$

Let $A = \begin{bmatrix} a_{11} & a_{12} \\ a_{21} & a_{22} \end{bmatrix}$, $X = \begin{bmatrix} x \\ y \end{bmatrix}$, $B = \begin{bmatrix} b_1 \\ b_2 \end{bmatrix}$

Then system (5.3) can be written in matrix form as

$$\begin{bmatrix} a_{11} & a_{12} \\ a_{21} & a_{22} \end{bmatrix}\begin{bmatrix} x \\ y \end{bmatrix} = \begin{bmatrix} b_1 \\ b_2 \end{bmatrix}$$

i.e. $AX = B$

If the R.H.S., namely B, is O then the system is called **homogeneous**, otherwise **non-homogeneous**.

Thus $2x + 3y = 0$,

$x - 4y = 0$

is a **homogeneous** system of two equations in two unknowns x and y and

$$3x - 4y = 7$$
$$2x + 9y = 0$$

is a **non-homogeneous** system of equations.

A system of three linear equations in three unknowns x, y, z is as follows :

$$\begin{aligned} a_{11}\,x + a_{12}\,y + a_{13}\,z &= b_1 \\ a_{21}\,x + a_{22}\,y + a_{23}\,z &= b_2 \\ a_{31}x + a_{32}\,y + a_{33}\,z &= b_3 \end{aligned} \right\} \qquad \ldots (5.4)$$

Which can also be written in matrix form as

$$\begin{bmatrix} a_{11} & a_{12} & a_{13} \\ a_{21} & a_{22} & a_{23} \\ a_{31} & a_{32} & a_{33} \end{bmatrix} \begin{bmatrix} x \\ y \\ z \end{bmatrix} = \begin{bmatrix} b_1 \\ b_2 \\ b_3 \end{bmatrix}$$

Let
$$A = \begin{bmatrix} a_{11} & a_{12} & a_{13} \\ a_{21} & a_{22} & a_{23} \\ a_{31} & a_{32} & a_{33} \end{bmatrix}, \quad X = \begin{bmatrix} x \\ y \\ z \end{bmatrix}, \quad B = \begin{bmatrix} b_1 \\ b_2 \\ b_3 \end{bmatrix}$$

Then the matrix form of given system is

$$AX = B$$

This system is, as before, homogeneous if B = 0 and non-homogeneous if B ≠ 0.

Solution of a System of equations :

Consider the system $2x - y = 1$ and $3x + 2y = 12$. We observe that $x = 2$ and $y = 3$ satisfy both the equations. (i.e. the system of equations.) Hence $x = 2$, $y = 3$ (or (2, 3)) is a **solution** of a given system.

A set of values of unknowns (x, y, z etc.) which satisfy all the equations in the system simultaneously is called a **solution** of given system.

Consistency of Equations :

Definition : A system of equations is said to be **consistent** if it has a solution.

Thus the system $2x - y = 1$ and $3x + 2y = 12$ is consistent.

Consider the equation $2x - 3y = 4$ we observe that $x = 8$, $y = 4$ is a solution of the equation. $x = 2$, $y = 0$ is also a solution of the given equation. In fact, it has infinitely many solutions. Hence this system (of only one equation) is consistent.

The system $2x - y = 4$ and $6x - 3y = 7$ is not consistent. (Why ? Try to find a solution).

This discussion leads us to find some criteria about existence of solution for a given system. In other words, we are interested in finding some condition/conditions which determines the consistency of equations.

Consistency of a Homogeneous System :

Consider the homogeneous system

$$a_{11} x + a_{12} y = 0$$

$$a_{21} x + a_{22} y = 0$$

of two equations in two unknowns x and y. We observe that, whatever be the values of $a_{11}, a_{12}, a_{21}, a_{22}$, x = 0, y = 0 always satisfy given system. Thus (0, 0) is always a solution of the given system and hence the system is consistent.

Similarly, the following system

$$a_{11} x + a_{12} y + a_{13} z = 0$$

$$a_{21} x + a_{22} y + a_{23} z = 0$$

$$a_{31} x + a_{32} y + a_{33} z = 0$$

is satisfied by x = 0, y = 0, z = 0. **Thus a homogeneous system is always consistent.**
In fact, it has a unique solution, namely x = 0, y = 0, z = 0 etc.

Consistency of Non-homogeneous System :

Consider the non-homogeneous system

$$a_{11} x + a_{12} y = b_1,$$

$$a_{21} x + a_{22} y = b_2$$

Let
$$A = \begin{bmatrix} a_{11} & a_{12} \\ a_{21} & a_{22} \end{bmatrix}, X = \begin{bmatrix} x \\ y \end{bmatrix}, B = \begin{bmatrix} b_1 \\ b_2 \end{bmatrix}$$

Then the system can be written in matrix form as AX = B. (B ≠ 0).

Pre-multiplying both sides by A^{-1}.

$$A^{-1} (AX) = A^{-1} B$$

∴
$$X = A^{-1} B$$

If A^{-1} exists the R.H.S. exists i.e. solution exists. Thus, existence of A^{-1} is necessary and sufficient condition for the system to be consistent.

But we know that A^{-1} exists if and only if $|A| \neq 0$.

Thus we have following result

Result : A system of equations AX = B (B ≠ 0) has unique solution if and only if A is non-singular i.e. $|A| \neq 0$. Since A^{-1} is unique, the solution $A^{-1}B$ is also unique.

Note that this result is true for a system of n linear equations in n unknowns. (However we shall confine ourselves to a system containing atmost three unknowns.)

Solution of a system of Non-homogeneous Equations :

Let $AX = B$ be a given non-homogeneous system of, n linear equations in n unknowns. Assuming existence of A^{-1}, $X = A^{-1} B$ is the solution.

Algorithm :

(1) Write the given system in the form of matrix equation as $AX = B$.

(2) If $|A| = 0$, A^{-1} does not exist so that solution does not exist. Write "System is not consistent".

(3) If A^{-1} exists find A^{-1}.

(4) Find $X = A^{-1} B$.

(5) Write values of x, y, z.

(6) Students are advised to verify the solution. i.e. whether the values of x, y, z so obtained satisfy given equations.

Illustrative Examples

Example 5.33 : *Solve the equations*

$$4x + 7y - 9 = 0$$
$$5x - 8y + 15 = 0$$

Solution : Given equations can be written as

$$4x + 7y = 9$$
$$5x - 8y = -15$$

Let, A
$$= \begin{bmatrix} 4 & 7 \\ 5 & -8 \end{bmatrix}, \quad X = \begin{bmatrix} x \\ y \end{bmatrix}, \quad B = \begin{bmatrix} 9 \\ -15 \end{bmatrix}$$

$\therefore$ Given system can be written as

$$AX = B$$

$\therefore$ $\qquad\qquad X = A^{-1}B$ $\qquad\qquad\qquad\qquad\qquad$ ... (1)

Let us find A^{-1}.

$$|A| = (4 \times -8) - (5 \times 7)$$
$$= -32 - 35$$
$$= -67$$

Minors and co-factors of matrix A are

$M_{11} = -8,$	$\therefore$	$C_{11} = -8$
$M_{12} = 5$	$\therefore$	$C_{12} = -5$
$M_{21} = 7$	$\therefore$	$C_{21} = -7$
$M_{22} = 4$	$\therefore$	$C_{22} = 4.$

$$\therefore \qquad \text{Co-factor matrix of A} = \begin{bmatrix} -8 & -5 \\ -7 & 4 \end{bmatrix}$$

$$\therefore \qquad \text{adj (A)} = \begin{bmatrix} -8 & -7 \\ -5 & 4 \end{bmatrix}$$

$$\therefore \qquad A^{-1} = \frac{1}{|A|} \text{ adj (A)}$$

$$= \frac{-1}{67} \begin{bmatrix} -8 & -7 \\ -5 & 4 \end{bmatrix}$$

From equation (1),

$$X = A^{-1}B$$

$$= -\frac{1}{67} \begin{bmatrix} -8 & -7 \\ -5 & 4 \end{bmatrix} \begin{bmatrix} 9 \\ -15 \end{bmatrix}$$

$$= -\frac{1}{67} \begin{bmatrix} -72 + 105 \\ -45 - 60 \end{bmatrix}$$

$$= -\frac{1}{67} \begin{bmatrix} 33 \\ -105 \end{bmatrix}$$

$$= \begin{bmatrix} -33/67 \\ 105/67 \end{bmatrix}$$

$$\therefore \quad X = -\frac{33}{67}, \quad y = \frac{105}{67}.$$

Example 5.34 : *Solve the system of linear equations by matrix method*

$$2x + y + 3z = 1$$
$$x + z \qquad = 2$$
$$2x + y + z = 3$$

Solution : Let $\qquad A = \begin{bmatrix} 2 & 1 & 3 \\ 1 & 0 & 1 \\ 2 & 1 & 1 \end{bmatrix}$, $X = \begin{bmatrix} x \\ y \\ z \end{bmatrix}$, $B = \begin{bmatrix} 1 \\ 2 \\ 3 \end{bmatrix}$

$\therefore$ Given equations can be written as

$$AX = B$$

$$\therefore \qquad X = A^{-1}B \qquad\qquad\qquad\qquad\qquad\qquad \text{... (1)}$$

Let us find A^{-1}

$$|A| = 2(0 - 1) - 1(1 - 2) + 3(1 - 0)$$
$$= -2 + 1 + 3$$
$$= 2 (\neq 0)$$

$\therefore$ A^{-1} exists.

Minors and cofactors of elements of A are

$$M_{11} = \begin{vmatrix} 0 & 1 \\ 1 & 1 \end{vmatrix} = 0 - 1 = -1 \qquad \therefore \quad C_{11} = -1$$

$$M_{12} = \begin{vmatrix} 1 & 1 \\ 2 & 1 \end{vmatrix} = 1 - 2 = -1 \qquad \therefore \quad C_{12} = 1$$

$$M_{13} = \begin{vmatrix} 1 & 0 \\ 2 & 1 \end{vmatrix} = -1 - 0 = 1 \qquad \therefore \quad C_{13} = 1$$

$$M_{21} = \begin{vmatrix} 1 & 3 \\ 1 & 1 \end{vmatrix} = 1 - 3 = -2 \qquad \therefore \quad C_{21} = 2$$

$$M_{22} = \begin{vmatrix} 2 & 3 \\ 2 & 1 \end{vmatrix} = 2 - 6 = -4 \qquad \therefore \quad C_{22} = -4$$

$$M_{23} = \begin{vmatrix} 2 & 1 \\ 2 & 1 \end{vmatrix} = 2 - 2 = 0 \qquad \therefore \quad C_{23} = 0$$

$$M_{31} = \begin{vmatrix} 1 & 3 \\ 0 & 1 \end{vmatrix} = 1 - 0 = 1 \qquad \therefore \quad C_{31} = 1$$

$$M_{32} = \begin{vmatrix} 2 & 3 \\ 1 & 1 \end{vmatrix} = 2 - 3 = -1 \qquad \therefore \quad C_{32} = -1$$

$$M_{33} = \begin{vmatrix} 2 & 1 \\ 1 & 0 \end{vmatrix} = 0 - 1 = -1 \qquad \therefore \quad C_{33} = 1$$

$$\therefore \quad \text{Cofactor matrix of A} = \begin{bmatrix} -1 & 1 & 1 \\ 2 & -4 & 0 \\ 1 & 1 & -1 \end{bmatrix}$$

$$\therefore \quad \text{adj (A)} = \begin{bmatrix} -1 & 2 & 1 \\ 1 & -4 & 1 \\ 1 & 0 & -1 \end{bmatrix}$$

$$\therefore \quad A^{-1} = \frac{1}{|A|} \text{ adj (A)}$$

$$= \frac{1}{2} \begin{bmatrix} -1 & 2 & 1 \\ 1 & -4 & 1 \\ 1 & 0 & -1 \end{bmatrix}$$

From equation (1),

$$X = A^{-1}B$$

$$X = \frac{1}{2}\begin{bmatrix} -1 & 2 & 1 \\ 1 & -4 & 1 \\ 1 & 0 & -1 \end{bmatrix}\begin{bmatrix} 1 \\ 2 \\ 3 \end{bmatrix}$$

$$X = \frac{1}{2}\begin{bmatrix} -1+4+3 \\ 1-8+3 \\ 1+0-3 \end{bmatrix}$$

$$X = \frac{1}{2}\begin{bmatrix} 6 \\ -4 \\ -2 \end{bmatrix}$$

$$X = \begin{bmatrix} 3 \\ -2 \\ -1 \end{bmatrix}$$

$\therefore$　$x = 3,\ y = -2,\ z = -1.$

Example 5.35 : *Solve the equations*

$$2x + y + z = 2,\ x + y + z = 0,\ 4x - y - 3z = 20$$

Solution : Let　　$A = \begin{bmatrix} 2 & 1 & 1 \\ 1 & 1 & 1 \\ 4 & -1 & -3 \end{bmatrix}$, $X = \begin{bmatrix} x \\ y \\ z \end{bmatrix}$, $B = \begin{bmatrix} 2 \\ 0 \\ 20 \end{bmatrix}$

$\therefore$　Given equations can be written as

$$AX = B$$

$\therefore$　　　　　　$X = A^{-1}\ B$ 　　　　　　　　... (1)

Let us find A^{-1}.

$$|A| = 2\,(-3+1) - 1\,(-3-4) + 1\,(-1-4)$$
$$= -4 + 7 - 5$$
$$= -2\ (\neq 0)$$

$\therefore$　　　　　　A^{-1} exists

Minors and cofactors of elements of A are

$$M_{11} = \begin{vmatrix} 1 & 1 \\ -1 & -3 \end{vmatrix} = -3 + 1 = -2 \qquad \therefore \quad C_{11} = -2$$

$$M_{12} = \begin{vmatrix} 1 & 1 \\ 4 & -3 \end{vmatrix} = -3 - 4 = -7 \qquad \therefore \quad C_{12} = 7$$

$$M_{13} = \begin{vmatrix} 1 & 1 \\ 4 & -1 \end{vmatrix} = -1 - 4 = 5 \qquad \therefore \quad C_{13} = -5$$

$$M_{21} = \begin{vmatrix} 1 & 1 \\ -1 & -3 \end{vmatrix} = -3 + 1 = -2 \qquad \therefore \quad C_{21} = 2$$

$$M_{22} = \begin{vmatrix} 2 & 1 \\ 4 & -3 \end{vmatrix} = -6 - 4 = -10 \qquad \therefore \quad C_{22} = -10$$

$$M_{23} = \begin{vmatrix} 2 & 1 \\ 4 & -1 \end{vmatrix} = -2 - 4 = -6 \qquad \therefore \quad C_{23} = 6$$

$$M_{31} = \begin{vmatrix} 1 & 1 \\ 1 & 1 \end{vmatrix} = 1 - 1 = 0 \qquad \therefore \quad C_{31} = 0$$

$$M_{32} = \begin{vmatrix} 2 & 1 \\ 1 & 1 \end{vmatrix} = 2 - 1 = 1 \qquad \therefore \quad C_{32} = -1$$

$$M_{33} = \begin{vmatrix} 2 & 1 \\ 1 & 1 \end{vmatrix} = 2 - 1 = 1 \qquad \therefore \quad C_{33} = 1$$

$$\therefore \quad \text{Cofactor matrix of A} = \begin{bmatrix} -2 & 7 & -5 \\ 2 & -10 & +6 \\ 0 & -1 & 1 \end{bmatrix}$$

$$\therefore \quad \text{adj (A)} = \begin{bmatrix} -2 & 2 & 0 \\ 7 & -10 & -1 \\ -5 & 6 & 1 \end{bmatrix}$$

$$\therefore \quad A^{-1} = \frac{1}{|A|} \text{ adj (A)}$$

$$= \frac{1}{-2} \begin{bmatrix} -2 & 2 & 0 \\ 7 & -10 & -1 \\ -5 & 6 & 1 \end{bmatrix}$$

From equation (1),

$$X = A^{-1}B$$

$$X = \frac{-1}{2} \begin{bmatrix} -2 & 2 & 0 \\ 7 & -10 & -1 \\ -5 & 6 & 1 \end{bmatrix} \begin{bmatrix} 2 \\ 0 \\ 20 \end{bmatrix}$$

$$X = \frac{-1}{2} \begin{bmatrix} -4+0+0 \\ 14+0-20 \\ -10+0+20 \end{bmatrix}$$

$$X = \frac{-1}{2} \begin{bmatrix} -4 \\ -6 \\ 10 \end{bmatrix}$$

$$X = \begin{bmatrix} 2 \\ 3 \\ -5 \end{bmatrix}$$

∴   x = 2, y = 3, z = – 5.

Example 5.36 : *Solve the system of linear equations*

$$5x + y = 8$$

$$2x + 3y = 11$$

using inverse of the coefficient matrix.   **(Oct. 2008)**

Solution : The given system of equations can be written as

$$\begin{bmatrix} 5 & 1 \\ 2 & 3 \end{bmatrix} \begin{bmatrix} x \\ y \end{bmatrix} = \begin{bmatrix} 8 \\ 11 \end{bmatrix}$$

i.e.   AX = B (say)

where $A = \begin{bmatrix} 5 & 1 \\ 2 & 3 \end{bmatrix}$, $X = \begin{bmatrix} x \\ y \end{bmatrix}$, $B = \begin{bmatrix} 8 \\ 11 \end{bmatrix}$.

∴   AX = B

∴   X = A⁻¹B   ... (1)

To find A⁻¹. |A| = 5 × 3 – 2 × 1 = 13

We shall find A⁻¹ by adjont method.

$$C_{11} = (-1)^{1+1}(3) = 3$$

$$C_{12} = (-1)^{1+2}(2) = -2$$

$$C_{21} = (-1)^{2+1}(1) = -1$$

$$C_{22} = (-1)^{2+2}(5) = 5$$

∴   Matrix of cofactor of A $= \begin{bmatrix} 3 & -2 \\ -1 & 5 \end{bmatrix}$

$\therefore$ $\qquad\qquad\qquad$ adj A $= \begin{bmatrix} 3 & -1 \\ -2 & 5 \end{bmatrix}$

$$A^{-1} = \frac{1}{|A|} \text{ adj A} = \frac{1}{13} \begin{bmatrix} 3 & -1 \\ -2 & 5 \end{bmatrix}$$

From equation (1) $\qquad$ X = A^{-1}B $= \frac{1}{13} \begin{bmatrix} 3 & -1 \\ -2 & 5 \end{bmatrix} \begin{bmatrix} 8 \\ 11 \end{bmatrix}$

$$= \frac{1}{13} \begin{bmatrix} 3 \times 8 - 1 \times 11 \\ -2 \times 8 + 5 \times 11 \end{bmatrix}$$

$$= \frac{1}{13} \begin{bmatrix} 24 - 11 \\ -16 + 55 \end{bmatrix} = \frac{1}{13} \begin{bmatrix} 13 \\ 39 \end{bmatrix} = \begin{bmatrix} 1 \\ 3 \end{bmatrix}$$

Thus, $\qquad\qquad\qquad \begin{bmatrix} x \\ y \end{bmatrix} = \begin{bmatrix} 1 \\ 3 \end{bmatrix}$

$\therefore$ $\qquad\qquad\qquad\qquad$ x = 1, y = 3.

Example 5.37 : *To control a crop disease, it is necessary to use 8 units of chemical A, 14 units of chemical B and 13 units of chemical C. One barrel of P contains 1 unit of A, 2 units of B and 3 units of C. One barrel of Q contains 2, 3, 2 units of chemicals A, B, C respectively. 1 barrel of R contains 1, 2, 2 units of A, B, C respectively. Find how many barrels of each type of spray be used to just meet the requirements.*

Let x, y, z be number of barrels of P, Q, R be used. Therefore the matrix form of the given problem is

$$\begin{array}{c} \\ \\ A \\ B \\ C \end{array} \begin{array}{ccc} P & Q & R \\ \end{array} \begin{bmatrix} 1 & 2 & 1 \\ 2 & 3 & 2 \\ 3 & 2 & 2 \end{bmatrix} \begin{bmatrix} x \\ y \\ z \end{bmatrix} = \begin{bmatrix} 8 \\ 14 \\ 13 \end{bmatrix}$$

i.e. $\qquad\qquad\qquad$ AX = B (say) $\qquad\qquad\qquad\qquad\qquad$ ... (1)

We find A^{-1} by adjoint method.

$$|A| = 1 (6 - 4) - 2 (4 - 6) + 1 (4 - 9)$$

$$= 1 (2) - 2 (-2) + 1 (1 - 5)$$

$$= 2 + 4 - 5$$

$$= 6 - 5$$

$$= 1$$

The co-factors are

$$A_{11} = \begin{vmatrix} 3 & 2 \\ 2 & 2 \end{vmatrix} = 6 - 4 = 2$$

$$A_{12} = - \begin{vmatrix} 2 & 2 \\ 3 & 2 \end{vmatrix} = -(4 - 6) = 2$$

$$A_{13} = \begin{vmatrix} 2 & 3 \\ 3 & 2 \end{vmatrix} = 4 - 9 = -5$$

$$A_{21} = - \begin{vmatrix} 2 & 1 \\ 2 & 2 \end{vmatrix} = -(4 - 2) = -2$$

$$A_{22} = \begin{vmatrix} 1 & 1 \\ 3 & 2 \end{vmatrix} = 2 - 3 = -1$$

$$A_{23} = - \begin{vmatrix} 1 & 2 \\ 3 & 2 \end{vmatrix} = -(2 - 6) = 4$$

$$A_{31} = \begin{vmatrix} 2 & 1 \\ 3 & 2 \end{vmatrix} = 4 - 3 = 1$$

$$A_{32} = - \begin{vmatrix} 1 & 1 \\ 2 & 2 \end{vmatrix} = -(2 - 2) = 0$$

$$A_{33} = \begin{vmatrix} 1 & 2 \\ 2 & 3 \end{vmatrix} = 3 - 4 = -1$$

$$\therefore \quad \text{Matrix of cofactors} = \begin{bmatrix} 2 & 2 & -5 \\ -2 & -1 & 4 \\ 1 & 0 & -1 \end{bmatrix}$$

$$\therefore \quad \text{adj A} = \begin{bmatrix} 2 & -2 & 1 \\ 2 & -1 & 0 \\ -5 & 4 & -1 \end{bmatrix}$$

$$A^{-1} = \frac{1}{|A|} \text{adj A} = \text{adj A} \qquad\qquad (\because |A| = 1)$$

From (1),

$$X = A^{-1}B$$

$$\therefore \quad \begin{bmatrix} x \\ y \\ z \end{bmatrix} = \begin{bmatrix} 2 & -2 & 1 \\ 2 & -1 & 0 \\ -5 & 4 & -1 \end{bmatrix} \begin{bmatrix} 8 \\ 14 \\ 13 \end{bmatrix}$$

$$= \begin{bmatrix} 16 - 28 + 13 \\ 16 - 14 + 0 \\ -40 + 56 - 13 \end{bmatrix} = \begin{bmatrix} 1 \\ 2 \\ 3 \end{bmatrix}$$

$$\therefore \quad x = 1, y = 2, z = 3.$$

Example 5.38 : *Solved the following system of equations x – 2y = 5, 2x + 3y = 2 by using inverse of coefficient matrix.*   **(April 2011)**

Solution : The given system can be written in matrix form as follows :

$$\begin{bmatrix} 1 & -2 \\ 2 & 3 \end{bmatrix} \begin{bmatrix} x \\ y \end{bmatrix} = \begin{bmatrix} 5 \\ 2 \end{bmatrix}$$

i.e. $$AX = B \text{ (say)}$$

$$\therefore \quad X = A^{-1}B \qquad \qquad \dots (1)$$

To find A^{-}. $$|A| = 1 \times 3 - (-2 \times 2) = 3 + 4 = 7$$

Cofactor of $1 = 3$

Cofactor of $-2 = -2$ (change in sign)

Cofactor of $2 = 2$ (change in sign)

Cofactor of $3 = 1$

$$\therefore \quad \text{Matrix of cofactors of A} = \begin{bmatrix} 3 & -2 \\ 2 & 1 \end{bmatrix}$$

$$\therefore \quad \text{adj A} = \begin{bmatrix} 3 & 2 \\ -2 & 1 \end{bmatrix}$$

$$A^{-1} = \frac{1}{|A|} \text{adj A} = \frac{1}{7} \begin{bmatrix} 3 & 2 \\ -2 & 1 \end{bmatrix}$$

From equation (1), $$X = A^{-1}B = \frac{1}{7} \begin{bmatrix} 3 & 2 \\ -2 & 1 \end{bmatrix} \begin{bmatrix} 5 \\ 2 \end{bmatrix}$$

$$\therefore \quad \begin{bmatrix} x \\ y \end{bmatrix} = \frac{1}{7} \begin{bmatrix} 3 \times 5 + 2 \times 2 \\ -2 \times 5 + 1 \times 2 \end{bmatrix}$$

$$= \frac{1}{7} \begin{bmatrix} 19 \\ -8 \end{bmatrix} = [\ 19/7 \quad -8/7\ ]$$

$$\therefore \quad x = \frac{19}{7}, y = \frac{-8}{7}$$

Exercise 5.8

Solve the following equations by matrix method.

1. $2x + 3y = 9$, $-x + y = -2$

2. $x + 3y = -2$, $3x + 5y = 4$ **(April 2010)**

3. $x + y = 1, 3y + 3z = 5, 3z + 3x = 4$

4. $x + y + z = 1$, $2x + y + 2z = 3$, $3x + 3y + 4z = 4$ **(April 2013)**

5. $x + y + z = 6$, $3x - y + 3z = 10$, $5x + 5y - 4z = 3$

6. Find the values of following determinants.

(i) $\begin{vmatrix} 1 & 2 & 3 \\ 8 & 4 & 6 \\ 4 & 2 & 3 \end{vmatrix}$ (ii) $\begin{vmatrix} 2 & 3 & 4 \\ 5 & 6 & 7 \\ 8 & 9 & 1 \end{vmatrix}$ (iii) $\begin{vmatrix} 5 & -2 & 0 \\ -1 & 4 & 8 \\ 0 & -9 & 6 \end{vmatrix}$

(iv) $\begin{vmatrix} x & 1 & 1 \\ 1 & x & 1 \\ 1 & 1 & x \end{vmatrix}$ (v) $\begin{vmatrix} 1 & 4 & 2 \\ 2 & -1 & 4 \\ -3 & 7 & -6 \end{vmatrix}$ (vi) $\begin{vmatrix} 0 & 1 & 1 \\ 1 & 0 & 1 \\ 1 & 1 & 0 \end{vmatrix}$

(vii) $\begin{vmatrix} 1 & a & b+c \\ 1 & b & c+a \\ 1 & c & a+b \end{vmatrix}$ (viii) $\begin{vmatrix} 1 & 1 & 1 \\ 1 & 1+x & 1 \\ 1 & 1 & 1+y \end{vmatrix}$

7. Solve the equations

(i) $\begin{vmatrix} x+1 & x+2 & x+3 \\ x+4 & x+5 & x+6 \\ x+7 & x+8 & 0 \end{vmatrix} = 0$ (ii) $\begin{vmatrix} x & 2 & x+3 \\ 3 & 5 & 8 \\ x+1 & 7-x & 12 \end{vmatrix} = 0$

8. Find x and y if

$$\begin{bmatrix} 2x+y & 4 \\ 5 & x+2y \end{bmatrix} = \begin{bmatrix} 2 & 4 \\ 5 & 5 \end{bmatrix}$$

9. If $A = \begin{bmatrix} 3 & 4 \\ 1 & -6 \end{bmatrix}$, $B = \begin{bmatrix} +1 & -2 \\ 1 & 2 \end{bmatrix}$ Find a matrix X satisfying the equation $A + 2X = B$.

10. If $A = \begin{bmatrix} 2 & 3 & 1 \\ 0 & -1 & 5 \end{bmatrix}$, $B = \begin{bmatrix} 0 & -1 & 3 \\ 1 & 2 & 1 \end{bmatrix}$,

Find $2A - 3B$.

11. If $A = \begin{bmatrix} 3 & 1 \\ -1 & 2 \end{bmatrix}$, show that $A^2 - 5A + 7I_2 = 0$

12. If $A = \begin{bmatrix} 3 & -2 \\ 4 & -2 \end{bmatrix}$ satisfies the matrix equation

    $A^2 - KA + 2I = 0$, find k.

13. If $A = \begin{bmatrix} 1 & -1 \\ 2 & 6 \end{bmatrix}$, find $|A - 2I|$

14. Solve for matrices X and Y if

    (i) $2X + 3Y = \begin{bmatrix} 3 & -2 \\ 5 & 6 \end{bmatrix}$ and $2X - 3Y = \begin{bmatrix} 4 & 2 \\ -5 & -6 \end{bmatrix}$

    (ii) $X - 2Y = \begin{bmatrix} 5 & 2 & 0 \\ -1 & 0 & 1 \end{bmatrix}$ and $2X + Y = \begin{bmatrix} -1 & -1 & 2 \\ 5 & 3 & 4 \end{bmatrix}$

15. If $A = \begin{bmatrix} 2 & -1 & 3 \\ 4 & 5 & 2 \end{bmatrix}$, $B = \begin{bmatrix} -1 & 1 \\ 0 & -2 \\ 3 & 6 \end{bmatrix}$

    Find AB and BA. Are they equal ?

16. If $A = \begin{bmatrix} 4 & -3 \\ -1 & 1 \end{bmatrix}$, show that $AA' = A'A = I_2$

17. If $A = \begin{bmatrix} 0 & 2 & 3 \\ 3 & 5 & 7 \end{bmatrix}$, $B = \begin{bmatrix} 1 & 3 & 7 \\ 2 & 4 & 1 \end{bmatrix}$

    Show that $BA' = (AB')'$.

18. If $A = \begin{bmatrix} 3 & 0 \\ -4 & -1 \end{bmatrix}$, $B = \begin{bmatrix} 3 & 5 & -7 \\ 0 & -1 & 8 \end{bmatrix}$, $C = \begin{bmatrix} 6 \\ -1 \\ 0 \end{bmatrix}$

    Verify that $A(BC) = (AB)C$.

19. Find x, y, z if $\left\{ \begin{bmatrix} 1 & 2 \\ 4 & 0 & 3 \\ -1 & 2 \end{bmatrix} - \begin{bmatrix} 3 & 2 \\ 1 & 4 \\ -2 & 4 \end{bmatrix} \right\} \begin{bmatrix} 0 \\ 2 \end{bmatrix} = \begin{bmatrix} x \\ y \\ z \end{bmatrix}$

20. Find the matrix X such that

    $$\begin{bmatrix} 2 \\ 4 \\ 1 \end{bmatrix} X = \begin{bmatrix} 6 & 2 & 4 \\ 12 & 4 & 8 \\ 3 & 1 & 2 \end{bmatrix}$$

21. If $\begin{bmatrix} x & 4 \\ 2 & 8 \end{bmatrix}$ is a singular matrix, find value of x.

22. If $A = \begin{bmatrix} 2 & 3 \\ -1 & 4 \end{bmatrix}$, $B = \begin{bmatrix} 1 & 0 \\ -1 & 2 \end{bmatrix}$, Verify that $|AB| = |A| |B|$.

23. Show that $A = \begin{bmatrix} 6 & 5 \\ 7 & 6 \end{bmatrix}$ satisfies the equation $A^2 - 12A + I = 0$. Hence find A^{-1}.

24. Find the adjoint of each of the following matrices.

(i) $\begin{bmatrix} 4 & -3 \\ 5 & -2 \end{bmatrix}$ (ii) $\begin{bmatrix} 3 & 2 \\ 7 & 5 \end{bmatrix}$ (iii) $\begin{bmatrix} 2 & -3 \\ 3 & 4 \end{bmatrix}$

(iv) $\begin{bmatrix} 1 & 2 & 2 \\ 2 & 1 & 2 \\ 2 & 2 & 1 \end{bmatrix}$ (v) $\begin{bmatrix} 2 & 0 & -1 \\ 5 & 1 & 0 \\ 1 & 1 & 3 \end{bmatrix}$ (vi) $\begin{bmatrix} 1 & 2 & 5 \\ 2 & 3 & 1 \\ -1 & 1 & 1 \end{bmatrix}$

25. Find the adjoint of the matrix.

$A = \begin{bmatrix} 1 & 2 & 3 \\ 0 & 5 & 0 \\ 2 & 4 & 3 \end{bmatrix}$ and verify that I_3. A (adj. A) = $|A| I_3$.

26. Find the inverse of the following matrices :

(i) $\begin{bmatrix} 0 & 1 \\ 1 & 0 \end{bmatrix}$ (ii) $\begin{bmatrix} 2 & 5 \\ -3 & 1 \end{bmatrix}$ (iii) $\begin{bmatrix} 2 & -1 & 1 \\ -1 & 2 & -1 \\ 1 & -1 & 2 \end{bmatrix}$

(iv) $\begin{bmatrix} 2 & 0 & -1 \\ 5 & 1 & 0 \\ 0 & 1 & 3 \end{bmatrix}$ (v) $\begin{bmatrix} 2 & 3 & 1 \\ 3 & 4 & 1 \\ 3 & 7 & 2 \end{bmatrix}$

27. If $A = \begin{bmatrix} 3 & 2 \\ 7 & 5 \end{bmatrix}$, $B = \begin{bmatrix} 4 & 6 \\ 3 & 2 \end{bmatrix}$

Verify $(AB)^{-1} = B^{-1} A^{-1}$.

28. Solve the following equations.

(i) $x + y + z = 6$, $2x + y + 2z = 10, 3x + 3y + 4z = 21$

(ii) $x + y + z = 1$, $2x - y + 7z = 7$ $3x + y + 2z = 2$

(iii) $x + y + z = 6$, $x - y + z = 2$, $2x + y - z = 1$

(iv) $2x - y + z = 1$, $x + 2y + 3z = 8$, $3x + y - 4z = 1$

(v) $2x - 4y + 3z = 1$, $x - 2y + 4z = 3$, $3x - y + 5z = 2$

(vi) $-3x + 2y + z = 3$, $4x - y + 3z = 11$, $x + y + 4z = 8$

Answers 5.8

1. $x = 3, y = 1$ 2. $x = \dfrac{1}{2}, y = \dfrac{1}{2}$ 3. $x = \dfrac{1}{3}, y = \dfrac{2}{3}, z = 1$

4. $x = 1, y = -1, z = 1$ 5. $x = 1, y = 2, z = 3$.

6. (i) 0   (ii) 27   (iii) 468   (iv) $(x - 1)^2 + (x + 2)$

   (v) 0   (vi) 2   (vii) 0   (viii) xy

7. (i) $x = -9$ (ii) $x = 2/3$

8. $x = -\dfrac{1}{3}, \; y = \dfrac{8}{3}$ 9. $X = \begin{bmatrix} -1 & -3 \\ 0 & 4 \end{bmatrix}$

10. $\begin{bmatrix} 4 & 9 & -7 \\ -3 & -8 & 7 \end{bmatrix}$ 12. $K = 1$

13. -2

14. (i) $X = \begin{bmatrix} \dfrac{7}{4} & 0 \\ 0 & 0 \end{bmatrix}, \; Y = \begin{bmatrix} \dfrac{1}{6} & \dfrac{-2}{3} \\ \dfrac{5}{3} & 2 \end{bmatrix}$

(ii) $X = \begin{bmatrix} \dfrac{3}{5} & 0 & \dfrac{4}{5} \\ \dfrac{9}{5} & \dfrac{6}{5} & \dfrac{9}{5} \end{bmatrix}, Y = \begin{bmatrix} \dfrac{-4}{5} & -1 & \dfrac{3}{5} \\ \dfrac{7}{5} & \dfrac{3}{5} & \dfrac{2}{5} \end{bmatrix}$

15. $AB = \begin{bmatrix} 1 & 22 \\ 2 & 12 \end{bmatrix}$, $BA = \begin{bmatrix} 2 & 6 & -1 \\ -8 & -10 & -4 \\ 30 & 27 & 27 \end{bmatrix}$, $AB \neq BA$.

19. $x = 12, y = 16, z = 8$ 20.   [3 1 2] 21. $x = 1$

23. $A^{-1} = \begin{bmatrix} 6 & -5 \\ -7 & 6 \end{bmatrix}$ 24. (i) $\begin{bmatrix} -2 & 3 \\ -5 & 4 \end{bmatrix}$ (ii) $\begin{bmatrix} 3 & -2 \\ -7 & 3 \end{bmatrix}$

(iii) $\begin{bmatrix} 4 & 3 \\ -3 & 2 \end{bmatrix}$ (iv) $\begin{bmatrix} -3 & 2 & 2 \\ 2 & -3 & 2 \\ 2 & 2 & -3 \end{bmatrix}$ (v) $\begin{bmatrix} 3 & -1 & 1 \\ -12 & 7 & -5 \\ 4 & -2 & 2 \end{bmatrix}$

(vi) $\begin{bmatrix} 2 & 3 & -13 \\ -3 & 6 & 9 \\ 5 & -3 & -1 \end{bmatrix}$ 25. $\begin{bmatrix} 15 & 6 & -15 \\ 0 & -3 & 0 \\ -10 & 0 & 5 \end{bmatrix}$

26. (i) $\begin{bmatrix} 0 & 1 \\ 1 & 0 \end{bmatrix}$ (ii) $\dfrac{1}{17}\begin{bmatrix} 1 & -5 \\ 3 & 2 \end{bmatrix}$ (iii) $\dfrac{1}{4}\begin{bmatrix} 3 & 1 & -1 \\ 1 & 3 & 1 \\ -1 & 1 & 3 \end{bmatrix}$

(iv) $\begin{bmatrix} 3 & -1 & 1 \\ -15 & 6 & -5 \\ 5 & -2 & 2 \end{bmatrix}$ (v) $\dfrac{1}{2}\begin{bmatrix} 1 & 1 & -1 \\ -3 & 1 & 1 \\ 9 & -5 & -1 \end{bmatrix}$

28. (i) x = 1, y = 2, z = 3   (ii) x = 0, y = 0, z = 1

(iii) x = 1, y = 2, z = 3   (iv) x = 1, y = 2, z = 1

(v) x = – 1, y = 0, z = 1   (vi) System has no solution.

Unit 6...

Functions

Contents ...

Learning Objectives:

Functions, Constants, Variables, Domain, Interval, Explicit function, Algebraic function, Polynomial function, Absolute value function, Inverse function, Rational and Irrational function, Monotone function, Even and Odd function, Supply/Demand function, Cost function, Total revenue function, Profit function, Utility function, Consumption function.

Chapter Objectives ...

To understand useful functions in business and economics.

6.1 Introduction   (Oct. 2013, April 2015)

The notion of function has been in use from 17th century introduced by mathematicians like Femat, Descartes and Newton. However, the term **"function"** was first used by Leibnitz in 1694. The latest definition given by George Cantor is based on set theory.

However, we shall use old definition which is sufficient to understand relationship between two variables and its applications to situations in Commerce and Economics.

6.2 Constant and Variables

A **constant** is a symbol which does not change its value throughout a set of mathematical operations.

For example, all numericals like $5, -\sqrt{7}, \frac{3}{17}$ etc.

Constants are generally denoted by the letters a, b, c, α, β etc.

A **variable** is a symbol, say x, which can assume any value out of a given set of values.

For example, profit, sale, height, weight etc.

Variables are usually denoted by x, y, z etc.

6.3 Continuous Variable

Let **a** and **b** be two given numbers where **a** < **b**. If variable **x** can take any value between **a** and **b** then **x** is called a **continuous variable**.

For example, temperature of a city on a given day, height of a plant during a given time interval.

Intervals are some special sets of real numbers. Let a and b be two real numbers such that a < b.

1.   The set $\{x \mid a \le x \le b\}$ is called a *closed interval* from a to b and is denoted by [a, b].

2.   The set $\{x \mid a < x < b\}$ is called an *open interval* from a to b and is denoted by (a, b).

3.   The set $\{x \mid a \le x < b\}$ is called a left closed-right open interval (or a semi-open interval or a semi-closed interval). It is denoted by [a, b).

4.   The set $\{x \mid a < x \le b\}$ is called a left open-right closed interval (or a semi-open interval or a semi-closed interval). It is denoted by {a, b].

The four types of intervals mentioned above are shown below geometrically.

Fig. 6.1

(Thick dot indicates that the particular number is included, circle indicates that the particular number is excluded.)

6.4 Functions   (Oct. 2013, April 2015)

If **x** and **y** are two variables such that value of y depends on value of **x** and for given value of **x** there exists a value of **y** then **y** is called function of **x** and it is written as **y = f(x)**.

The set of values of **x** is called **domain** of the function and set of values of **y** is called **co-domain** of the function. x is called **independent variable** and y is **dependent variable**.

If domain is set A and Codomain is set B then function f defined from A to B is written as $f : A \to B$.

Note : Let $x_1 \in A$ (domain) and $y_1 = f(x_1)$ then it is also written as $(x_1, y_1) \in f$. (x_1, y_1) is called **ordered of air**. The order of elements is important.

Different methods of representing a function :

Consider the function f : A → B whose arrow diagram is given below :

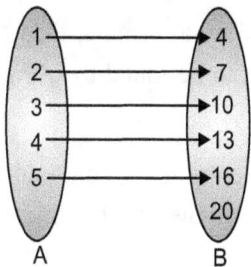

Fig. 6.2

(1) Arrow diagram : Drawing the arrow diagram is itself one simple method of representing a function. It has, however limited utility.

(2) Set of ordered pairs : A function f : A → B can be represented by writing down the set of all ordered pairs (x y) such that x ∈ A, y ∈ B and y = f(x). In the above illustration, we have,

$$f = \{(1, 4), (2, 7), (3, 10), (4, 13), (5, 16)\}$$

The set denoted by f represents the function f.

(3) Tabular form : A function f : A → B may be represented by tabulating the values of x, y such that x ∈ A, y ∈ B and y = f(x). In the above illustration, we may tabulate the values of x, y as follows :

x	1	2	3	4	5
y	4	7	10	13	16

This table of values of x, y represents the function f.

The above three methods of representing a function are useful only when the number of elements in the domain of the function is small. For a number of well known functions, domain is R (the set of all real numbers). In such a case, obviously, none of the above three methods can be used.

(4) Formula : This is the most useful method of representing the function. It can be used even when the domain of the function is an infinite set. Here the image y of an element x in the domain is expressed in terms of x by a formula for all x in the domain. In the above illustration, observe that

$$f(1) = 4 = 3 \times 1 + 1, \quad f(2) = 7 = 3 \times 2 + 1, \quad f(3) = 10 = 3 \times 3 + 1$$

$$f(4) = 13 = 3 \times 4 + 1, \quad f(5) = 16 = 3 \times 5 + 1$$

We immediately see that, $f(x) = 3 \times x + 1 = 3x + 1$ for all $x \in A$. Thus the formula $y = f(x) = 3x + 1$ represents the function f.

(1) If a function is represented by a formula, then the values of the function at all the elements x of the domain can be found by using the formula and thus we know the range of the function.

(2) If a function is represented by a formula and the domain of the function is not explicitly given, we take it as the set of elements for which f(x) can be found from the formula.

For example,

(1) $y = f(x) = x^2 + x + 1$. Here f(x) can be found for all $x \in R$.

Therefore, the domain of f is R, the set of real numbers.

(2) $y = f(x) = \sqrt{4 - x^2}$. Here for y to be real, $4 - x^2 \geq 0 \therefore x^2 \leq 4$

$$\therefore |x| \leq 2 \therefore -2 \leq x < 2.$$

Therefore, the domain of f is [–2, 2].

(3) $y = f(x) = \dfrac{x+4}{x-1}$. Here we cannot find y if $x = 1$. We can find y for all other real values of x. Therefore, the domain of f is $R - \{1\}$.

Range of a Function :

Definition : If $f : A \to B$, then the range of the function f is defined as the set of images of all elements in A.

i.e. range $= \{y \mid y = f(x), x \in A\}$

For example,

(i) Consider the function $f : N \to N$ defined by $f(x) = x^2$.

Then the range $= \{1, 4, 9, 16, ...\}$

(ii) If $f : [-4, 4] \to [0, 10]$ is defined by $f(x) = |x|$.

Then range $= [0, 4]$, which is a proper subset of [0, 10].

(iii) If $f : \{0, 1, 2\} \to \{2, 5, 8\}$ is defined by $f(x) = 3x + 2$.

Then the range $= \{2, 5, 8\} =$ co-domain,

These examples show that the *range is always a proper or improper subset of the co-domain.*

Illustrative Examples

Example 6.1 : *Exhibit each of the following relations as a set of ordered pairs. Which of them are functions ? Justify your answer.*

(i) $\{(x, x + 3) \,/\, x \in N, 4 \leq x \leq 8\}$

(ii) $\{(x, y) \,/\, y^2 = x^2 + 1, x \in Z, -1 \leq x \leq 1\}$ **(April 2015)**

Solution : (i) The relation is given by the set $\{(4, 7), (5, 8), (6, 9), (7, 10), (8, 11)\}$. It is clearly a function since every x has unique image.

(ii) The relation is given by the set $\{(-1, \sqrt{2}\,), (-1, -\sqrt{2}\,), (0, 1), (0, -1), (1, \sqrt{2}\,), (1, -\sqrt{2}\,)\}$

Since -1 has two images (in fact every element of the domain has two images, the relation is not a function.

Example 6.2 : *Find the domain and range of the following functions :*

(i) $\dfrac{x^2}{1 + x^2}$,   (ii) $\sqrt{9 - x^2}$ **(Oct. 2013, 2014)**

Solution : (i) $f(x) = \dfrac{x^2}{1 + x^2}$ is defined for all real x and hence domain is R. Since numerator of $f(x)$ is non-negative and denominator is positive, $f(x) \geq 0$.

Since numerator < denominator for every x, $f(x) < 1$.

Therefore, range $= [0, 1)$.

(ii) $f(x) = \sqrt{9 - x^2}$. For $f(x)$ to be real, we have $9 - x^2 \geq 0$. $\therefore$ $9 \geq x^2$ i.e. $x^2 \leq 9$

$\therefore$ $-3 \leq x \leq 3$. Therefore domain $= [-3, 3]$. At $x = \pm 3$, $y = 0$. At $x = 0$, $y = 3$

Therefore, range $= [0, 3]$.

Example 6.3 : *(a) If $f(x) = x + \dfrac{1}{x}$, find $f(-3)$, $f(\sqrt{2})$, $f\left(\dfrac{9}{11}\right)$. Also show that $f\left(\dfrac{1}{x}\right) = f(x)$.*

(b) If $f(x) = \dfrac{x - 1}{x + 1}$, find $f(0)$, $f(6)$. Also show that $f\left(\dfrac{x - 1}{x + 1}\right) = -\dfrac{1}{x}$

Solution : (a) $f(-3) = (-3) + \dfrac{1}{-3} = -3 - \dfrac{1}{3} = \dfrac{-10}{3}$

$f(\sqrt{2}) = \sqrt{2} + \dfrac{1}{\sqrt{2}} = \dfrac{2 + 1}{\sqrt{2}} = \dfrac{3}{\sqrt{2}}$

$f\left(\dfrac{9}{11}\right) = \dfrac{9}{11} + \dfrac{1}{\dfrac{9}{11}} = \dfrac{9}{11} + \dfrac{11}{9} = \dfrac{81 + 121}{99} = \dfrac{202}{99}$

$f\left(\dfrac{1}{x}\right) = \dfrac{1}{x} + \dfrac{1}{1/x} = \dfrac{1}{x} + x = f(x)$

(b)
$$f(0) = \frac{0-1}{0+1} = -1$$

$$f(6) = \frac{6-1}{6+1} = \frac{5}{7}$$

$$f\left(\frac{x-1}{x+1}\right) = \frac{\frac{x-1}{x+1}-1}{\frac{x-1}{x+1}+1} = \frac{[(x-1)-(x+1)]/(x+1)}{[(x-1)+(x+1)]/(x+1)} = \frac{-2}{2x} = -\frac{1}{x}$$

6.5 Types of Functions   (April 2015)

1. **One valued function :** If a function has only one value corresponding to each value of independent variable then the function is called a one valued function. For example, for every value of **x**, there is a unique value of y. Then y = f(x) is called a **single valued function**. For example, $y = x^2 + 2$, $y = \log x$, $y = 10^x$.

Note : A function which is not a single valued is called **multiple valued function**. For example, $y = \sqrt{x}$ $(x > 0)$.

2. **Explicit function :** Consider the function $ax + by + c = 0$, which can also be written as $y = \frac{-ax-c}{b}$. This is of the form $y = f(x)$. This is called explicit form of the function.

Thus, when the dependent variable (y) can be expressed entirely in terms of independent variable (**x**) then it is called explicit form of the function.

For example, $y = x^3 - 3x + 2$, $y = 2^x + x^2$ etc.

Remark : Following are not explicit functions $x^2 + y^2 + 2xy = \log(xy)$, $\log(x+y) = x^3 y^3$.

3. **Algebraic functions :** Consider the following functions :

$$y = 2x^3 - 5x^2 + 17, \quad y = \frac{2x^2-3}{5x^3+4}, \quad y = \sqrt[3]{x^2+4x+1}$$

We observe that these functions involve basic operations like addition, subtraction, multiplication, division and root. Such functions are called **algebraic functions**.

Remark : Following functions are **not** algebraic

$$y = \log x, \quad y = \sin x + \cos x, \quad y = x^2 + 5^x \text{ etc.}$$

4. **Polynomial function :** A function of the type $f = f(x) = a_n x^n + a_{n-1} x^{n-1} + \ldots + a_1 x + a_0$ where, $a_n \neq 0$ and a_i's are all integers is called a polynomial function.

For example, $y = 2x^3 - 3x + 6$, $y = 4x^7 - 3x^4 + 52x^2 - 18$.

Note that a constant is a polynomial of degree 0.

5. **Absolute value function :** A function defined by $y = |x|$ is called **absolute value function**.

Recall that
$$|x| = x \quad ; \quad \text{if } x \geq 0$$
$$\quad = -x \quad ; \quad \text{if } x < 0$$

The graph of y = |x| in [–3, 3] is plotted below.

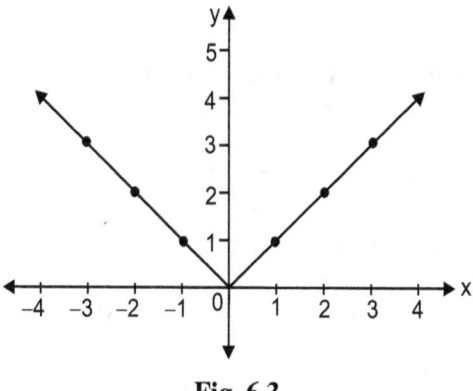

Fig. 6.3

6.   Inverse function : Let y = f(x) be a function such that for each value of **x** there corresponds a unique value of **y** and for every value of **y** there corresponds a unique value of **x**. In this case **x** can be expressed as a function of **y**, say x = g(y). Then g is called inverse of f and it is denoted by f⁻¹.

For example, consider the function y = 2x – 3, x∈ **R**.

Clearly for given a value of x there is only one value of y and for a given value of y and for a given value of y there is unique value of x.

y = 2x – 3 implies x = $\dfrac{y+3}{2}$ this is called inverse of the given function.

7.   Rational and Irrational function (Oct. 2013) : Let P(x) and Q(x) be two polynomials in x then $\dfrac{P(x)}{Q(x)}$ is called a rational function.

For example, $\dfrac{x+2}{3x^3-7}$, $\dfrac{4x^4-3x^2+6x-2}{2x^2-7x+6}$, $\dfrac{1}{x^3+1}$, x^5-7. $\left(\text{Note that } x^5-7 = \dfrac{x^5-7}{1}\right)$

An expression involving root of a rational function is called irrational function.

For example, $\sqrt{\dfrac{x^3-2}{x^2+6}}$, $\sqrt{x^3+x^2+x+2}$ etc.

8.   Monotone function (Oct. 2013) : Consider the function y = 3x + 2. We observe that an increase in the value of **x** cause an increase in value of **y** and a reduction in the value of **x** causes reduction in the value of **y** such a function is called **monotone increasing function**.

On the other hand consider the function y = $\dfrac{1}{x}$ (x > 0). An increase in the value of x cause a reduction in the value of **y** such a function is called **monotone decreasing function**.

Now we give mathematical definition of monotone increasing and monotone decreasing function.

Definition : A function $y = f(x)$ is called monotone increasing if $x_1 < x_2$ implies $f(x_1) \leq f(x_2)$.

Definition : A function $y = f(x)$ is called monotone decreasing if $x_1 < x_2$ implies $f(x_1) \geq f(x_2)$.

The inequality sign ($<$ or $>$) gets reversed in two cases :

(i) Taking reciprocals i.e. it $x_1 < x_2$ then $\dfrac{1}{x_1} > \dfrac{1}{x_2}$.

(ii) Multiplying by a negative number i.e. if $x_1 < x_2$ then $-kx_1 > kx_2$ $(k > 0)$.

For example, (i) $y = f(x) = x^2 + 2$ is increasing in $[0, 10]$.

Let $x_1, x_2 \in [0, 10]$ such that $x_1 < x_2$.

Then $\qquad\qquad\qquad\qquad\qquad x_1^2 < x_2^2$

$\therefore \qquad\qquad\qquad\qquad\quad x_1^2 + 2 < x_2^2 + 2$

i.e. $\qquad\qquad\qquad\qquad\quad f(x_1) < f(x_2)$

Thus, $x_1 < x_2$ implies $f(x_1) < f(x_2)$.

$\therefore$ $f(x)$ is monotone increasing in $[0, 10]$.

(ii) $f(x) = y = 3 - 2x$ is decreasing in $[1, 8]$.

Let $x_1, x_2 \in [1, 8]$. Such that $x_1 < x_2$.

$\therefore \qquad\qquad\qquad\qquad\qquad 2x_1 < 2x_2$

$\therefore \qquad\qquad\qquad\qquad\quad -2x_1 > -2x_2$

$\therefore \qquad\qquad\qquad\qquad 3 - 2x_1 > 3 - 2x_2$

$\therefore \qquad\qquad\qquad\qquad\quad f(x_1) > f(x_2)$

Thus, $x_1 < x_2$ implies $f(x_1) > f(x_2)$.

$\therefore$ $f(x)$ is monotone decreasing in $[1, 8]$.

9. Even and Odd function : Consider the function $y = x^2$. Replacing x by $-x$ we see that x^2 is not changed.

that is y remains same if x is replaced by $-x$. Such a function is called an **even function**.

Definition : A function $y = f(x)$ is called **even** if $f(x) = f(-x)$.

For example, $y = x^4 - 2x^2 + 1$, $y = |x|$.

Consider the function $y = f(x) = x^3 - 2x$.

Replacing x by –x we get

$$(-x)^3 - 2(-x) = -x^3 + 2x = -(x^3 - 2x) = -f(x)$$

Such a function is called **odd function**.

Definition : A function $y = f(x)$ is called **odd** if $f(-x) = -f(x)$.

Illustrative Examples

Example 6.4 : *Draw the graphs of following functions :*

(i) $y = x$ (ii) $\dfrac{x}{2} + \dfrac{y}{3} = 1$ (iii) $f(x) = |3 - x|$

(iv) $f(x) = 3 + 2x$,   *when $x > 0$*

               $= 3 - x$,   *when $x < 0$*   **(Oct. 2013)**

(v) $y = x^2$.   **(April 2015)**

Solution : (i) The graph of $y = x$ is plotted below :

x	– 4	– 3	– 2	– 1	0	1	2	3
y	– 4	– 3	– 2	– 1	0	1	2	3

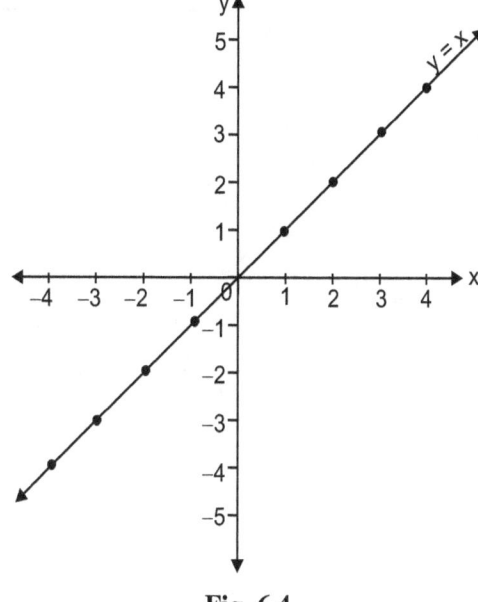

Fig. 6.4

(ii) The graph of $\dfrac{x}{2} + \dfrac{y}{3} = 1$ i.e. $3x + 2y = 6$ is plotted below.

x	– 2	0	2
$y = \dfrac{6 - 3x}{2}$	6	3	0

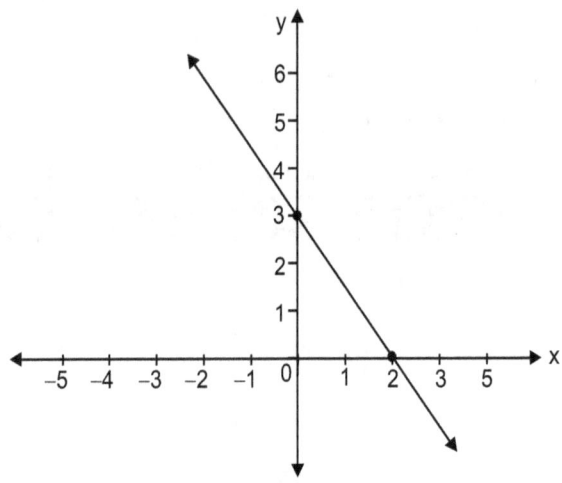

Fig. 6.5

(iii) The graph of $f(x) = |3 - x|$ is plotted below.

x	– 2	– 1	0	1	2	3	4	5
y	5	4	3	2	1	0	1	2

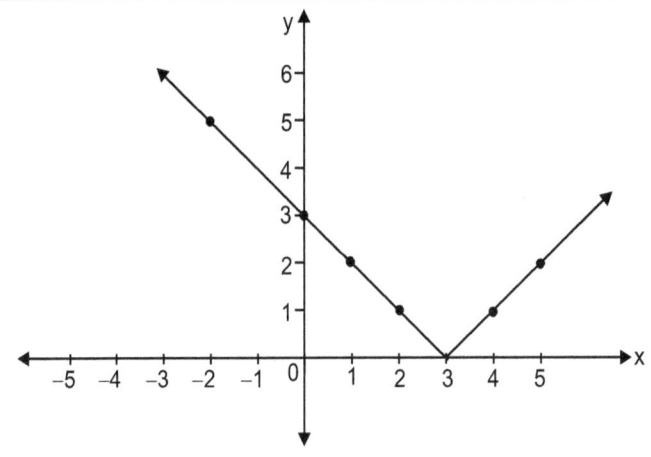

Fig. 6.6

(iv) The graph of $f(x) = 3 + 2x$; when $x \geq 0$

$= 3 - x$; when $x < 0$.

is plotted below.

x	– 2	– 1	0	1	2
f(x)	5	4	3	5	7

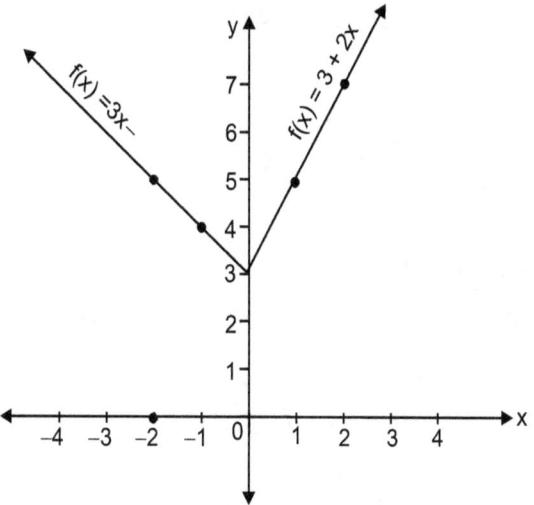

Fig. 6.7

(v) The graph of y $=$ x² is plotted below.   **(Oct. 2015)**

x	− 2	− 1	0	1	2
y	4	1	0	1	4

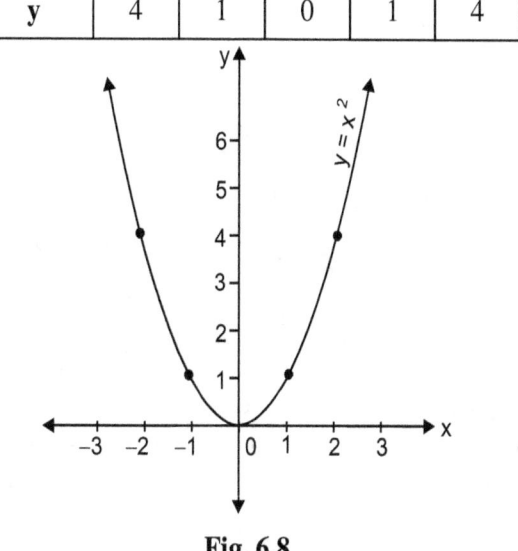

Fig. 6.8

Example 6.5 : *If f(x)* $= 3x^2 - 5x^4$ *and g(x)* $= 6x^3 + 11x$ *show that f(x) is an even function and g(x) is an odd function.*   **(April 2015)**

Solution : $f(x) = 3x^2 - 5x^4$

∴ $f(-x) = 3(-x)^2 - 5(-x)^4$

          $= 3x^2 - 5x^4 = f(x)$

∴   f(x) is an **even** function of x.

Now,　　　　　　　　　　　　$g(x) = 6x^3 + 11x$

∴　　　　　　　　　　　　$g(-x) = 6(-x)^3 + 11(-x)$

　　　　　　　　　　　　　　　$= -6x^3 - 11x$

　　　　　　　　　　　　　　　$= -(6x^3 + 11x)$

　　　　　　　　　　　　　　　$= -g(x)$

$g(x)$ is an **odd** function of x.

Example 6.6 : *If f(x)* $= |3x - 1|$, *find the values of x for which* $f(x) = f(2x - 3)$.

(Oct. 2013, 2014)

Solution : Since,　　　　　$f(x) = |3x - 1|$

　　　　　　　$f(2x - 3) = |3(2x - 3) - 1| = |6x - 9 - 1|$

　　　　　　　　　　　　　$= |6x - 10|$

Now,　　　　　　　　　　$f(x) = f(2x - 3)$

∴　　　　　　　　　$|3x - 1| = |6x - 10|$

∴　　　　　　　　　$3x - 1 = \pm(6x - 10)$

$3x - 1 = 6x - 10$ gives $6x - 3x = 10 - 1$

∴　　　　　　　　　　　$3x = 9$

　　　　　　　　　　　　$x = 3$

and　　　　　　　　$3x - 1 = -(6x - 10)$ gives

　　　　　　　　　$3x + 6x = 10 + 1$

∴　　　　　　　　　　　$9x = 11$

∴　　　　　　　　　　　$x = \dfrac{11}{9}$

∴　　$x = 3$ and $\dfrac{11}{9}$ are two values.

Example 6.7 : *Show that the function* $f(x) = x^2 + 2x + 1$ *is increasing in* [1, 20].

Solution :　　　　　　　$f(x) = x^2 + 2x + 1$

Let $x_1, x_2 \in [1, 20]$ such that $x_1 < x_2$.

∴　　　　　　　　　　　$x_1^2 < x_2^2$

∴　　　　　　$x_1^2 + 2x_1 + 1 < x_2^2 + 2x_2 + 1$

∴　　　　　　　　$f(x_1) < f(x_2)$

Thus, $x_1 < x_2$ implies $f(x_1) < f(x_2)$.

∴　　$f(x)$ is monotone increasing in [1, 20].

Example 6.8 : *Show that $x^2 - 5x + 6$ is decreasing in (0, 2).*

Solution : Let $\qquad\qquad$ $f(x) \;=\; x^2 - 5x + 6 \;=\; (x - 2)(x - 3)$

Let $x_1, x_2 \in (0, 2)$ such that $x_1 < x_2$.

$\therefore$ $\qquad\qquad\qquad\qquad$ $- x_1 \;>\; - x_2$

$\therefore$ $\qquad\qquad\qquad\qquad$ $2 - x_1 \;>\; 2 - x_2$

Similarly, $\qquad\qquad\qquad$ $3 - x_1 \;>\; 3 - x_2$

$\therefore$ $\qquad\qquad$ $(2 - x_1)(3 - x_1) \;>\; (2 - x_2)(3 - x_2)$

$\therefore$ $\qquad\qquad\qquad\qquad$ $f(x_1) \;>\; f(x_2)$

Thus, $x_1 < x_2$ implies $f(x_1) > f(x_2)$.

$\therefore$ $f(x)$ is monotone decreasing in (0, 2).

Exercise 6.1

1. Find the domain and range of the following functions :

 (i) $y = x^2$ (ii) $y = \dfrac{1}{x - 2}$ (iii) $y = \sqrt{x^2 - 4}$.

2. If $f(x) = 8x^6 - 3x^4 + 1$ and $g(x) = \dfrac{x}{1 - x^2}$ show that $f(x)$ is an even function and $g(x)$ is an odd function.

3. If $f(x) = x^2 + x$, find the value of $f(x + 1) - f(x - 2)$.

4. If $f(x) = ax^2 + bx + c$ and $f(1) = 6$, $f(2) = 11$ and $f(3) = 18$, find the values of a, b and c and hence find $f(-1)$.

5. Draw the graph of the following functions :

 (i) $x = 3$ (ii) $y = 3x + 2$ (iii) $\dfrac{x}{4} + \dfrac{y}{3} = 1$ (iv) $y = 2x^2 + 4x + 3$

 (v) $\qquad\qquad\qquad\qquad$ $f(x) \;=\; x - 1 \qquad ; \qquad$ when $x > 0$

 $\qquad\qquad\qquad\qquad\qquad\quad = -\dfrac{1}{2} \qquad ; \qquad$ when $x = 0$

 $\qquad\qquad\qquad\qquad\qquad\quad = x + 1 \qquad ; \qquad$ when $x < 0$

 (vi) $y = 1 - |x|$.

6. If $f(x) = \dfrac{3x + 2}{3x - 2}$, prove that $\dfrac{f(x) + 1}{f(x) - 1} = \dfrac{3x}{2}$.

7. Show that the function $f(x) = x^2 - x - 6$ is monotone increasing in [2, 5].

8. Show that the function $f(x) = 1 - 3x$ is monotone decreasing in [–2, 7].

Answers 6.1

(1) (i) **Domain :** The set **R** of all real numbers.

Range : The set of all positive real number including zero.

(ii) **Domain :** The set of all real numbers except 2.

Range : The set of all real numbers.

(iii) **Domain :** The set of all real numbers except the number between – 2 and 2.

Range : The set of all real numbers x, $x \geq 2$ or $x \leq 2$.

(3) 6x   (4) a = 1, b = 2, c = 3, f(– 1) = 2.

(5) (i)   (ii)

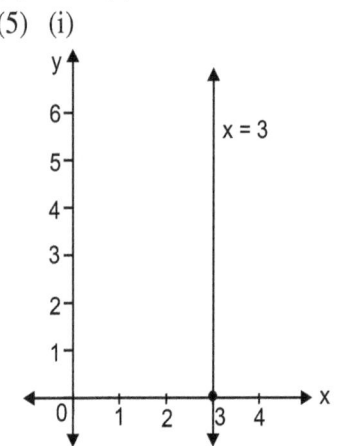 

Fig. 6.9   Fig. 6.10

(iii)   (iv)

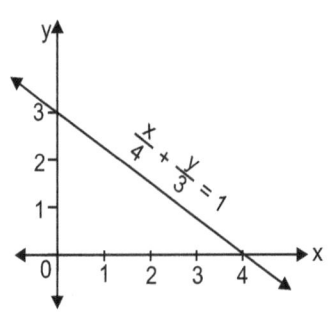   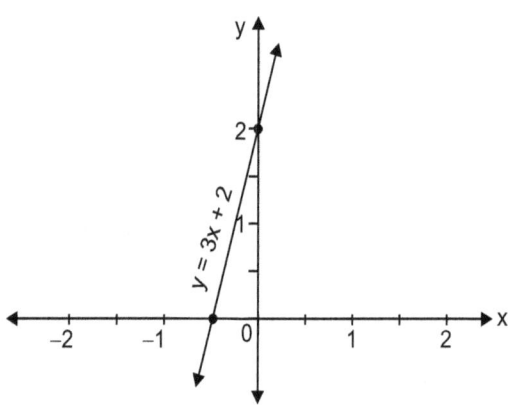

Fig. 6.11   Fig. 6.12

(v)   (vi)

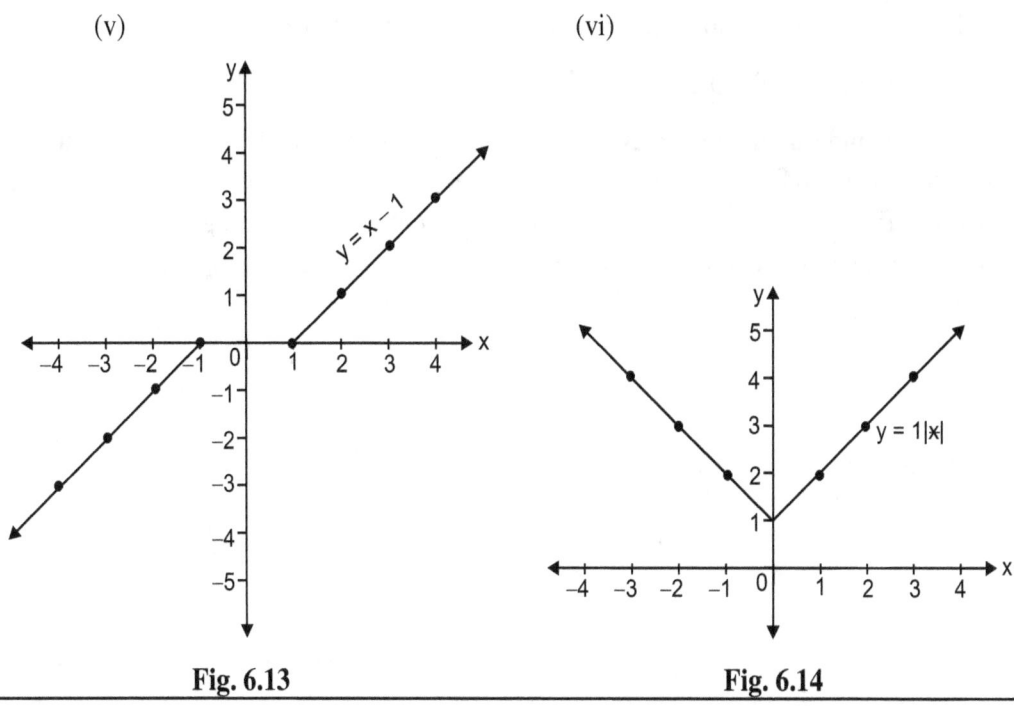

Fig. 6.13   Fig. 6.14

6.6 Important Functions in Commerce and Economics   (Oct. 2014)

The following functions are extensively used in commerce, economics and decision-making in business.

1.   Supply Function (Oct. 2013) :   This function, denoted by S, is used to specify the quantities of a particular commodity available for sale in the market at different prices.

Since, for higher price, supply in likely to be more, supply curve, normally rises from left to right (see Fig. 6.15).

For example, its slope is positive. In other words, it is monotone increasing function.

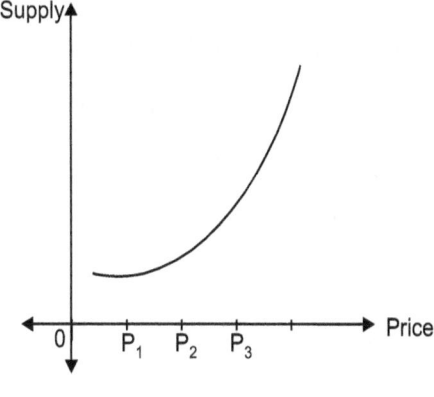

Fig. 6.15

Normally, supply functions are polynomials in p (p : price).

For example, $S = p^2 + p + 2$, $S = 4p - 1$ etc.

2. Demand Function (Oct. 2013) : This function denoted by D, specifies quantities of a particular commodity that buyers are willing to purchase at different prices. Since, an increase in the price causes a fall in demand, it is a **monotone decreasing function**. In other words, demand curve normally tapers down from left to right (See Fig. 6.16). i.e. its slope is negative.

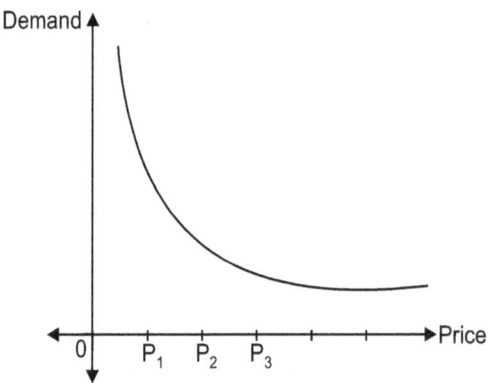

Fig. 6.16

Normally, demand functions are polynomials in p (p : price).

For example, $D = 40 + 2p - 3p^2$, $D = \dfrac{20}{2p + 1}$.

Remark : If at a price p, demand equals supply i.e. D = S, then p is called equilibrium price.

3. Cost function : Suppose that a firm produces motor-bikes. It is clear that bigger the production, more the cost. You know that the cost of manufacturing, say C consists of two parts (i) fixed cost, which is independent of x. (ii) variable cost V(x), which depends on x.

Fixed cost includes expenditure on security, insurance, minimum electricity bill etc.

Variable cost V(x) depends on x, the number of units produced.

Thus, $C(x) = F + V(x)$

Average cost of production or cost per unit is found by dividing total cost by number of units produced.

i.e. $A(x) = \dfrac{C(x)}{x}$.

Since, the cost of production is directly proportional to the number of units produced, cost curve has a positive slope. (Refer Fig. 6.17).

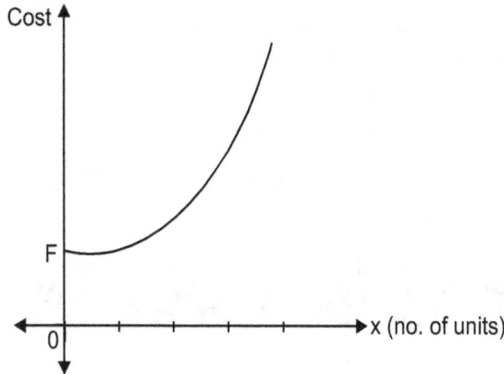

Fig. 6.17

4.   Total Revenue Function :   The total amount of money realised by sailing a particular commodity is called **revenue**.

Clearly, revenue depends on the price of the commodity and quantity sold. If D is the demand and price per unit is p, then revenue

$$R(x) \ = \ p \cdot D(x) \ \ (x : \text{no. of articles})$$

∴
$$p \ = \ \frac{R(x)}{D(x)}$$

i.e. p is the average revenue of the firm (per unit).

5.   Profit Function : Suppose that a company produces x items and sells all of them in the market. If C(x) is the total cost of production and R(x) is the revenue then profit function P(x) is given by

$$P(x) \ = \ R(x) - C(x)$$

6.   Production Function :   Production of a firm depends on several variables like man-power, availability of time, availability of capital etc., production function cannot be expressed as a function of only one variable. Since, labour (L) and capital (K) are dominant factors for production, Cobb-Douglas production function defined as follows is generally used.

$$P \ = \ c \, K^{\alpha} \, L^{\beta}, \ \ \alpha + \beta \ = 1$$

i.e.
$$P \ = \ 100 \, K^{1/2} \, L^{1/2}$$

7.   Utility Function : Consider the case of an individual who buys x and y units of two commodities say A and B. The satisfaction that the gets by this purchase is called utility function, denoted by U(x, y), examples of such functions are

$$U \ = \ (x + k) \, (y + h) \qquad\qquad \text{where, h and k constants}$$

or
$$U \ = \ kx + hy$$

Note that this concept can be extended to any number of commodities.

8.   Overall Consumption Function : Suppose that a family/community/country has propensity (special behaviour) to consume c and its income is Y, then total consumption function is given by

$$C = a + cY$$

The quantity **a** stands for minimum consumption a family (or community) needs irrespective to income.

Since income is Y and consumption is C, Y – C is the saving of the community.

Illustrative Examples

Example 6.9 : *For a new product, a manufacturer sets-up an infrastructure which costs him ₹1,50,000. The variable cost (labour, materials etc.) is estimated at ₹125 for each unit of the product. The sale price per unit is fixed at ₹ 160. Write down the cost function, revenue function and profit function.*   **(Oct. 2015)**

Solution : Let x be the number of units produced by the company.

∴   The revenue received by the company is R(x) = 160x.

Total cost of production of x units

$$C(x) = 1,50,000 + 125x$$

∴   The profit function $= P(x) =$ Revenue – Cost

$$= R(x) - C(x)$$

$$= 160x - (150000 + 125x)$$

$$= 35x - 150000$$

Example 6.10 : *Find equilibrium price given : the demand and supply function is :*

$$D = \frac{8p}{p-2}, \quad S = p^2 \qquad \text{(Oct. 2013)}$$

Solution :   For equilibrium price

$$D = S$$

$$\frac{8p}{p-2} = p^2$$

∴ $8p = p^2(p-2)$

∴ $8 = p(p-2) = p^2 - 2p$

∴ $p^2 - 2p - 8 = 0$

∴ $(p-4)(p+2) = 0$

∴ $p = 4 \quad \text{or} \quad p = -2$

Since price cannot be negative, p = 4.

This equilibrium price is 4.

Example 6.11 : *Assume that for a closed economy, E = C + I + G, where, E is total expenditure, C is expenditure on consumption goods, I is expenditure on investment goods and G is government spending. For equilibrium, we must have E ≡ Y, where Y is total income received.*

For a certain economy, it is given that C = 15 + 0.9Y, I = 20 + 0.05Y and G = 25.

Find the equilibrium values of Y, C and I. How will these change if there is no Government spending ?

Solution : We are given that

$$E \ = \ C + I + G \qquad\qquad \dots (1)$$

and for equilibrium, $\qquad\quad E \ = \ Y \qquad\qquad \dots (2)$

From (1) and (2), we have

$$Y \ = \ C + I + G \qquad\qquad \dots (3)$$

Substituting the given values of C, I and G in (3), we get

$$Y \ = \ (15 + 0.9Y) + (20 + 0.05Y) + 25$$
$$= \ 60 + 0.95\ Y$$

∴ $\qquad\qquad Y - 0.95\ Y \ = \ 60$

∴ $\qquad\qquad 0.05\ Y \ = \ 60$

$$Y \ = \ \frac{60}{0.05} \ = \ 1200$$

∴ $\qquad C = 15 + 0.9\ Y \ = \ 15 + 0.9 \times 1200 \ = \ 1095$

and $\qquad I = 20 + 0.05\ Y \ = \ 20 + 0.05 \times 1200 \ = \ 80$

If there is no Government spending then G = 0 and the equilibrium equation takes the form.

$$Y \ = \ C + I \qquad\qquad \dots (4)$$

Substituting the given values of C and I in (4), we get

$$Y \ = \ (15 + 0.9\ Y) + (20 + 0.05\ Y)$$
$$= \ 35 + 0.95\ Y$$

∴ $\qquad\qquad Y - 0.95\ Y \ = \ 35$

∴ $\qquad\qquad 0.05\ Y \ = \ 35$

∴ $\qquad\qquad Y \ = \ \frac{35}{0.05} \ = \ 700$

∴ $\qquad C = 15 + 0.9\ Y \ = \ 15 + 0.9 \infty\ 700 \ = \ 645$

$$I = 20 + 0.05\ Y \ = \ 20 + 0.05 \infty\ 700 \ = \ 55$$

∴ The changed values of Y, C and I, if there is no government spending, are respectively 700, 645 and 55.

Exercise 6.2

1. A shoe manufacturer is planning production of a new variety of shoes. For the first year the fixed costs for setting-up the new production line are ₹ 1.25 lacs. Variable cost for producing each pair of shoes is ₹ 35. The sales department projects that 1,500 pairs can be sold in the first year at the rate of ₹ 160 per pair.

    (i)   Determine the cost function $C(x)$ for producing x pairs of shoes.

    (ii) Determine the revenue function $R(x)$ for the total revenue from the sale of x pairs of shoes.

    (iii) Determine the profit function $P(x)$ for the profit from the sale of x pairs of shoes.

    (iv) If 1,500 pairs are actually sold what profit or loss the company will incur ?

2. Find equilibrium price given that demand and supply functions are :

    $D = 2 - 0.02 \, p, \quad S = 0.2 + 0.07 \, p.$

3. A garment manufacturer is planning production of new variety of shirts. It involves initially a fixed cost of ₹ 2.5 lacs and a variable cost of ₹ 200 for producing each shirt. If each shirt can be sold at ₹ 350 then find cost function, revenue function, profit function.

4. A publishing house finds that the production of cost directly attributed to each book is ₹ 35 and that the fixed costs are ₹ 15,000. If each book can be sold for ₹ 50, then determine the cost function, the revenue function, profit function.

5. $C(x) = 5x + 350$ and $R(x) = 50x - x^2$ are respectively the total cost and the total revenue functions for a company that produces and sells x units of a particular product find

    (i)   the value of x that produce a profit.

    (ii) the value of x that result in a loss.

Answers 6.2

(1) (i) $C(x) = 1,25,000 + 35x$

    (ii) $R(x) = 160x$, (iii) $P(x) = 125 \, (x - 1000)$

    (iv) Profit of ₹ 62,500.

(2) 20

(3) $C(x) = 2,50,000 + 200 x$, $R(x) = 350 x$

   $P(x) = 150 x - 2,50,000$

(4) $C(x) = 15,000 + 35x$, $R(x) = 50x$, $P(x) = 15 (x - 1,000)$.

(5) (i) $10 \leq x \leq 35$ (ii) $x < 10$ or $x > 35$.

Miscellaneous Exercise 6

1. If $f(x) = \dfrac{1 + x}{1 - x}$, find $f(x) \times f\left(-\dfrac{1}{x}\right)$.

2. If $f(x + 3) = 2x^2 - 3x - 1$, find $f(x + 1)$. Also find the value of x, if $f(x + 1) = f(x + 3)$.

3. Find domain and range of following functions :

   (i) $y = \dfrac{3}{x - 3}$ (ii) $y = -x^4$ (iii) $y = \sqrt{x - 5}$ (iv) $f(x) = -3x + 100$.

4. A watch company is to produce a cheaper variety of wrist watches. It involves initially a fixed cost of ₹ 1.25 lacs and a variable cost of ₹ 150 for each wrist watch. If each wrist watch be sold at ₹ 600, then find (i) cost function, (ii) revenue function, (iii) profit function.

5. Total cost of producing 100 items of a commodity is ₹ 205000, while total cost of producing 25 items is ₹ 40000. Assuming that the cost function is a linear function, find the cost function.

6. A company sells x pens each day at ₹ 30 per pen. The cost of manufacturing is ₹ 20 per pen and the distributor charges are ₹ 2 per pen. Besides, the daily overhead cost comes to ₹ 840. Determine the profit function. What is the profit, if 1,000 pens are manufactured and sold in a day ?

Answers

(1) -1

(2) $f(x + 1) = 2x^2 - 11x + 4$, $x = \dfrac{5}{8}$

(3) (i)   **Domain :** Set of all real numbers except 3.

       Range : Set of all real numbers except zero.

    (ii)   **Domain :** Set of all real numbers.

       Range : Set of all negative numbers including zero.

(iii) **Domain :** Set of all real numbers greater than or equal to 5.

Range : Set of all positive numbers including zero.

(iv) **Domain :** Set of all real numbers.

Range : Set of all real numbers.

(4) (i) $C(x) = 1,25,000 + 150x$

(ii) $R(x) = 600\,x$ (iii) $P(x) = 450\,x - 1,25,000$

(5) $C(x) = 100\,(22x - 15)$

(6) $C(x) = 840 + 22x$, $R(x) = 30$, $P(x) = 8x - 840$, ₹ 7160.

1. **Attempt any four :** (4 × 4 = 16)

(1) The rate of commission in increased from 6% to 8% still the income of an agent is the same. Find the percentage change in his sale.

(2) In a certain company 12 operators can perform a certain job work involving manufacturing of 900 units of a product. If the operators work for 15 hours a day for 36 days, how many days would be required by 16 operators working 12 hours a day to manufacture 1200 units of the product.

(3) Sunil sold a car to Pradeep at 20% profit. Pradeep sold the car to Milind at 10% profit for ₹ 2,65,000. Find the price at which Sunil has purchased the car.

(4) Income of A, B and C in the ratio 2 : 3 : 4 and their expenditure are in the ratio 5 : 7 : 9. If A saves $\frac{1}{5}^{th}$ of his income, find the ratio of their income of saving.

(5) The sum of the present ages of 3 persons is 66 years. Five years ago their ages are in the ratio of 4 : 6 : 7. Find their present ages.

(6) A dealer in furniture buys chairs at 340 each. At what price should be mark them for sale, so that he may earn a profit of 25% after giving 15% discount ?

2. **Solve any four :** (4 × 4 = 16)

(1) Explain the terms :

   (a) Proportion.

   (b) Continued proportion.

   (c) Direct proportion.

   (d) Inverse proportion.

(2) Find the present value of an annuity of ₹ 500 payable at the end of every half year for 10 years at 10% per annum compound interest.

(3) Milind deposits ₹ 20,000 in a bank at 15% p.a. to give scholarship to needy students every years. Find the amount of yearly scholarship.

(4) Explain the terms 'commission' and 'commission agent'.

(5) A plot was sold and the owner received ₹ 10,000 after the payment of commission at 8% on the cost of land, find the cost of land.

(6) Aditya sold the share of 6% at ₹ 90 of ₹ 10,000 and invests the proceeds in 10% at ₹ 120. What is the change in his income ?

3. **Attempt any four :** $(4 \times 4 = 16)$

   (1) Exhibit each of the following relations as a set of ordered pairs. Which of term are functions ? Justify your answer :

      (i) $[(x, x + 3)|x \in N, 4 \leq x \leq 8]$

      (ii) $[(x, y)|y^2 = x^2 + 1 \ x \in Z, -1 \leq x \leq 1]$.

   (2) Write the important formulae of simple interest. Amount and compound interest.

   (3) Evaluate : $D = \begin{bmatrix} 28 & 45 & 63 \\ 20 & 34 & 48 \\ 31 & 36 & 51 \end{bmatrix}$.

   (4) Define matrix different types of matrices. Write any two in detail.

   (5) Anita purchased 50 shares of ₹ 100 each at ₹ 120 per share. Company declared 10% divided. Find total income of Anita and return on her investment.

   (6) $A = \begin{bmatrix} 1 & 2 \\ 3 & 4 \end{bmatrix}$, $B = \begin{bmatrix} 1 & 0 \\ 2 & 3 \end{bmatrix}$ and $C = \begin{bmatrix} 1 & -1 \\ 0 & 1 \end{bmatrix}$.

      Show that $A (B + C) = AB + AC$.

4. **Attempt any four :** $(4 \times 4 = 16)$

   (1) If $f(x) = 3x^2 - 5x^4$ and $g(x) = 6x^3 + 11x$, show that $f(x)$ is an even function and $g(x)$ is an odd function.

   (2) Draw the graph of $y = x^2$.

   (3) Find inverse of A. Given : $A = \begin{bmatrix} 7 & 2 \\ 5 & 4 \end{bmatrix}$.

   (4) Define function. What are different methods of representing a function ?

   (5) Find the difference between simple interest and compound interest on ₹ 2,500 for 3 years at 10% p.a.

   (6) If $A = \begin{bmatrix} 3 & -2 \\ 4 & -2 \end{bmatrix}$.

      Satisfy the matrix equation $A^2 - KA - 2I = 0$.

5. **Attempt any two :** $(8 \times 2 = 16)$

   (1) A washing machine worth ₹ 20,000 is purchased on installment basis under equal 20 monthly installments including compound interest at 18% p.a. Find equated monthly installment by reducing method.

   (2) Ravi holds 500 shares of ₹ 100 each of a company. The company issued bonus shares in the ratio 5 : 2. Thereafter company declared a dividend of 10% on enlarged capital. Find the return on investment which Ravi gets ?

   (3) Find compound interest on ₹ 1,200 at 5% p.a. for 3 years and 4 months compounded annually.

◻◻◻